The Mabamba Return
A Historical Novel

John B. Franz
Author of *Congo Shadows*

First Edition Design Publishing
Sarasota, Florida USA

The Mabamba Return
Copyright ©2020 John B. Franz

ISBN 978-1506-909-49-3 PBK
ISBN 978-1506-909-50-9 EBK

LCCN 2020913636

August 2020

Published and Distributed by
First Edition Design Publishing, Inc.
P.O. Box 17646, Sarasota, FL 34276-3217
www.firsteditiondesignpublishing.com

Prologue

Metamorphosis of the Mabamba

The Common Glider or *Cymothoe caenis* is a beautiful white African butterfly with black wing tips reaching nearly four inches across. It is a living ornament that periodically decorates the rainforests of Kwilu Province in the Democratic Republic of Congo (DRC). Locally known as *Mabamba,* [Ma-BAHM-ba] the villagers welcome the lovely, fluttering swarms that inundate their community annually.

As a migratory species, the *Mabamba* are drawn back to the region by mysterious forces lodged deep within their DNA. But even more, as is true for all others of the species, their compulsion is to return to a very specific locale, to a particular type of tree to complete their circle of life. The *Mabamba* lay their eggs exclusively on the leaves of the Oncoba Welwitchii. It is a medium sized tree typically found in splotchy light on the edge of the forest. Its leaves are shaped like elongated hearts, and it bears small orange spiky fruit capsules. Access to foliage from this specific tree is crucial for the species' survival.

When the tiny *Mabamba* eggs hatch, the larva or caterpillars that emerge are occupied with a single-minded purpose: to eat and grow. And do they ever grow! They daily consume up to double their body weight of their essential food source. The caterpillars molt or shed their exoskeleton on five successive occasions, each stage becoming a new "instar." The *Mabamba's* identity during this period differs greatly from a butterfly: it is a leaf-eating tree dweller with limited mobility. Youthful caterpillars are vulnerable to a plethora of life-threatening circumstances. Drought, fire and loss of habitat; birds, other insects, monkeys, and a variety of forest tree creatures are among its predators. Villagers collect tubs of green *Mabamba* caterpillars in season to sell for food in the local markets.

When mature *Mabamba* caterpillars have reached their full length and weight, they crawl to the underside of a leaf, secreting a substance that quickly hardens into a protective shell or chrysalis. It provides both camouflage and protection as they

1

hang from beneath the leaf or branch. During this pupa stage it appears from the outside that not much is happening, but that is far from true. Major transformations are occurring internally. A series of hormones direct the dissolving and redeployment of cells in the right sequence and at the right time. Clearly, the larva has no control or say-so in the matter. Should the pupa emerge too soon, disaster would result. The process of change proceeds at its own pace until it is fully completed.

The final stage of development occurs as the chrysalis is broken open by an emerging butterfly. Fluid from the pupa is injected into newly formed veins of newly formed wings. It quickly hardens and the butterfly exercises its wings with newly formed muscles. Then, it takes to the air. The *Mabamba's* true identity is finally revealed: it is a highly mobile, nectar-consuming flier, whose first task upon emerging is to find a mate.

Metamorphosis of the *Mabamba*: vulnerability, protection, transformation

Character & Term List
in order of appearance

Part I: Vulnerability

- **Kisambo** – (Kee-SAHM-bo) – The key village in the story
- **MMC** = Mennonite Mission Congo – the novel's hypothetical mission organization
- **Phonie** = short wave radio
- **Hal (Harold) Schroeder** – this is his story; aka "**Lumwenu**" (loo-MWHEN-oo) = the clairvoyant one, the seer
- **Martha Schroeder** – Hal's mother, his advocate
- **Calvin Schroeder** – Hal's father, missionary Bible teacher
- **Patty Schroeder** – Hal's older sister, eventually lives in San Jose
- **Rhonda Schroeder** – Hal's older sister, eventually lives in Texas
- **Kuyantika (aka Tika)** – (koo-yahn-TEEK-a) - Hal's childhood friend; son of Kinbumba
- **Kinbumba** – (keen-BOOM-ba) - Tika's father, the original Kisambo pastor
- **Nsukula (aka Nsuka)** – (n-SOOK-oola) - Hal's childhood friend, son of Museka Adoko
- **Muzeka Adoko** – (moo-ZECK-a, ah-DOH-ko) -Nsuka's father, the original Kisambo shaman
- **Ilunga** – (ee-LOON-ga) - Hal's childhood friend; remains in Kisambo as a teacher
- **Ntotilla** – (n-toe-TEE-la) – the original Kisambo village chief
- **Barb** (Barbara) **Clausen** (Jones) – Hal's childhood Kisambo friend; eventually lives in DRC as a nurse
- **Elizabeth Clausen** – Barb's mother
- **Larry Clausen** – Barb's father; school administrator at Kisambo
- **Elsie Buller** – single missionary nurse at Kisambo; rescued at evacuation
- **Thomas, Rosine, Kintuntu, Alongi, Muteba, Cécile** = Kisambo station workers
- **Biungu** – (bee-YOON-goo) - Nsuka's older brother; joined the *Jeunesse*
- **Njoli** = rebel friend of Biungu
- **Mulele** (moo-LAY-lee) **Pierre** & **Gizenga** (gee-ZENG-a) **Antoine** – the founders of the *Jeunesse* rebellion
- **MAF** = Missionary Aviation Fellowship – bush plane transport in Congo's back country
- **Paul Gingrich** – MMC Legal Representative, resided in Tshikapa
- **Marvin Elrich** – missionary colleague, Kindambo; rescued at evacuation
- **Philip Bartel** – missionary colleague, Kindambo; rescued at evacuation

1

- **Martin & Sarah Yoder** – missionary colleagues, guest house hosts, Kindambo
- **George Kimball** – MAF pilot

Part II: Protection
- **Tricia** – Hal's youngest daughter, lives in LA with **Emmie** (4); Starbucks barrister
- **Cal**– Hal's son, lives in Portland, OR; is an attorney
- **Judy** – Hal's daughter; lives in Vancouver, WA; is a 5th grade teacher
- **Phyllis**– Hal's ex-wife, lives in Portland, OR with husband **Greg** (new spouse)
- **TCKs =** Third Culture Kids – youth raised in foreign countries who together create a unique culture & identity that differs from either passport or host country cultures
- **Brad Waterhouse** – Hal's best friend from USC Anthropology; TCK from Ghana
- **TASOK =** The American School of Kinshasa; Hal's high school in Congo
- **Lindsey Franklin** – Hal's therapist; Psychologist and TCK from Papua New Guinea
- **Darrel & Bonnie Baylor** – guesthouse hosts, Kinshasa
- **TASOK Classmates:**
  - **-Tim McClennon** (AZ), electrical engineer
  - **-Paul Bannon** (IN), owner, high end foreign auto repair shop
  - **-Tyrone Williams** (MO), lawyer
  - **-Oscar Peters** (TX), owner, welding shop
  - **-Monica Conrad** (CO), board member, World Wildlife Fund
  - **-Lawanda Jones** (WA), insurance manager
  - **-Alice Broadbent** (UK), HR manager, textile firm
  - **-Joanna Brubaker** (PA), high school social studies teacher
  - **-Muhammed Kukazi** (Australia), owner import-export business
  - **-Abdul Malik** (BC), osteopathic surgeon
  - **-Carl Cooper** (IL), travel agent
  - **-Kasandra Taylor** (OK), nurse
  - **-Shirley Hansen Bond** (FL), X-ray technician

Part III: Transformation
- **MCC =** Mennonite Central Committee – a Mennonite relief & development agency
- **Michael & Shirley Friesen** – MCC Country Directors, DRC
- **Bobozo** (bo-BO-zo) **Henri** – DRC education official

- **Mukana** (moo-KAHN-a) **Jonas** – Regional church legal representative
- **Sgt. Mpika** – (m-PEEK-a) - Friend of Tika; military escort
- **Kamanga Nsapo** (ka-MAHN-ga, n-SAH-po)– current Kisambo shaman, anti-missionary
- **Munzele Zacharie** – (moon-ZELLY) - niece to former shaman, current resident of Kisambo
- **Mansuaki** – (man-SWAH-kee) - eldest son of Ntotilla; current Kisambo chief
- **Lumingu** – (loo-MEEN-goo) - current pastor of Kisambo village
- **Muwana** (moo-WAH-na) **Pierre** – Tika's friend, member of Congo's National Assembly (politician)
- **Brian Clausen** – Barb's older brother
- **Shawna Jones** – Barb's daughter
- **Lumwenu Abongwami** – (loo-MWHEN-oo; ah-BOHNG-wamee) = the seer who has changed, is healed or is whole; the new name ascribed to Hal

Part I
Vulnerability

#1 Kisambo Station

January 1964

"Hal? It's time to come in and clean up, son. Don't make me send Thomas for you."

The warm light of late afternoon was dimming. The familiar voice rang out across the yard where a small number of churning black arms and legs was fully engaged in a major battle before an even larger crowd of cheering fans. Sweaty limbs whirled about in clouds of dust and squeals of delight. Twelve-year-old Hal and his three best friends were fully engrossed in an intense soccer match against an equal number of their village friends – the fantasy finals of the *Coup du Monde* (World Cup). It was Congo versus Brazil. Never had more been at stake.

"Hey Kalala, pass it here!" Clashing exertion, shouts and taunts of the young players, "bula...chobo...mouf," all but drowned out the repeated calls from within the cement block, tin roofed residence that bordered the playing field. The caller's annoyance was obvious – obvious, had anyone been paying attention. None of the young competitors looked up, however. The only sign of notice-taking came from inside the house. In the corner of the kitchen, the dark eyes of the family's quiet African cook, Thomas, briefly flicked up. The corners of his mouth turned ever so slightly in a smile. He remained otherwise without expression, concentrating on his potato pealing duties.

Martha strained her neck in each direction and leaned across the sink to look out the open barred window, searching for some sign of acknowledgment from the lightest skinned competitor in the yard. *"Ack! The dust! By now he's become the same color as his friends,"* she thought, slowly shaking her head at the writhing brown, dust-caked figure flying across the yard. Sighing, Martha placed the rabbit carcass she had been working on in the sink, freshly harvested from the hutch behind the house. In one continuous motion, she rinsed and dried her hands, flung the hand towel across the tiled counter and marched out the door.

The corners of Thomas' mouth turned up once again. *This ought to be good.*

The back-yard championship match screeched to a halt as the high official strode into the midst of the action. "Stop! Now! *Sesepi yai!*" she exclaimed with as much authority as any World Cup referee. Instead of holding up a red card, however, Martha grasped the offending competitor by his left ear, dragging him sideways behind her toward the house.

"Awww, c'mon Mama, just a few minutes more...we were winning!" The whining voice came from behind the tow of a very determined mother. The entire collection of barefoot African friends stood still watching, wide-eyed, sweaty arms at their side as the dust settled. Mama-*mpasi* (trouble) would not happen this way in the village. Just before she reached the screen door, their white friend's frowning mama stopped. Spinning around, she gestured with a sweep of her free hand. "And the rest of you...home now. Back to the village! *Kwenda!* (go)" The crowd of young Africans immediately scampered off: no flicker of hesitation, no backward glances.

"What am I going to do with you, young man? You are filthy! And you just ignore me when I call. This has been happening way too often lately. I'm not happy with you."

"But Mama, I didn't hear you. We were..." A raised finger silenced the protest.

"No more excuses. That one is all used up. Get yourself into the tub. Now! Use some soap this time. I don't want to see all that dirt left on the towel when you're done. We'll find out what your father thinks about your "hearing problem" when he gets home. *Luzitu ve!* (No respect)"

"But..."

"I really don't want to hear it, Harold. To the tub," Martha pointed in the direction of the bathroom. "I already had Thomas add a tea kettle of heated water so it's all ready for you."

"'Harold?' Jeez, I guess I really did it this time," Hal mumbled quietly to himself. Mama only used his full name when she was really ticked off. He shuffled down the hall shoulders drooping, and head slumped. At the entrance to his bedroom Hal paused to pull his dust-caked tee shirt over a mop of thick, black hair. Next, his shorts and underwear dropped to the floor. Then, wadding his clothes into a ball, he propelled the bundle into the corner of the room. Wrist bent in follow through, it was a perfect two-point shot. *"I supposed she'll want me to put them in the hamper, later"* he thought. *"Well, later is later..."* and he swung around the corner into the bathroom leaving a dusty handprint on the doorframe.

***

The distant rumble of thunder could be heard, and occasional flashes of lightening were seen through the open, barred windows as the three Schroeders sat down at the dinner table for supper. An evening thunder squall was on its way.

"I sure miss Patty and Rhonda," Hal volunteered. "It's so quiet around here without them. I can't wait 'til next year when I can go to boarding school instead of home schooling." *Sometimes when you know you are going to 'get it' after supper,* he told himself, *it helps to establish a little rapport ahead of time. Mama is not likely to bring up any unpleasant topics during the meal.*

"Yes, it's hard to believe they're already back at school, Hal. It's a lot quieter around here without them. Probably too quiet for you," replied Hal's father with a smiling pause between bites of rabbit stew. It was a good switch from *luku,* (manioc balls) *saka-saka* (greens) and *muamba* (palm oil gravy) and he was relishing the meal.

Calvin Schroeder was a slender, even-tempered man of medium height, tanned from his nearly twenty years of missionary work in the Congo interior. A Bible teacher and pastor, he tended to be more reflective than reactive. The wrinkles at the corners of his eyes, however, revealed him to also be in possession of a quick smile and a ready sense of humor.

Hal continued his rapport-building strategy. "Why did you take them to Mukedi to fly back to school last week instead of to Gungu, Daddy? Gungu is a lot closer, right?"

A dark shadow appeared to cross the face of Hal's father. He flicked a quick glance in the direction of his frowning wife, who had paused, fork-in-air, awaiting his reply. Hal could tell he had hit the target with that question.... some kind of target, anyway. Calvin ran his fingers through his salt-and-pepper hair, a familiar sign of worry, before offering a quiet response.

"Well, son, the short answer is that MAF suggested we do so. That was their advice via phonie after a Gungu fly over. Apparently, they consider Mukedi a safer location for flights in and out of our area these days."

"Safer? Safer from what, Daddy?" Hal put down his fork and

reached for a glass of water. He tried to act nonchalant, but something was going on here that wasn't being said. He tried to read his parents' faces.

"Um...Calvin, I don't know if it's all that helpful to go into this with...with young ears and fears." Martha's fork was now on the table. Mama's eyes expressed something Hal couldn't clearly interpret. Was it worry? Fear?

"No...Martha, I disagree. This time I think we need to be open with our son about these things. Remember what happened following Independence...the chaos of evacuation? That was only three and a half years ago. Looking back, I don't think it helped to keep the unfolding trouble from our girls. I think Hal needs to be made aware of what's happening at present around here."

Martha sighed deeply, "I suppose you're right, dear. I just hate to create anxieties if nothing ends up coming of it this time."

"What're you two talking about?" blurted Hal. *I can't believe they think I'm just a scared little kid*, he thought. *I'll change that!*

"What *aren't* you telling me?" Without waiting for a response, eyes sparkling, in excited, rapid disclosure, he continued. "So, it's true what they're saying. But I already know more than either of you think. My friends have told me stuff." It was a secret he'd been dying to let out for some time now.

"My friends say that people in the village are not happy with Independence. They think they got cheated. Some of them even think we missionaries are helping the bad government people keep them poor. My buddies told me that some of the older guys, their brothers and cousins, have been sneaking off into the forest for training with the rebels. They call themselves '*Jeunesse*'. Even their families don't know exactly where they are going or what they're doing."

The adults were speechless. Both parents sat silent, mouths at half-mast, brows raised, and eyes locked on the agitated young speaker. Meanwhile, Thomas had slipped away from his meal prep duties in the kitchen and edged closer to the conversation. He stood just out of sight behind the doorway to the dining room hoping to catch more of what was being said. *It's true what they say*, he thought, "*Little pots have ears.*"

Hal's father cleared his throat as he regained his composure. "Who told you these things, son? How long have you known them?" Since his questions were posed in Dad's rarely used no-

nonsense tone, Hal figured he'd better come clean.

"Kuyantika – we guys call him Tika – first told me about this stuff a couple of weeks ago. Then, today Nsukula told us guys that his father is mad at his older brother for sneaking off to meet strangers in the forest. I guess almost everyone in the village is upset with things, especially after hearing from the visitors."

"Visitors? What visitors?"

"*Kuzaba ve*...I dunno. They didn't say who they are. Just some strangers who showed up a while back. They don't like the leaders in Leo."

"Kuyantika is pastor Kinbumba's boy," Martha reminded herself out loud. Turning to her husband, she puzzled, "I thought you told me, Cal, that when you asked the pastor about the *Jeunesse*, he indicated that he didn't know anything about it, that he thought the rebels were somewhere far from here."

"Yes, it's true. So, this is troubling news. Actually, Nsukula's father told me the same thing and so did some of the other village elders I've approached recently. If what Hal's telling us is true...well, I'm not sure what to make of those replies." Calvin frowned. His hand went up, fingers automatically combing back through his hair as if to smooth the unsettling thoughts.

Impatient with this exchange, Hal pressed his question. "Okay, Daddy, so what is going on that I need to be told about? Is it what I just told you?"

Calvin pushed his chair back from the table and wiped his mouth, carefully placing his napkin on the table. Facing Hal, he began. "It's true we have also heard that many Congolese expected their lives to be far better after Independence. They have gradually become disappointed and angry because things have not in fact improved-- at least not here in the interior. Some unhappy folks have recently stirred up trouble in Idiofa, 100 miles north. We've heard that there have already been violent clashes between government supporters and those who want to overthrow the people in charge in Leopoldville."

"But my friends think there are *Jeunesse* near here, not a hundred miles away," Hal protested.

"If so, that's the first I've heard of it," Calvin continued. "I learned last week that the Portuguese palm oil factory just south of Idiofa was burned. Government troops were killed and driven off...or they ran away. Then, just a couple of days ago we received word that three school buildings at Gungu were set afire, and the teachers were roughed up. That's only 35 miles away. That's why MAF advised us to take your sisters further east to Mukedi to fly off to school. They think that Gungu is too dangerous."

Martha jumped in, "But you don't have to worry, sweetheart, we are still very safe here. Our local church friends have assured us that we are not in any danger from the rebels." She reached over to take Hal's hand. He ignored his mother's comment and withdrew his hand from hers as diplomatically as he could without signaling his annoyance.

"So, Daddy, what do *you* think? Will we have trouble here at Kisambo? The *Jeunesse* may be training guys from our own village, and you didn't even know about it. The elders know it's happening, but they don't know where."

"Ahem," Thomas entered the room, interrupting the family's discussion. As he set about clearing the dinner dishes, Martha addressed him in Kituba. *"Thomas, ba Jeunesse ikele pene pene awa?* (Are *Jeunesse* rebels training near here?) Are any of our villagers joining them?"

"No, mam, the *Jeunesse* are *ntama* (far away)," was his reply. Thomas continued picking up the silverware as he spoke, not looking up.

"Are you sure? Hal's friends tell him some of the young men from our village have been training with the rebels."

"They are just little boys telling stories, mam. Any *Jeunesse* in this region are a long way from Kisambo, *ntama.*" Thomas went about his duties without making eye contact with his employers. Hands full of dirty dishes, he returned to the kitchen.

Martha frowned, deep in thought. Casting a quizzical glance at her spouse, she mused, "Do you think Thomas can understand English?"

2 Kisambo Village

January 1964

Three small, dusty brown torsos, sweat-lined and attired only in ragged cutoffs shuffled down the rutted trail through the edge of the forest toward the village. The intense tropical sun and still air meant that few others – man or beast – were moving about at this oppressive time of day. Blotchy shadows from dense foliage had just begun their afternoon migration. High above, white and gray thunderheads spiked up into a clear blue sky, making a typical afternoon appearance during this season of the year. Today, however, the celestial billows had formed over the forest a good distance away. It looked like the three friends would not have to dash for shelter from a downpour after all.

The boys had avoided discussing the previous afternoon's abrupt dispatching by the mother of their friend, Hal. Nsukula, aka Nsuka, the oldest of the trio was the first to broach the topic. "*Mindeles* are strange. Our mamas would not drag us off like that. Hal's mama looked angry, but for nothing. Do you think she'll beat him, for not hearing her? Or will she get Rev. Schroeder to do it?" Half spinning around, he batted at a cluster of white butterflies fluttering around a bush by the path.

Ilunga, following right on his heals, smiled as he gave his friend a hardy, two-handed shove, causing him to stumble off the path. "Not your mama, anyway. She had too many little ones to keep in line before you came along. That's why she named you Nsukula (the end)." That reference to the Kituba meaning of his name brought giggles all around.

"You'd think *Lumwenu* (the clairvoyant one) would have seen his mama's *mpasi* (trouble) coming," chimed in Tika, still chuckling.

"*Keba* (careful) using that name. Hal would have *mpasi mingi* (lots of trouble) if his parents or the other *mindele* (whites) missionaries knew he has the gift." Nsuka circled around catching Tika in a neck hold as he spoke. He rapped his friend sharply on the forehead with his knuckles to emphasize his point. "And that's no joke."

"Eiyee! Hey, *Lumwenu* is the Kikongo name your *tata* (father) calls him. He's the one who discovered it. He's the one who's showing him how to use the gift."

"Yeah, but if Hal got ears pulled just for not listening, guess what his mama would do if she knew he's learned some of my *tata's kindoki* (sorcery). *Tata* says Hal is special. He warned me that we must be very careful not to reveal this secret. That goes especially for you, Tika, since your *tata* is pastor and close with the *mindeles*."

By this time, the threesome had arrived at the wide, sandy lane that marked the center of the village. Rows of mud and stick structures lined each side of the street. Most had thatched roofs and carefully swept dirt yards, permitting their residents to identify any nighttime visitors, human or animal, welcome or not. Here and there stood low cement walls where a few prosperous villagers had begun to construct more substantial homes, Congo-style. That is, the structures rose very slowly, a few blocks at a time, whenever the owners could save enough for a sack of cement.

Two huge mango trees shaded the only completed block building in the village. Its rusty tin roof and central location identified it as the village chief's domicile. Chickens pecked at fallen mangos in the front yard, squeals and snorts sounded from the side, giving further evidence of the headman's wealth and status. The front of the building was painted sky blue, but only the one wall. Apparently, the supply of paint, money, and motivation - or all three - had impeded completion of the project.

As the boys approached, a loud rumble of diesel engines sounded from the edge of the village, halting them in their tracks. Three large, green trucks - a huge Mercedes followed by two Land Rovers – came roaring down the broad street in a billowing cloud of dust. Chickens squawked and flew out of the way; mamas grabbed their small children; dogs barked and joined the chase. Brakes squealing, the trucks stopped directly in front of Chief Ntotilla's home. By the time the dust began to settle, a bevy of uniformed soldiers had descended from all three vehicles, rifles in hand.

The passenger door of the big Mercedes opened slowly. All eyes in the assembling group of soldiers turned toward a short, stocky figure that slowly descended to the street. He was clad in a

crisply ironed sweat-stained military uniform. It barely contained his ample girth. The officer sported mirrored sunglasses and a maroon beret. His authority was immediately evident to all. By now, the "all" included virtually the entire village that had gathered in response to the visitors' sudden and unexpected arrival.

The trio of boys crept around the side of the big Mercedes to get a better look. Their village was seldom visited by any vehicles let alone military ones. This surprise appearance was cause for great interest. At that moment, however, it was a toss-up whether curiosity or alarm was the stronger draw for the growing circle of residents. Two squads of soldiers, just short of twenty in total, stood by quietly while the villagers noisily chattered among themselves in nervous expectation. Something important was happening right in the center of their little world, but what?

Ntotilla, the village's patriarch emerged from his residence having hastily donned his chiefly garb: a special beaded hat, a beaded scepter in hand, topped with a long tuft of zebra hair, and a dark, ill-fitting, western style suit coat. He greeted the thickset officer and offered him a chair and a cup of palm wine. The visitor accepted the vessel, took a sip and spit it out at the chief's feet. "Summon the elders!" *Benga bango nyoki-nyoki!* (call them immediately!) he demanded.

Wide-eyed, the boys looked at one another and shrunk back slightly. "This isn't going to go well," whispered Nsuka to his companions who nodded in silent reply.

Chief Ntotilla beckoned the village elders to step forward. As each emerged from the crowd he was immediately gripped by waiting soldiers and positioned before the officer. Others of the military men performed crowd control, moving the village onlookers back. "*Attention! Bozonga nsima!*" (move back!)

"Tell me about the *Jeunesse*," demanded the burly officer in a loud voice. "When did they visit your village? What did they tell you? How many of your young men have they recruited?" Sunglasses hid any expression from the headman's face but his booming, angry tone and stubby finger, jabbing in their faces, made the elders tremble. The crowd grew silent.

Most of the village leaders just shook their heads or lifted shoulders and palms to indicate ignorance. Two of their number managed to squeak out, "*Na yebi te*" (I don't know). Finally, Chief

Ntotilla spoke up, "We know nothing of the *Jeunesse* in this village. We are told they are far from here. Idiofa, perhaps. Not Kisambo. I would know if they came here."

Scoffing, the stout interrogator once again turned to the village elders. This time he stalked down the line of older men being held firmly in place by his soldiers. Glaring directly into the eyes of each in turn, he demanded, "Tell me what you know about the *Jeunesse!*" One by one the trembling figures stared down or to one side shaking their heads and swearing their ignorance of rebels and rebellion.

As he came to the last elder, the officer sharply pivoted. Grasping the startled Ntotilla's jacket with both hands by the lapel, he pulled him forward until his face was directly in front of the shiny sunglasses on his nose. "You listen well, chief. If I find out you and your elders have not told me the truth, you are going to pay. We will first break your legs, then have our way with your women and finally we will burn your village. The *Jeunesse* and their friends will soon discover it does not pay to oppose the government." Pausing for effect, he continued, "And now, it is time for my soldiers to collect payment for their hard work keeping Congo free of rebels."

With that, the officer raised his right hand and with a circular motion, signaled to his men. He then turned and deliberately made his way back into the Mercedes. On cue, the army regulars dashed about the village in search of livestock. Here and there could be seen short pursuits: burly men in military uniforms chasing after fleeing pigs, goats and chickens. In the end, a menagerie of squealing, grunting and squawking animals were captured, bound and tossed into the back of the army vehicles. Having completed their mission, the soldiers piled in behind their bounty. Engines roared to life and the small invading caravan departed the same way it had arrived, rapidly, in a cloud of dust.

Nsuka had tears in his eyes. Tika reached for his arm, "Are you scared, *mpangi* (friend)?" The older boy nodded. "But not for me, Tika, for my brother. Now, *Tata* is going to be really mad. My brother will *never* come home when he hears about the soldiers' visit. What he's doing is not just dangerous for him. It may also bring harm to the elders. He won't return any time soon, for sure. I'm afraid he's into something really bad."

#3 Kisambo Station

January 1964

Elizabeth Clausen hummed a familiar hymn as she stacked the bandages on the clinic shelf. *"Oh, the deep, deep love of Jesus; Vast, unmeasured, boundless free..."* Her dark hair was pulled into a bun, and her blue eyes sparkled as she went about her duties. This was the part of her day that she enjoyed the most...helping out the nursing staff. Organizing came easy for her and as the good Lord knew, they could surely use her help in that busy medical clinic. It was a constant challenge to keep track of things. Misplaced supplies had a way of quickly disappearing, but not nearly as frequently under the watchful eye of this orderly missionary.

"Hey Beth. I was hoping I'd find you here." Elsie Buller, the clinic's veteran missionary nurse stuck her head and shoulders around the door. She was dressed in a white uniform and had her trademark nurses' cap on. The hat was an unnecessary touch in that rural location, but Elsie felt it communicated a measure of professionalism and authority to her patients. Never married, she had spent the last half of her 50-something years working in small out of the way medical clinics in the Congo. In contrast to some of the other single ladies in her mission, she was far from somber and colorless. Her graying hair and wiry frame offered no hint of the boundless energy and enthusiasm they barely contained. Elsie was constantly in motion. Today was no exception.

"Barbara was looking for you. She seemed upset. It appears the girls from the village are not being allowed to come to the station to play. She said that she's finished her homework and is bored...wants her Momma to come home." With that, Elsie made a quick wave and headed off in her usual brisk pace, calling out over her shoulder, "Just passing along the message. Gotta go!"

The smile slowly faded from Elizabeth's face as she paused in her duties to glance out the window in the direction of her house. She wondered if she should heed Barbara's request and head for home or continue on and complete her duties. Just then, one of the nurses' aides walked in with a stack of towels. Elizabeth turned to take the armload from her African colleague. In Kituba she asked, "Kintuntu, do you know why the village girls aren't being allowed to come play with Barbara?"

The uniformed worker shook her head and offered a quick reply. "No, Mme. Elizabeth. Perhaps they have extra duties at home." She did not linger for further conversation but hurried off in the direction she had come.

"That's curious," Elizabeth thought to herself. *"Kintuntu is usually very chatty. I wonder if the village folk are starting to feel uneasy from the reports of trouble we've been hearing about."*

She finished stacking the bandages, arranged the towels in their place in the cabinet and headed to the front of the clinic. There, waiting patiently in the lobby, were a handful of village mamas attired in colorful pagnes with babies wrapped to their backs. Young children chased around them in front of the counter. "I wonder where all the patients are," she reflected out loud. "It's pediatric clinic day and there's usually a crowd filling the reception area with a line out the door."

"Where are all the patients today, Rosine? We don't seem to have much business," she inquired of the receptionist seated behind the sign-in counter.

"Most people are staying home, Mme. Elizabeth. There's been some trouble nearby," was the reply.

Elizabeth rested a friendly hand on her colleague's shoulder. "I'm leaving a bit early today, myself. I need to check on my daughter." The young woman looked up, smiling and waved an acknowledgement in silent reply before resuming her duties with the patient before her.

Elizabeth left the clinic cutting across the grass to the stone-lined dirt pathway leading to her residence. She walked with rapid, purposeful strides, just short of breaking into a jog. Between Barbara's grounded friends, the missing clinic patients, Kintutu's terse reply and Rosine's comment about trouble, her head was spinning. What is happening around here?

She had no sooner reached the stone porch steps of her house than she heard her name being called from behind. "Beth, wait up!" It was the familiar sound of her husband's voice. She turned just in time to catch his arrival from the Schroeder's place and to return a hurried hug. Breathless, he tugged at her elbow, motioning in the direction of the corner of the house. "I wanted to catch you before you went in. Let's talk in private over here."

"What's up, Larry? Something's wrong around here, isn't it!"

"A little while ago I sat in on the afternoon's short-wave net at the Schroeder's place. Only yesterday we heard about those three Gungu classrooms being burned. Now, it appears an attack has taken place at the small government outpost in Vudi, just to the west of us. The report is that the agents fled, and the buildings were torched. There may have even been a killing there as well, though that's not been confirmed. We have been advised to be alert. I'm thinking we may need to be ready to leave Kisambo on short notice."

Larry Clausen's balding head was creased with worry and beaded with sweat. His shirttail had come out. The white shirt bore sweat lines in front and back. His sleeves were rolled up, collar open. Wrinkled kaki chinos and dusty, sandal-clad feet completed his crumpled school administrator's attire. He clearly occupied the opposite end of the "organized" scale from his neatly dressed spouse.

The two of them moved to the shade at the corner of their residence. Larry lowered his voice. "Yes, Beth. I'd say trouble is clearly escalating. I thought I'd better alert you before we say much to Barbara. She's such a little worry-wart."

"There are some troubling signals at the clinic as well, Larry. That's why I headed home early." Elizabeth told him of her concerns about the absence of village folk at the station, the denials and lack of openness she perceived from clinic staff. "How serious is this? Do you think we are in any immediate danger?"

Larry pulled a wrinkled and well-used handkerchief from his back pocket and wiped his forehead. Before he could answer her question, Elizabeth reached out and snatched the cloth from his hand. "Good night, Larry! Give me that dirty rag. We have clean handkerchiefs in the drawer." He briefly rolled his eyes, before returning to the conversation.

"Cal tells me he has had assurances from our local church leaders that we are safe, and that if trouble comes this way they will look after us missionaries, but he also said that he has been getting mixed messages about the rebellion. Most claim to know nothing about it. He thinks a good deal more rebel activity is happening here locally than we have been led to believe. I've gotten the same impression from the teaching staff I've talked to."

At that moment, the front screen door banged open and eleven-year-old Barbara came flying down the front steps, blond ponytail flying, and words streaming out. "Mommy, Daddy...I thought I heard you out here. I'm so glad you're home. I was getting worried. I told Alongi to go to the clinic and have Elsie find you and have you come home. My friends have to stay in the village. They won't say why. I don't want to be at home alone." She clasped her parents in a three-way hug as they exchanged uneasy glances above her.

"Let's go inside where it's cooler," Larry proposed. "We can talk better there."

The three Clausens moved up the front steps, Barbara in between, holding her parents' hands. It was noticeably cooler in the high-ceilinged living room of their cement block residence. Elizabeth pointed in the direction of the couch and big chair. "You two sit. I'll get the lemonade."

"And cookies too?" Barbara called out as her mother left the room.

In his usual direct way, without further small talk Larry got right to the subject at hand. "Barb, honey, I think I know why your friends couldn't come to the station today."

"Really? Why, daddy?" Barbara scrunched her face in a puzzled look.

Larry sat forward, elbows on his knees. He looked straight into his daughter's inquiring blue eyes. "I think it's because their parents are worried about the reports of rebel activity near here."

"What is 'rebel activity' and what does it have to do with my friends staying home?"

"The rebels are people who think the Congo government is bad. They think the leaders have made things worse since Independence – that they have lied and stolen wealth that was supposed to go to the people. The rebels want to throw them out, to take over and put their own people in charge."

"But..." Barbara began, as her father held up his hand to interrupt. "They have already used violence north of here, in Idiofa and more recently near Gungu. People are worried that they might do the same here."

"We're not the government, Daddy. Why would they bother us?"

Elizabeth entered the living room with a tray containing three

19

glasses of lemonade and a small plate of cookies. "This sounds like a verrry serious conversation," she said with animation. Her slight smile signaled mock seriousness. "Can I join in as well?"

"Of course, Mommy, don't be silly," said the ponytailed child reaching for a cookie.

When all three had glasses and oatmeal treats in hand, Larry continued. "Barbara, because some of our mission leaders are concerned for our safety, they have asked us to each pack a small bag in case we have to leave in a hurry. Your mother and I don't think we'll have to go - we have good African friends who are looking out for us - but we'd better do what our leaders say and be prepared."

Barbara stopped eating and put her glass down. Her eyes filled with tears and her chin was quivering. "That sounds really scary, Daddy. Maybe the rebels will try to hurt us because we live in a big house like the rich government folks in Leopoldville. But we're here to help the people, aren't we?"

Elizabeth moved over next to her daughter on the couch and pulled her close in a hug. "You don't have to be afraid, sweetheart. If trouble comes closer, we'll just move out of the way. We can talk to Jesus about this. He loves us and told us not to fear."

Barbara hugged her mother with both arms, pressing her face into her bosom. "Maybe you can just talk to Jesus and not be scared but I can't." Mother and Father exchanged silent glances.

#4 The Forest

January 1964

Biungu slowed his pace, moving even more cautiously along the narrow game path through the deepening afternoon shadows of the jungle. Soon, he reasoned, he and his companion, Njoli, would have to leave the path entirely and use extra care as they neared the edge of the forest. It would not do for them to encounter anyone from the village. If word got back to Tata that they were nearby, he would surely pursue them day and night. That would end any participation in the *"La Deuxième Indépendence,"* (the Second Independence), as their cause was known. It would end participation...or worse.

The two young Congolese glided along through the forest making steady progress, barefoot, legs slightly bent, machetes adeptly slicing as they crouched and twisted, stepping carefully to avoid brushing overhanging leaves and branches, silent shadows in motion. Both were dressed in tattered khaki shorts and baggy tee shirts with faded logos, long ago acquired from the missionaries.

Leading the way, Biungu was at high alert, listening for any subtle shift in the sounds of the jungle. Bird calls, chattering of monkeys overhead, shifts in the background tones of insect hums, anything that might signal the presence of others was a cause for concern. At several points he paused, holding his hand up to signal Njoli to stop, tilting his head to listen before proceeding. Fluttering above in the mottled sunlight were scores of migrating white Mabamba butterflies. At last, they came to a large tree stump covered with multicolored mushrooms. Biungu paused, pointing out the familiar signpost to his companion. Still silent, he then signaled to the right and parting the bushes, headed off in that direction.

A few minutes later the dense forest foliage opened up to a small clearing roughly five meters across. It was a cave-like setting with thick surrounding bushes and vines hanging overhead under the forest canopy high above. Two low flat slab chairs had been placed alongside several sizeable wood blocks providing seating. The seats were arranged in a semi-circle around a small black fire ring at the center.

"This is where I have arranged to meet my brother," Biungu said to his partner, in low tones as he lowered himself into one of the chairs. "He should be here shortly." He reached for the gourd at his waist to take a sip of water.

""You knew exactly where to come. What is this place?" asked Njoli, glancing slowly around the clearing.

"This is our secret spot. It's where some of us kids from the village used to sneak away and meet. When I was younger, sometimes one of our group would bring some *malafu* (palm wine) or smokes. None of our parents knew about it." Njoli smiled and nodded as he sat in one of the slab chairs and picked at a chigger in his big toe.

The two friends rested in the dim light and visited quietly for several minutes before Biungu stopped mid-sentence and held up his hand. "*Shhhh...wa* (listen)!" Twigs snapped and leaves rustled. Someone was headed their way.

The rustling stopped, bushes parted, and a young head and shoulders emerged, peering cautiously into the clearing.

"Nsukula, *ndeko!*" Biungu was on his feet in an instant, crying out as he pulled his brother into the clearing with a hearty two-handed clasp in greeting. He motioned in the direction of his companion, who had also jumped to his feet, "This is my good friend, Njoli. We have been together in the training camp. His village is near Gungu." Holding his brother at arm's length, he declared, "And this is my little brother, Nsuka, who...is no longer so little."

Njoli smiled, "He is as tall as you, friend. Watch out for soon, *ye akobula yo, ya solo* (he will certainly beat you up), instead of vice versa." The two spoke in Lingala, a requirement of their *Jeunesse* membership.

Nsuka moved to the side as two more slender figures made their way through the thick bushes into the cave-like setting. "I hope you don't mind, brother, but I brought Tika and Ilunga with me. It's okay for them to be here, isn't it? The three of us have visited this place before. We've never told anyone about it."

Biungu frowned, then sighed and slapped his brother on the back. "Yeah, I guess it's okay. But they cannot let anyone know that we were here. Not anyone!" He looked back and forth into each boy's eyes. Both of Nsuka's young companions shook their heads. "*Ata muntu ve* (No one!)," they said in unison, responding in Kituba.

"So how are Mama and sister Makiese? And our animals...are all well?" Biungu put off inquiring about Tata. That was likely to be a more difficult report.

"Everyone is fine. But we miss you. The soldiers that came to the village a few days ago took our best goat and one of the pigs."

Nsuka abruptly changed the subject. "Biungu, Tata is very angry with you. Mama is worried but Tata is mad. He thinks that you and the others from our village who joined the *Jeunesse* have put us all in danger." Nsuka held his brother's hand as he spoke. His eyes radiated fear and anxiety, clearly evident even in the dim light.

"What is so important about this *Jeunesse* thing, *mbuta* (older brother), that you stay away and stir up Tata's anger? I don't understand."

The older brother led his younger sibling to one of the wood blocks and gestured. "*Fanda* (Sit), brother. I will explain to you and your friends why I am a part of this movement. But before I do so I want to let you know why I asked you to meet me here today. You see, I need your help in getting some of my things from our home. I can't take the chance of being seen by Tata or his friends. They would keep me from my mission."

"What do you want me to get?" Nsuka asked, cringing with apprehension. He had only triggered their father's anger on a couple of occasions in the past, but his back still bore the marks of those whippings. Father's anger was a fearsome thing, and he wasn't anxious to repeat the experience. Not even by fulfilling his elder brother's request.

"I need my hunting bow and arrows and my favorite bush knife. Oh yes, I'd also like you to bring my extra pair of shorts under the sleeping mat. Can you get them out of the house and bring them to me without anyone seeing you? I don't want to get you in trouble." The last part he added as an afterthought.

Nsuka scratched at a bug bite on his arm, looked at the ground and furrowed a crease between his eyebrows as he considered Biungu's request. It could be difficult to get those items out of their small house without being noticed. Tata would clearly not approve of him furnishing weapons to his estranged brother. He sighed deeply before responding.

"For you, Biungu, I will take the chance, but I don't like it. Tell me why you need those things, why you are willing to place us both on the path of trouble."

"It is worth the risk to take back our country from the thieves and crooked officials in Leopoldville. In the past three years they have robbed us of the fruits of Independence and left us with mere scraps. They drive their Mercedes, but when have you seen a new bicycle around here? They dress in fine clothes and eat in restaurants, but we can't buy cloth for a pagne or salt for our greens. They send their children to be educated in other countries, but we have no money to even attend the village school. They prosper from the work of others, like the *mbembele* (mosquito) sucks the blood of men. It is time for a second independence. We true Congolese must throw out the blood suckers and their Belgian backers if we ever want to enjoy the riches of Independence."

Biungu was on his feet, gesturing with sweeping motions, eyes blazing. His companion, Njoli sat quietly, arms folded, an admiring smile on his face. The three young members of Biungu's audience looked on with open mouths and rapt attention.

"The father of our movement is a fellow MuPende from the Kwilu, Gizenga Antoine. Have you heard that name?" The young listeners shook their heads. "He is President of the PSA, the *Parti Solidaire Africain*, the official name of our group. Most people call us simply *Jeunesse* because so many of us are young. Gizenga's friend, Mulele Pierre, is the one who has been teaching us the ways of revolution, showing us how to defeat the crooked government. He is a BaMbunda from Idiofa, and also a spiritual man, well versed in the ways of our ancestors."

While Biungu was speaking, Ilunga rose from his seat, picked up a dead branch and began to break off and stack small twigs into a cone in the center of the fire ring. Taking a flint from the pouch at his waist, he chipped at it with his knife until a small shower of sparks flew into the dry grass at the center of the cone. After several hardy puffs the smoldering embers burst into flame, illuminating the dim clearing. Larger pieces of wood were added to the fire circle and soon the flames were well established. The flickering firelight added to the intimacy of the occasion. Biungu paused in his discourse to poke at the flames with a stick.

Tika broke the silence. "What is this 'revolution training' you spoke of? What are the *Jeunesse* planning to do to defeat the bad government? They are too strong. Aren't you just looking for sausage in the dog's house?"

"Well, young friend, we have learned that the ancestors will smile upon us as long as we carefully follow the instructions of our leaders. In order to remove the miseries of the Leopoldville thieves and their *"bampangi na bo"* (partners in crime), all the common people of Congo must rise up, village by village. We must refuse to pay taxes and refuse to obey bad chiefs, soldiers and police. If they come after us, as they are now doing, we must enter into combat and repel them with force. Mulele says we must rid the land of all reminders of our former Belgium oppressors. This means that we destroy bridges and ferries, burn state posts and take back the goods from wealthy merchants, goods that belong to the people."

The three young friends exchanged nervous glances. This was sounding scary...and dangerous. Tika repeated his question. "So how are the *Jeunesse* – how are you – going to defeat the army?"

Biungu, standing, placed his foot on the chair and leaned forward with one elbow on his knee. "Each village in the Kwilu has a *'quipe'* (*equipe* or team), and each 'quipe, a leader. Larger villages have several 'quipes. There are a dozen of us in the Kisambo village 'quipe. Njoli here was appointed as our leader. He has had extra training and he successfully carried out a mission near his home."

Ilunga leaned into Nsuka and whispered, "Yeah, he probably was the one who burned down the school in Gungu." Nsuka did not reply. He waved off the comment, keeping his eyes fixed on his brother, who continued talking.

"At our camps we are also instructed in combat. We learn how to fight hand-to-hand. We practice with bows and arrows. Eventually, we will have guns to use. We have learned lots of things: how to make "Molotov cocktails," how to set trucks and buildings on fire, how to hide in the forest, how to confuse trackers who might try to follow us, how to cut cables on a ferry, and how to dig hidden pits to stop army trucks. We have rules for combat. We always go barefoot on missions in order to keep in touch with ancestral earth at all times. We live only with fellow comrades, tolerate no fighting among us, no sex before battles, always work hard and obey our leaders. We only use Lingala...no French. When we go into battle we chant 'Mai, Mulele' (Mulele's water) and any bullets shot at us by the military turn to harmless drops of water, just like they did for our leader. So, you see we can be outnumbered but not defeated... as long as we carefully follow all the rules."

"What's a 'Molotov cocktail?'" asked Tika.

Biungu replied, "It's a glass bottle filled with gasoline. A gauze rag is placed in the neck and lit. It is then thrown at a house or vehicle. Fire spreads instantly when the glass shatters. It's a great way to burn something down."

"What happens if someone doesn't follow the rules?" Ilunga interjected.

"Well, that person risks losing the protection that surrounds all of us who are faithful."

Nsuka shifted on his log seat and rubbed his toes that had gotten quite warm from the crackling fire. "What about the *mindeles* (white people) at Kisambo Station and other places? Are they bad? Will they be sent away...or harmed?" The crease between his eyebrows deepened into a straight line.

Njoli, who had remained silent until then, spoke up. "The missionary *mindeles* do some good things for the people, it is true, but they also are friends with Leopoldville who permits them to come here. They live in big houses filled with expensive goods that few of our people possess. When the Second Independence is successful, we will replace all their village schools and clinics with something much better. They have to go." In a quieter voice he added, "We do not have instruction on how this is to happen...*ntete ve* (not yet)."

Biungu clapped as if suddenly realizing the lateness of the hour. He stepped over to Nsuka, extended his hand and pulled him to his feet. "It's getting dark, brother, *kwenda, basika* (get out of here!). You and your friends must hurry back to the village before you are missed. Njoli and I will move to another spot we have located to spend the night and then return to this place tomorrow at the same time. Bring my things to me then. And if you can sneak out any of Mama's *chikwanga* (fermented manioc), bring that too. Now go."

With that, Nsuka and his two friends parted the bushes and headed back for the village, filled with new knowledge, but troubled at what it might mean for them and for their families and friends.

#5 Kisambo Station

January 1964

Blackness covered everything, an ebony blanket on a moonless night in the depths of the jungle, still and humid, radiating deadly menace. There was a hint of movement in the darkness, nothing that could actually be seen yet faint motion, nevertheless. Was it the soft rustling of leaves in multiple locations? The impending sense of danger was palpable.

A shaft of light from a small flame brought the blindness of the dark night to an abrupt end. Another and another followed it until a wide circle of flickering lights had formed. At the center of the wavering fire ring a group of shadowy dwellings became visible -- village huts. Chanting began: *"Mai, Mulele, mai Mulele."* The rhythmic words were repeated over and over, louder and louder until at last a high-pitched scream shattered the scene. The circle of flames began to move. In rapid succession, one after another, huts burst into flame as the torches were extended to dry thatch that ignited. Just as suddenly the entire scene exploded into chaos. Screams and war cries comingled, dark shadows and silhouettes tangled in desperate action, the ghosts of death and war dancing, fully at play.

"Nooo...help, stop!" Hal bellowed out at full voice, springing up in bed, sheets tangled about his slender frame, sweat dripping from his brow. Darkness fled from the bedroom as his mother rounded the corner carrying a brightly lit kerosene lamp in hand.

"It's okay, honey. It was just a bad dream." Her comforting words both subdued his alarm and brought him to full consciousness. Martha set the lamp on the table and sat beside her son on the bed wrapping him in a big hug. Hal was still trembling. Setting aside his pre-teen male pride, he hugged her back, eagerly wrapping both arms around her shoulders.

They sat in the embrace for several minutes without speaking. Hal continued to tremble. Martha finally reached over to untangle the sheets from his legs. "My, Hal that must have been some scary nightmare."

"It was awful, Mama. So real." In hesitant sentences he described the still vivid images that had invaded his sleep. "It's almost like I was actually there, watching it all happen. People were being killed...the village burned." He shuddered. "It was really creepy."

"Nightmares are like that, sweetheart. But it was just a dream and it's still the middle of the night. Why don't you get a drink of water, use the bathroom if you need to, and then I'll rub your back a little and we'll see if you can get back to sleep. Sweet dreams are in order for this round, okay?" Hal nodded with a weak smile and headed off to the bathroom. He was far from convinced that he'd do much sleeping through the remainder of this night, however.

Restless though the night proved to be, Hal did manage to drift off again. When he next opened his eyes, the bedroom was filled with light. Morning sun flooded through the window frame projecting a bright patterned replica on his bedroom wall. Hal rubbed the sleep out of his eyes and rolled out of bed. He could hear loud voices nearby speaking in Kituba. They seemed to be coming from the direction of the kitchen. He hastily pulled on his cut offs and tee shirt and headed down the hall.

Both Mama and Papa were listening intently to Thomas. He was clearly agitated, speaking loudly and gesturing with both hands. Though fluent in Kituba, Hal was unable to follow much of Thomas' rapid and loud exclamations. He picked up enough key words, however – "fire...*Jeunesse*... killed... blood" – to more than explain the expressions of alarm and horror on his parents' faces.

"What has happened?" he blurted out as he entered the kitchen, "What's wrong?"

Martha immediately drew Hal close in a hug, while Calvin held up a hand to halt Thomas' ranting. In a calm, steady voice he replied. "Thomas tells us that last night the village of Buta just over the hill was burned. His sister lives there and she managed to escape with her children, but it appears that her husband and several of his family members did not."

Hal glanced at Thomas' anguished face. Tears were streaming down. He swayed as he held his head with both hands, eyes closed, moaning.

"What happened, Papa? Was it...was it *Jeunesse*?"

"Yes, Hal, it appears it was." Cal spoke directly, candidly, without buffering the reality. "The village was surrounded. The people awoke to a circle of torches and chants, and then their homes were set ablaze. Many of the villagers were shot and wounded as they fled. Injured people have apparently been streaming to our clinic all night."

"Are we in danger, Papa?"

"That remains to be seen, Hal. No *Jeunesse* have shown up at Kisambo so far, but we need to contact our mission leaders right away to see what they recommend. According to Thomas, the chief at Buta and some of the village elders angered the *Jeunesse* by disciplining young men from the village who had joined their cause. Their violent and bloody response is a very serious development, especially since it has happened so close to us."

Cal turned to Thomas and placing a hand on his shoulder, addressed him in Kituba. "Can I pray for you and your family?" Thomas nodded, his body shaking from sobs.

"Father God, we are in need of your mercy and your protection. Evil has arisen and great harm has visited our brother Thomas and his family. We don't understand such things, how you can permit injury and death to innocents. We know you love us and care about our burdens, so we ask for your Spirit's tender comfort and care for Thomas' family and the others from Buta village as they grieve their great injuries and losses. We ask for your strong arm of protection in these dangerous times. Help us all to know how best to respond in the days to come. Amen."

Thomas grasped Calvin's hands in both of his. "Merci, Tata Calvin."

Cal gently guided him to the door. "You are needed at home today, Thomas. Go and care for your family." Thomas nodded and flicked a pained smile in reply as he headed out the door.

Cal ran his hand through his hair, his signature sign of worrying, before turning back to face his wife and son. "I think I'd better go now to check on our neighbors and bring them up to speed on what's happened. I'm pretty sure that Elsie already knows. No doubt she is busy working at the clinic. I'll be back shortly for our 8 AM phonie net with the other stations. You two plan to stay close to home today. Also, let's keep things closed up as a precaution, okay?"

After Cal left, both mother and son sat at the kitchen table for a long time without speaking, each one deep in thought. Hal stared at the tabletop as if his vision could bore a hole through it. He couldn't believe his father's words. They were like a perfect echo of his nightmare.

Martha stared at Hal, a strange, quizzical expression covering her face. Finally, in a quiet voice she observed, "You saw it all happen in your dream, didn't you, Hal?"

He looked up, with a start, shocked that she had seemingly read his mind. "What? No...I mean, sort of." His eyes pooled. "I didn't know it was going to be real," he stammered. "Maybe I could have...I should..." His voice trailed off. Shoulders shaking with silent sobs, he could no longer contain the tears.

Martha rose and put her arms around him. "Don't even go there, Hal. It was just a coincidence. You couldn't know what was going to happen. There's nothing you could do about it."

Hal's body shook with silent sobs. He did not want to tell Mama that this wasn't the first time his dreams had turned into reality.

***

The morning's phonie net prompted new plans for Calvin underscoring the mission administration's concern for the safety and well-being of Kisambo Station and its residents. At the conclusion of the morning's inter-station consult, Calvin was asked to participate in an emergency meeting of the field executive committee at Kindambo Station, a day's drive to the east. Its purpose was to assess the current situation in the Kwilu region generally, and at Kisambo Station in particular and to make plans accordingly.

Martha was heavy-hearted as she placed a food bag on the front seat of the light green Jeep Wagoneer for her husband's long drive -- sandwiches, pineapple slices and plantain chips in a cloth sack alongside a thermos of coffee. "Cal, this could be a very dangerous trip. I'm surprised that the other executive committee members actually expect you to make it. I'm glad at least you're taking Elsie's worker, Muteba with you in case of car trouble...or other trouble."

"Yes, sweetheart, I'll admit I'm a bit nervous as well about heading out right now, but Muteba will be good company. He has family in Kindambo and has traveled the road many times." Calvin checked to see his shovel and extra jerry can of gas were in the back as he threw in his overnight bag as well. "I guess I'll just have to tell any villagers who want a ride that it's too dangerous to take passengers and this is an emergency, because it's true."

He walked over to Martha and put his hands on her shoulders. Anxiety clouded his face. "I feel particularly uneasy leaving you and the others here when trouble has sprung up so close and so recently. But, as was pointed out to me, the executive committee really does need to hear directly about our situation in order to assess just how dangerous this *Jeunesse* threat may be. No one wants to leave the field this time if we don't have to. It was very disruptive and not well received when all of us evacuated so suddenly at Independence. Some of our Congolese friends felt then – and probably still feel – that we abandoned them, that we put our personal security above our commitment to them. We shouldn't be too hasty to repeat that experience."

"The 'too hasty' part I understand, but staying in harm's way is dangerous, even foolhardy if things continue to unravel. We shouldn't risk our lives unnecessarily, Cal." Martha, on the verge of tears, ended their exchange by clasping her husband in a tight embrace.

After the intense hug, Cal continued holding his wife, while he gently stroked her hair. "We've prayed about it, Martha, and we know the Lord is fully aware of our concerns...and our needs. Let's trust him for our safety on this journey, as we have for all our years together." Martha nodded, tearfully maintaining her grasp as if it could be their last.

A short time later, Calvin waved goodbye to his wife and son and to the three Clausens who had joined them on the porch and drove off the station grounds. He had a long wait at the Kwilu River crossing just below Kisambo. No less than a dozen vehicles were lined up on the steep road that descended to the water's edge. This was not a welcome sight. A relatively small ferry or "bac" as it was known, departed from there, accommodating only two vehicles at a time. The boat traversed the swiftly flowing river by means of cables attached to secure posts on each side, with the strong current providing the moving force. River crossings were thus by nature annoyingly slow, further compounded by a normal backlog of waiting vehicles.

It was midafternoon when Calvin finally drove up the ramp and onto the ferry, and nearly an hour later when he exited the floating transport on the other side of the river. He shifted down to ascend the steep hill that led from the ferry. Over the whine of the engine came the clamor of excited voices behind him. He stopped, pulled the emergency brake, swung open the door and stepped down to check out what was happening back at the river. *"Inki mambo, Muteba?"* (What's happening?)

What they saw was alarming. The bac was not at the loading site but floating offshore several hundred yards down river. It held a full load of vehicles and a small cluster of frantically waving passengers. The cables no longer held the craft in place. They had been severed. Whether the disabling was intentional or accidental, it was obvious to Calvin that there would be no more ferry crossings made at this point for some time to come. No returning back the way he had come. Though it had barely begun, this trip was already getting complicated. He slowly climbed back into the Jeep, whispered a silent prayer, turned on the engine and headed off.

#6 Kisambo Station

January 1964

The rest of the morning Hal tried to do his math homework, but he just couldn't concentrate. He kept thinking about the fire and burning huts, the screams and chants of *"Mai, Mulele."* And the dream that was real. It was confusing and troubling. Not something an adult could figure out, let alone a twelve-year old mind. And Papa was now heading out alone to his meeting with the other missionaries. It felt so...scary to have him gone.

Hal sat at his little desk mulling these thoughts over, absent-mindedly bouncing his scuffed-up soccer ball against the wall. "Ko-Ko" came a soft voice from outside the bars of his open window. He jumped up and rushed to the sill, grasping the crisscrossed bars with both hands as he looked down to find the smiling face of Tika looking back at him. *"Kweza, nduku*; come on in, friend."

Hal rushed down the hall to open the front door, calling out as he passed the kitchen, "It's Tika, Mama. I'm going to let him in."

Martha was in the middle of mixing some cookies and started to object but had second thoughts. Hal could probably use the distraction. That's what her cookie making was about as well. "Okay, sweetheart, but close the door after you let him in, won't you please?"

When Hal opened the door, Tika was not alone. Ilunga was with him as well. The boys greeted one another with the special handshake and hip bounce that they had invented, giggling as they inevitably did when employing it. "Let's go to my room," Hal announced. Martha greeted the two familiar visitors as they passed by, "I'll have some fresh cookies for you boys in a few minutes." That brought a smile to all three faces.

The friends settled down on the bedroom floor in a tight triangle cross-legged, facing one another, knees nearly touching. Tika immediately launched into conversation. "Have you heard, *Lumwenu*? Buta village was burned last night. Some people were killed, many wounded by the *Jeunesse*. Everyone is alarmed. Perhaps Kisambo will be next."

"We heard about it from Thomas first thing this morning," Hal replied. "His brother-in-law was killed. My father spoke with our mission people on the phonie net this morning and now he's on his way to Kindambo to meet with the other leaders and figure out what to do."

Tika and Ilunga both nodded, somberly. After a pause Ilunga volunteered, "We're actually here because Muzeka Adoko sent us. He would have sent Nsukula, but he doesn't want him to leave home because he's afraid that Biungu will take him away to join him with the *Jeunesse*. So, he sent us to see you. Our fathers don't know we're here."

Hal sat back with his hands flat on the floor, arms locked. "Why did he send you to see me?" The hair began to rise on the back of his neck. He was not getting a good feeling about this visit. He really did not want to hear the answer but had to ask anyway.

Tika responded. "You need to know that we met with Biungu and a *Jeunesse* friend of his at our secret forest spot. He asked Nsuka to get some of his things from his hut including his arrows and bush knife. They told us all about the *Jeunesse*. They have recruits from every village in the Kwilu. They plan to take back Congo and make things better. Unfortunately, Muzeka found out about our meeting. He suspects Biungu was part of the Buta raiding party. He wants to know if Kisambo is going to be next. He thinks you can tell us."

Hal swallowed hard. A cold shiver coursed through his body as he looked first at one and then the other set of expectant eyes. He wanted to run away and hide. What should he say? Finally, he managed to mumble, "Um, how...? I don't know anything about..." His voice trailed off.

Tika leaned forward and looked directly into Hal's eyes. "*Lumwenu*," using the nickname given by Muzeka, "Did you see the Buta raid before it happened?"

Hal flushed. He couldn't deny it, especially to his friends. Tears began to flow. "I can't help it. It's not my fault. It just happened. It was a nightmare. When morning came, I found out it was real. The village burned, the people...it was awful." He covered his face with his hands. His body shook.

The two Congolese friends looked at one another and nodded in acknowledgment. After a short pause, Tika turned to Hal, "Have you seen anything of Kisambo? Muzeka said that if you haven't yet seen it in a dream you should toss the bones in the way he showed you and tell us what you learn from them, from the ancestors. He is very worried. Biungu may be about to shed the blood of his own people or be killed by them."

"I...I haven't dreamed anything having to do with Kisambo." Hal blurted out as he rose to his feet. He ran his hand through his hair. "And I don't know about the bones thing...what if I get it wrong? What if someone finds out...like your father, Tika...or mine? I'd really be in big trouble."

"But Muzeka has confidence in you. Nsuka is counting on you, too. It could be the difference of life and death in their family...for ours as well! You've got to do it, *Lumwenu*...you have been given a gift."

"I don't know...I'm not sure it's okay," Hal said in an unconvincing tone as he moved toward his closet where he kept the bones hidden.

At that moment, Martha stepped into the room with a plate of warm cookies. All three boys jumped as if stuck with a pin. Their reaction was so dramatic that she stopped and frowned. "What's going on here? Are you boys doing something you shouldn't?"

Hal spun around with the bones bag behind his back. "No, Mama, we were just talking about the Buta thing and it's got us all jumpy. It's pretty scary, you know."

Martha set the cookie plate down. Her face relaxed at Hal's response. "Yes, it is an upsetting thing for all of us. We're trusting the Lord to protect us and at the same time being wise and careful. I'm sure your parents are doing the same, boys. Now I've brought you some fresh cookies to take those worries away. Enjoy." And with that, she headed back down the hall.

The boys eagerly helped themselves to the cookie plate. In between bites, Ilunga whispered, "Whew, that was close. Now we need to head *nyoki* (immediately) for the sacred spot in the forest. Push your bone-things out the window so your mama doesn't see them."

Hal opened the screen and pushed a small burlap sack and a rolled-up animal skin through the bars that crossed the open bedroom window. Then the three friends headed down the hall, cookies in hand. "We're going to check the rabbit hutch in the back, mama. Ilunga's mama asked him to see if we've got a good breeder for them to buy. Then we're just gonna mess around out back."

Martha smiled. "Okay, but don't wander far. I'd feel better if you stay close by, Hal."

Hal picked up the bag and skin he'd dropped and after checking that they were not seen, the three bee-lined for the nearby tree line at a full gallop. Tika led the trio into the thick foliage, whacking leaves here and there with his machete as they made their way along a faint forest path. Shortly, they came to a small clearing with packed earth that signaled it had seen frequent visitors. A half-dozen or more tree stumps that bordered the clearing appeared to be coated with old candle wax; stubs of burned incense sticks stuck out of the wax.

Ilunga smiled and said in a hushed voice, "This is the place, for sure. I can feel the presence of the ancestors here."

Hal carried the small burlap sack and a rolled-up animal skin to the center of the shady clearing. He unfurled the soft skin. It formed an uneven circle about a meter across. Next, he placed a small candle on one of the tree stumps and lit it with the matches he had brought from his room. He also lit a short stick of incense that he pressed into the wax on the side of the candle. Finally, he withdrew a small mirror, *tala-tala*, through which the ancestors supposedly communicated. Kneeling before the skin, he emptied out the bony contents from the sack. He then paused and quietly repeated the chant to the ancestors that Muzeka had taught him. Picking up each piece, Hal arranged them between his two hands in the manner his mentor had shown him. Quietly, but speaking aloud, Hal asked the question: "Will Kisambo be attacked by the *Jeunesse*?" Holding his arms straight out, he released the bones.

Tika moved in to get a better look. Ilunga took a couple of steps closer, leaning over Hal's shoulder to view the bones. The handful of brittle white objects fell with a soft clatter just in front of Hal. He stared at them and then at the *tala-tala* for a long time before speaking.

"Most of the bones fell very close to me. That means something is to occur soon. The three forming an upside-down triangle means something is going away. The bones closest to me that are all lined straight up and down mean a definite "Yes" to my question. Finally, the upside down "U" shape of those remaining bones means...bad luck." The color had drained from Hal's face and his eyes were narrowed. Grimacing, he looked up at first one and then the other of his friends. "I'm pretty sure the bones say that Kisambo is going to be attacked, and it will happen soon."

The three friends all remained motionless for what seemed like a long time, though in reality it was just a moment or two. Then, without saying another word, Ilunga blew out the candle, and wetting his thumb and finger snuffed out the incense stick. Tika scooped up the bones and returned them to the sack while Hal rolled up the throwing skin. Without further discussion, the boys walked silently back down the trail, parting at the edge of the forest. Somberly, they exchanged their *"Kwenda Mbote"* goodbyes and the two young Congolese scurried off in the direction of the village.

Hal headed slowly back to his home, eyes glistening.

#7 Kindambo Station

January 1964

The short but colorful sunset was fading to soft pastels when Calvin and Muteba finally drove onto the grounds of Kindambo Station. It was a rough but thankfully, uneventful day. Villagers in the small settlements he passed through merely waved at his dust-clouded vehicle and showed little interest in halting him or expressing displeasure at the *mundele* in the jeep. No signs of *Jeunesse* along the way. He only encountered one army roadblock on the entire day's drive and even that stop was benign. After the usual banter and short delay, he was amiably waved through without any attempt to shake loose some sort of toll. That was surely cause for rejoicing in his mind.

Muteba scurried off to his relatives' place in the village nearby. Calvin was directed to the station's guesthouse, where he stashed his bag and washed up before heading across the compound to the Yoder's place for dinner. The others on the mission executive committee would join them there later. Sarah Yoder was full of questions regarding Martha, Hal and the girls who were away at school as she passed the beans and potatoes. Martin, on the other hand, wanted to hear details about the *Jeunesse* and the burning of Buta village. Calvin barely had time to finish his fried chicken as the first of the committee members arrived at the door.

Interest was high in Calvin's report on conditions at Kisambo. The other four men fired questions at him. What have you seen? Heard? Are the *Jeunesse* organized in the village? Do the rebels have local support? Do the missionaries? What's the position of the village elders regarding the rebellion? Have you or Larry Clausen received any complaints about wages from teachers or medical staff? What's the status of the station's fuel supply? How reliable are the vehicles and the phonie? If rebels threaten the station, what can be done to protect the safety of mission personnel and the non-Bapende Bible school students in residence?

At the end of the evening the executive committee arrived at consensus on several points. First, the safety of the non-local students and mission personnel was primary. Calvin was encouraged to return home and meet with the Kisambo church elders to solicit their assurance of protection.

Second, additional fuel was needed in case of an emergency evacuation. Two of the men from Kindambo were directed to purchase fuel in Gungu and drive it down in the next couple of days. It was determined that they should also deliver a new short-wave radio that could be operated off of a car battery. The present short-wave radio ran off the station's diesel generator and that could be vulnerable in emergency conditions.

Finally, the committee concluded that they should consult via phonie the next morning with the mission's legal representative, Paul Gingrich. He lived in Tshikapa, a city 110 kms distance from the station. His was the final word regarding any evacuation decision since he was in regular contact with Congolese political and military authorities.

Calvin spent a very restless night. His head was spinning. He was perplexed that he did not know more about the imminent threat of the *Jeunesse*. He had found himself responding to many of his colleagues' questions with, "I'm just not sure. It's not clear. Our Congolese neighbors claim that they know nothing of the rebels, that they are but a distant threat at best." The Gungu attacks and now the Buta situation seemed to indicate otherwise. Are they intentionally withholding information? If so, why?

The next morning Calvin headed back to the Yoder's for breakfast and to participate in the daily inter-station phonie net. Kindambo's phonie was housed there. The various stations were still checking in when Larry Clausen's gravelly voice interrupted the process. "This is an urgent message from Kisambo station to Calvin Schroeder at Kindambo. Conditions here are deteriorating rapidly. We request your immediate return."

That message sent a cold chill down Calvin's spine. It prompted statements of alarm and prayerful concern from all of the mission stations on the net. Clausen did not elaborate his request with any details but repeated it a second time. Martin Yoder was still in the process of signing off as Cal dashed out the door to grab his things from the guesthouse, summon Muteba and head for home.

"What are the deteriorating conditions Larry referenced? With the Kisambo bac out I'm going to have to take the Gungu ferry.

Will I run into *Jeunesse* on the way back? Are Martha, Hal and the others safe? What kind of help or support can they expect from our church friends? This will no doubt be a real test of our relationships in Kisambo."

These and many more such thoughts and questions kept Calvin company on the long day's drive home.

***

The midafternoon thunderheads climbed upwards in irregular pillars as Calvin's green Wagoneer bumped down the dusty main street of Gungu. It was humid and stifling hot. So far, no rain showers had descended, but the dark base of the anvil-shaped clouds suggested that things could change at any moment. Sweat lines coursed down Calvin's cheeks and dripped off his chin. Even the resident town mutts that typically chased vehicles, yipping and snapping, had retreated to shady hideouts at this hour of the day. They merely glanced up at the passing jeep, disinterested, ears flicking at the ever-present collection of circling flies.

As uncomfortable as it was to travel in the heat, Calvin found that there was also an ironic upside. The intense afternoon sun meant that the road was virtually clear of foot traffic and other impediments. No soliciting of rides, requests for favors or other distractions to deal with. To underscore this fact, he had driven right through the last army checkpoint on the far side of town without even stopping. The guard post's occupants were all fast asleep.

Calvin passed the last of Gungu's commercial buildings, whitewashed cement walled structures stained amber with years of dust and rain. Faded color remained on some of the doorsills and on the barely visible store names painted on the walls. The barred windows and open doorways were dark and empty. As he drove toward the tree line a quarter mile ahead, a loud noise sounded above him, and a large dark shadow zipped across his path. Calvin pulled over, startled.

Muteba stuck his head out of the window and looked up. *"Avion!"* he called out, pointing. It had already dawned on Calvin that a small airplane had just buzzed them. Stepping out of his vehicle, he shaded his eyes, squinting toward the retreating sound. He immediately recognized the familiar sight of an MAF Cessna in the distance banking to the right for another pass.

He waved as the plane once again passed low overhead. This time it dropped an object as it swooped by. Muteba ran to retrieve it...a soup can. The note inside read, *"Calvin, please turn around and head back to the Gungu airstrip. Your legal rep Paul Gingrich is with me & wants to ride with you to Kisambo. George Kimble, MAF"*

Calvin was both nervous and relieved to see Paul Gingrich. He was glad to have additional company for this last lap of his drive. It was in all probability the most dangerous segment of the journey because of the hostile *Jeunesse* activity in the area and because of the virtual absence of any army forces. But he was also nervous about what Paul's presence might mean for Kisambo. Would it tip the scales toward evacuation? If Larry's urgent request for his return and his report of "deteriorating circumstances" signaled a serious threat was imminent, would Paul's presence provide added incentive for hostile action by the rebels? Besides all that, Calvin never quite knew how to read Paul, so he wasn't sure what to make of this unexpected visit by the top man in his mission.

Paul Gingrich turned out to be good company. He was pleasant, cordial and appropriately concerned with present events in Kisambo. Calvin was relieved. After greetings were exchanged with Muteba and Calvin, Gingrich clarified that his sudden visit was in response to both the executive committee's hastily called meeting and to Larry's urgent morning request on the phonie. Since the MAF plane just happened to be in Tshikapa for other reasons, he thought he'd take the opportunity to fly up and get a first-hand picture of the evolving situation.

The drive from Gungu to Kisambo was uneventful, without incident, much to the relief of all three travelers and their anxious greeting party at the other end. As Calvin's jeep rattled onto the station grounds in a cloud of dust, Martha, Hal, and all three Clausens came rushing up. They had obviously been watching for the jeep's arrival. Greetings, hugs, handshakes and smiles filled the first moments before Larry launched into an update.

"The Buta attack was brutal. So far, we're aware of eight villagers killed and at least fifteen injured, some very seriously. We have heard reports of additional attacks and kidnappings in the forest. Rumors are flying about. Everyone seems to be on edge. We're on edge!"

The small group headed for the Schroeder's residence. Paul

Gingrich rested one hand on young Barbara's shoulder as they made their way up the path and ascended the steps to the porch. She smiled, pleased at the attention it signaled from someone as important as Rev. Gingrich. He glanced over to Calvin. "Can you send for Pastor Kinbumba and the church elders? I'd like to see what they have to say."

***

The same evening, all of the missionary personnel from the station joined the local Congolese church leaders, clinic and school staff and their friends and families for a standing-room-only meeting in the Kisambo chapel. It seemed the entire community had gathered. Kerosene lanterns were hung at intervals above the heads of the attendees, creating a dim but intimate glow across the sanctuary. Occasional dark flashes above signaled that bats were at work soaring about the beams chasing insects attracted by the lanterns. The combination of a packed room and minimal air circulation created an intense aesthetic experience – sounds, colors and odors.

Pastor Kinbumba took charge of the assembly. He first offered a long prayer before making a short speech and extending a warm welcome to the station's honored guest, Rev. Gingrich. When finally called upon to speak, Gingrich began by expressing his condolences to those who had lost friends and family in the recent Buta village attack. The crowd was unusually quiet as he spoke. He continued, "I am here tonight concerned for the safety of all of the members of this community – villagers, students, staff, their families and our missionary family. The terrible events nearby have prompted my unplanned visit to see first-hand just how dangerous things may have become in your community. Now I'd like to hear from you."

At this, Rev. Gingrich paused and waited. There was a long, awkward silence. At first, no one responded. Glances exchanged and gradually a low murmuring rippled across the crowded church. Finally, Pastor Kinbumba slowly stood and spoke.

"We were surprised and saddened by the attack at Buta. Whoever the *Jeunesse* are, they must be people who have come to our community from a distance. No local people would be foolish enough to threaten or destroy our medical and educational resources. These *Jeunesse* have no reason to do any harm to our people or to the facilities at Kisambo."

Muted voices of assent to the pastor's declaration could be heard here and there across the crowded room, but the audience's response was far from a groundswell of assent. Many glances were exchanged. Rev. Gingrich attempted several more times to gain more specifics. "Are you sure no local people are involved? Other than at the Buta attack, have any *Jeunesse* been spotted in the area? How concerned should we be about the safety of our Bible school students who have come from outside the region and for our missionaries and their families?"

Gingrich's questions produced little in terms of either information or reassurance. Headshakes, denials, expressions of ignorance, and platitudes re safety and protection met his queries. Finally, Pastor Kinbumba brought the evening to a close. He called upon several of the elders to pray. Paul Gingrich and Calvin Schroeder joined in representing the mission community. The prayers offered were for wisdom and courage to face the uncertainties that surrounded them as well as expressions of faith and confidence in God's care and protection. It was a positive ending...on the surface.

As they walked back to the Schroeder home however, Paul Gingrich turned to Calvin with a somber expression and a quiet comment. "I'm not sure I learned much of anything tonight, Cal, except that there's probably more going on around here than your Congolese friends are prepared to admit."

"I agree," Calvin replied, looking about to make sure they were not overheard. "Did you see all the looks being exchanged in the audience? And the elders were consistently vague in their replies to your questions. I really don't know what to make of it, Paul."

"I'd keep alert. And make sure that short wave radio is in good working order."

#8 Kisambo Station

January 1964

"Mama, there's something I need to tell you." Hal sat at the breakfast table staring at his toast and soursop jam. An egg, over easy – his preference, sat on the plate as well, untouched, getting cold. The adults had already finished their breakfast and were off somewhere else. He didn't have much of an appetite this morning. *How should I say this?* He kept wondering to himself.

Wiping her hands on a towel, Martha pulled out a chair and sat down across from her somber son. "So, what's up with the serious face, sweetheart? Aren't you feeling well? You haven't touched your breakfast."

"You know the meeting last night with Rev. Gingrich and the elders?" he began, taking a deep breath. "Well...they weren't telling the truth, Mama."

"And you know this for a fact...how?" his mother replied looking at him with a sidelong glance.

Hal pushed back from the table. "I...I don't want to get anyone in trouble. But they said they thought all the *Jeunesse* are from somewhere far from here. That's not true. I told you before. In fact, there are several guys from the village who have joined up with the *Jeunesse*. They know this. Nsuka's brother Biungu is one of them. Tata Museka Adoko is really angry with him. He is worried that he might have been in on the Buta attack. Mama, it's very possible that the next attack could happen right here at Kisambo."

Martha frowned and pulled her head back, skeptically. "Your friends told you all this?"

"Yes, it's true! I'm not making it up." Hal stood up and mirroring his father's habit, ran an anxious hand through his hair. "You know I had that nightmare and the next morning we found out that it was true? Well, I have a really bad feeling about what's going to happen next. I think something awful is going to happen right here, and soon."

"Come here, Hal." Martha held her arms out to him. Hal slowly approached her welcoming hug. "That nightmare was just a coincidence. It's got you all riled up and worried. Your father and the others are concerned but not alarmed. They are confident our Congolese neighbors will prevent any problems from developing here at Kisambo." She added with a reassuring smile, "But perhaps you should go ahead and tell him any new details you heard from your friends."

Hal hugged his mother. It felt safe there for the moment. He pondered her suggestion and thought to himself, *I'll tell Papa about Biungu, and my fears but I can't tell him all I've learned, that's for sure. I wonder if sharing this will be enough to keep us safe?*

***

Later that same day the distinct growl of a Land Rover was heard as it made its way up the hill to Kisambo Station. The doors swung open. Philip Bartel and Marvin Elrich, missionary colleagues from Kindambo stepped out, sweat stained and parched after their long drive. They pounded the dust from their clothes and stretched as Calvin and Paul hailed them from across the yard at the front of Schroeder's house.

"Welcome friends. You made good time." Calvin extended a hand and a warm smile. Philip pulled him into a hug. The others shook hands.

"Yes, we were most fortunate, blessed as it were." Philip said as he resumed rubbing his stiff back muscles with the heels of his hands.

"I'm going to assume that means that you did not run into any trouble on your way." Calvin grasped Philip's elbow and turned him motioning in the direction of his residence. "Let's get you something cool to drink and you can freshen up a bit as well." They started for the house. "It looks like you were also successful in getting the extra petrol." He pointed to the row of ten-liter gasoline cans strapped together in the back of the Land Rover. "We can unload them after you rest up."

"We were thankfully able to complete this first part of our trip without incident, but we can't call it entirely a success. Unfortunately, the MAF flight bringing your new short-wave unit was unable to make it to Gungu today because of bad weather. George told us he'd try again tomorrow, and so will we. You do need that upgraded equipment." The four men climbed the steps and greeted Martha who stood at the door.

She pointed Philip and Marvin to the bathroom. Calvin and Paul continued on into the living room and settled down on the comfortable chairs there. "You know, the timing is going to work out well here," Paul mused to his host. A note of relief could be detected in his voice. "It looks like now I'll be able to ride back to Gungu with the fellows in the morning and pick up a lift from MAF back home." As an afterthought he added, "I don't envy the men their mission tomorrow. All the back and forth on those terrible roads, is no picnic."

***

Following dinner that evening, the three Clausens and Elsie Buller joined the visitors for dessert at the Schroeder's home. Such gatherings had become a virtual tradition whenever guests came to the station. Thomas had prepared a delicious mango cobbler that was a big hit. Coffee and tea were served, and conversation flowed freely. After a round of updates and exchanges on the status of family members and ministries, the discussion turned to the local scene and the recent developments at Kisambo. Elsie was the first to express her concerns. She tended to use her hands when speaking. Hal thought that watching her speak was more interesting than listening to what she had to say. Like watching an orchestra conductor, he mused.

"We have had quite a challenge the past few days at the clinic, taking care of the wounded from the Buta attack. It was a brutal event. Since much of the village was burned, our own Pastor Kinbumba has been urging the church folk to take in survivors and care for them. They'll need help rebuilding the village...and their lives. Chief Ntotilla and the elders are concerned that Kisambo may be next on the *Jeunesse* list."

Paul Gingrich set his coffee mug down on the table and leaned forward to speak. "I realize that the reality of the *Jeunesse* threat is not lost on you folks. That's quite clear. Last night's meeting plus other conversations we had with your Congolese friends and colleagues, however, have not provided much clarity about where things stand at present. We're neither reassured nor convinced you're in immediate danger. They claim ignorance of any knowledge of local rebel activity other than the obvious event at Buta. Until we know otherwise, we'll have to take them at their word."

Hal had been quietly standing behind the couch listening to the adults' conversations. At Gingrich's words he turned beet red. He had told himself that he would just keep silent and listen to what they all had to say. But earlier that afternoon, he had been very disappointed in Papa's reaction to his fears about a Kisambo attack. Papa had heard him out – that part was good – but he had then replied that he was "more inclined to believe the adults then to put my faith in the reports of your young friends." That hurt. So, now Hal felt he'd burst if he didn't say something to refute those...those *lies* that the missionary men had swallowed.

"No! They're not telling you the truth." Hal blurted out in a loud voice. Martha, standing nearby instinctively reached out for his arm, but he shrugged off her grasp and stepped forward. All eyes turned to him and the room became quiet. In a rapid stream of consciousness, he continued.

"My friends told me that a number of the young men from the village have joined the *Jeunesse*, including some of their brothers. Their parents and the elders know about it and are worried, but the young men are avoiding them, hiding and training in the forest. We are in danger. We are! They want to defeat the Congo government – to have a second independence – and to rid the country of all who are friends with them. That includes missionaries. Us!"

The room sat in silence for a long moment. Paul Gingrich finally turned to Calvin. "What do you make of your son's words, Cal?"

By that time, Calvin had risen from his chair, stepped over to Hal and pulled him close. Sobs shaking his body, Hal eagerly responded to his father's gesture by pressing tightly to his father, wrapping both arms around his waist.

Holding his son with one arm, Calvin ran his other hand through his hair, "Hal shared these thoughts with me this afternoon. It is possible his friends are telling the truth. On the other hand, we have received repeated reassurances from the adults in the village, including his friends' parents and the leaders, that they know nothing of the rebellion. It would seem really out of character for them to mislead us in something this serious, but there's lots of room for doubt."

Hal's head, buried in his father's chest, turned toward the room. "I'm not lying! My friends have told me the truth."

Paul Gingrich slowly stood. "I think on this note the best thing we can do is gather for a time of prayer. The Apostle James tells us, 'If any of you lacks wisdom, he should ask God who gives generously to all without finding fault, and it will be given to you.' These words are for us. I believe wisdom is clearly called for here."

The evening ended with the entire group participating in an extended time of prayer. Hal felt somewhat better as the gathering broke up and people headed off in various directions for the night. The opportunity to voice a warning, and the prayers of the adults were at least a partial validation, an improvement over Papa's afternoon dismissal. Still, the reality of a hidden, looming threat left him feeling anxious and tense. Which will prove to be true? The bones or the prayers...or both?

#9 Gungu Air Strip

January 1964

Having left Kisambo at first light, it was mid-morning when Philip Bartel turned his station's Land Rover off the main road and headed toward the airstrip just outside of Gungu. A familiar MAF Cessna 185 workhorse was anchored at one end of the flat grassy runway, standing alone in the bright, hot sun. Adjacent to it was a small cement structure that served as the flight operations center. It housed fuel barrels, lanterns and other equipment that serviced visiting aircraft. George Kimball, assisted by two Congolese men and a cluster of young onlookers, appeared to be loading *pondu* (manioc greens) sacks into the plane's cargo area.

The Rover's dusty brakes squealed as they came to a stop. Aware of their arrival for the first time, George turned sharply from his duties, and with a smile called out, "Hey guys, you made good time. I just landed a short while ago, myself. We're almost finished loading right now. We can head for Tshikapa shortly." After hefting another sack, he continued, "You're probably ready to get back home, Paul. I think I can promise you a smoother ride on this segment than the one you just completed."

The three men approached him glad to feel the blood reach their lower limbs once again. "It took us longer than we anticipated to get here, George." Paul reached out to shake the pilot's hand. "Several times we had to haul out the planks the boys brought along to make it across freshly dug ditches in the road."

"Oh-oh. Sounds like the rebels have been busy. That's not a good sign." George frowned and put his hands on his hips, stretching his sore back.

By then the cluster of children had surrounded them. They chattered away, laughing, pointing and scuffling with one another in excited animation. Their antics brought instant smiles to the faces of the newly arrived *mindeles*. Raising his voice above the noise, Marvin Elrich asked, "Did you bring along something special for us, George?"

"Ah, yes." George stepped back to the plane and reached into the open door to slide out two long cardboard boxes stacked in the back. He then climbed up into the cockpit, reaching back between the seats. "Could one of you fellows help me here? These are heavy." He handed two car batteries down, one at a time commenting, "I'm glad the weather cooperated this morning. I understand that there's some urgency to get this phonie equipment to Kisambo right away."

"That's why we're here," Marvin replied with a smile. He and Philip proceeded to carry the boxes to their vehicle while Paul chatted further with George about the flight ahead. The two Kindambo missionaries then returned to the plane and said their goodbyes.

"We won't wait to see you two off. We have a lot of road to cover so I think we'd better just head out. It was good to see you again, Paul. Have a safe flight. Greet the missus for us." With that, they climbed back into their Land Rover and headed off in the direction they had come, chased by a cloud of dust and a score of laughing children.

The two men drove for nearly an hour without seeing a single person along the side of the road, unusual as they were so close to the town. They would have expected to pass numerous persons coming or going from the area's commercial center. "What do you make of the empty road, Marv?"

The words had no sooner left Philip's mouth than the road before them was filled with angry looking young men who had suddenly appeared from the tall grass at one side. Most were bare-chested, in ragged shorts. All carried some sort of weapon: long bush knives, arrows or spears. Philip slammed on the brakes and the dust cloud that had followed them continued forward, before settling onto the human blockade. A loud voice demanded, *"Bima mindele!"* (Come out, white men) The two missionaries looked at one another and slowly stepped out of the vehicle.

They were immediately surrounded by a clamoring horde of excited warriors. Roughly pressed against their Land Rover, knives and sharpened spears were pushed against the men's necks and backs, nearly breaking the skin. Neither dared move a muscle. The shouting and animation continued for several minutes before a wiry man with a clear sense of authority stepped to the side and raised his arms. With this action, the noise dropped sharply. He had a wisp of a goatee and some flecks of gray at his temples revealing that he was older than the majority of the mostly adolescent youth surrounding the captives. Loudly, in Lingala he yelled, "*Bato nyonso! Kanga maboko na bango!*" (Everyone. Tie their arms).

His orders were swiftly obeyed. The two missionary men shortly found themselves with their arms snugly tied behind, stumbling after the "*President,*" as the leader was referred to, in a rebel procession that headed off the road and along a path into the forest.

Surrounded as they were, and prodded with weapons, neither spoke. They just followed. The warrior band walked for the better part of an hour through the forest. The intense mid-day sun was filtered by the canopy above creating blotchy contrasts of light and shade that seemed to further animate the steadily moving line of men. The white men's sunglasses and hats had been quickly appropriated by their captors causing them to squint as they passed through sunny gaps along the trail. One hat/glasses set now adorned the *President* at the head of the procession. The line slowed as they approached a small village. Dogs barked, naked children scrambled about, and loose chickens fluttered off the path.

The line of young rebels came to a halt near the center of the village. The *President* and several of his comrades engaged in animated conversation with one of the village's older residents seated in front of a thatched hut. Both missionaries were nearly beside themselves with fear and shock. "Can you make out what's happening, Phil?" Marvin asked. "I think he just demanded food for his troops," was the reply.

"*Silence!*" rang out behind the men. Whack! A spear shaft cracked across the back of Philip's head propelling him to his knees and opening a nasty gash. Marvin moved to assist, but his bound hands and arms prevented any aid. "*Yo...kanga munoko!*" (shut your mouth).

The negotiations for provisions came to a predictable end. The village chief protested that it would be very difficult to find food for the sizable group on short notice. The *President* countered with a simple question. "Do you wish for us to burn your village?" At that, the chief, trembling, quickly fell to his knees before him, begging him to allow them to serve the invading '*quipe*. It was no small task to take on, since the entire village census was fewer than the head count of their visitors. Nodding assent with closed eyes and a barely perceptible dip of the chin, the *President* then signaled to his soldiers to gather around and find shady places to rest while waiting to be served.

Marvin and Philip were untied so that they could eat along with their captors. The soldiers were fed fufu (manioc balls) and greens with peanuts and palm oil sauce. It took almost an hour for the women of the village to prepare the meal. The two missionary men were given small bowls of mush and over-ripe bananas, but they were thankful for even this minimal sustenance and especially for the gourd full of water that accompanied their food. They bowed their heads to pray before they ate, and their guards permitted them to speak out loud.

Philip prayed (in English), "Lord we know that our lives are in your hands. If it pleases you to do so, we ask for deliverance, for help. We also ask you for courage and trust as we face this present danger. We pray for our enemies, that you will restrain their violent intent. Thank you for being with us and for providing us this food." The guards were by that time so focused on eating that little notice was given to the *mindeles'* prayer or to the low exchanges between the two men that followed as they ate.

After the meal, the *Jeunesse* column continued on through the forest as the afternoon shadows grew longer. The missionary captives' hands were once again bound behind them, adding to the difficulty they had in keeping up with the group's rapid pace. They passed through two other small villages, and in each instance the *President* demanded foodstuffs and his warriors made threats, before they resumed their march.

The sun finally dropped below the tree line. Darkness was rapidly descending when they finally arrived at the banks of the mighty Kwilu River. Its dark, smooth and rapid flow was as ominous and unpredictable as the circumstances facing the two missionaries. Small ripples picked up lines of color from the sky that was just completing the last of its evening technicolor display. In short order, dugout canoes appeared, and the group proceeded to make a crossing.

While the boatmen guiding the long canoes stood at the rear with their long poles, the *Jeunesse* and their captives kneeled, the latter, with hands bound behind their backs. Some in the center of the tippy transports baled water as they moved across. A number of the young warriors who were non-swimmers, clutched the sides of the dugouts with desperate wild-eyed clenches. *"Keba bangubu!"* (watch out for hippos) The Kwilu was known for hippos, so perhaps they had reason for concern.

As their dugout wobbled and sliced its way across the quarter mile of river, Marvin whispered to Philip, "Look upstream by the bend. You can see where the ferry used to be. Cal said the cables were cut. It was likely this bunch that did it."

The *Jeunesse* band reassembled on the other side and continued uphill on a narrow forest path. As they stumbled along in the increasing darkness, both of the men took note of a glow shining through the trees at the top of the hill.

Marvin whispered low, "Oh-oh. That doesn't look good." Philip responded with a muffled, "Mmmm." The glow increased in brightness as they continued on the uphill path. Emerging from the trees, flames were clearly visible dancing just behind the top of the ridge. Philip turned to the young guard on his right, *"Mboka nini?"* (what village?) motioning in African style with his chin lifted in the direction of the light.

"Kisambo," was the reply.

#10 Kisambo Station

January 1964

Dinner was over, dishes were done, and Hal noted that Papa had retreated to reading in his favorite chair in the living room. Mama was still finishing up in the kitchen. He picked up his copy of *The Clue of the Screeching Owl*, a Hardy Boys novel that grandma just sent, and adjusted the kerosene lamp by his bed. The station's diesel generator could be heard in the distance, chugging away but since the electric light in the center of his room tended to flicker, Hal preferred the familiar old-fashioned lamp for reading.

He had looked forward to diving into this latest mystery in his favorite series but now that he sat down to do it, he couldn't concentrate. It was hard to put his finger on it, but something just didn't seem right. Hal's mind kept returning to the dinner table discussion. Anxious glances exchanged between Mama and Papa were obvious even though they had tried to keep the conversation positive, *probably to protect me,* he reasoned to himself. Likewise, their worried looks reflected concern for the two men from Kindambo who had not returned from their round trip to Gungu by dark. That was a serious thing in these tense times. Deep in his guts, Hal had this mounting feeling of dread.

"Eeek! Calvin look!"

Mama's scream carried down the hall, shattering Hal's reflections. He leaped up as if poked by an electric prod. In one motion he dashed full speed toward the living room. His parents stood in the open front door. Mama's one arm was wrapped around Papa and the other was pointing in the direction of the village.

Crackling flames leapt skyward illuminating the dark sky as one after another, nearby village huts exploded into fiery balls, the red and yellow wall of flames expanding before them. Excited shouts and screams could be heard and against the flaming backdrop, numerous figures could be seen running about, some carrying torches, others with bows and arrows, bush knives and spears.

"Hal, come...now!" Papa's no-nonsense voice sent a chill down his spine, but he did as ordered, and joined his parents on the porch. Papa turned, slammed and locked the door. He grabbed Hal's hand in one of his, and Mama's in the other and the three of them ran down the steps and across the grass to the Clausen home. It was located at the center of the station compound and by previous arrangement it served as the designated assembly point in the event of a station emergency. This definitely qualified.

The Schroeder trio arrived just as Elsie rounded the corner from the opposite direction. Larry opened the door wide for his colleagues. Beth was right behind him, and the terrified Barbara was tightly clutching her mother. He slammed the door closed and locked it.

"Our sentry just came by warning us of the attack," Larry blurted out. "I told him to look for Pastor Kinbumba and have him come quickly before I sent him off. Maybe Pastor K or others of the elders can convince the rebels..."

Boom!

Something heavy hit the door, interrupting Larry's comments.

Crash! Crash!

First one window and then another shattered as rocks were hurled through them. Glass fragments flew about the huddled missionaries.

After a quick calculation, Calvin called out, "Larry, open the door. Let's get out of here. Hands raised, everyone. We've got to leave if we don't want to be burned alive in this place."

Needing no further encouragement, Larry swung open the front door and the small group of *mindeles* cautiously ventured out onto the porch with hands raised. They were greeted by a screaming, jeering mob that grew in number even as they exited. A rock hit Martha on the shoulder. She briefly lowered her arms to rub the sore spot, before returning them to their upright position.

Three wild-eyed attackers rushed up the porch steps, pulling and prodding the cowering group of missionaries down to the yard. Screaming, bare-chested youth closed in around them, reaching over one another to poke and slap them with their hands and hit them with the flat edges of their bush knives. Barbara screeched with each blow, sobbing in between yelps. The two mothers bent over; protective arms wrapped about their children.

The men futilely attempted to position themselves between the mob and their women and children. Hal ducked down but still managed to feel the sting of a rope whip across the back of his neck. Hostile hands pushed and herded him to and fro. Other hands wrenched off glasses, shoes, and watches and emptied the pockets of each of the white captives.

"Where is the gas? What are you doing in our politics? Why have you ruined our land? Why have you called the soldiers?" A cacophony of loud accusations rang out, interspersed with shouts of *"Boma bango!"* (Kill them!)

They stood huddled together, barefoot in the dim flickering firelight, amidst a surreal drama. All about them were the sounds of chaos: roofs crashing in, fuel barrels exploding, glass shattering, fire crackling, everywhere voices screamed and raged. A young rebel appeared with a gasoline can and began to pour a circle around the missionaries.

At that point, a dark figure holding a torch in one hand and a machete in the other stepped forward and called out in a loud authoritative voice. The din continued unabated, but the crowd shuffled back. "Take them to that house" he called out, pointing toward the station's last remaining dwelling that hadn't burned. Two from the surrounding mob leaped forward and tugged on Calvin's arms, pulling him in the direction of Elsie Buller's residence that stood undamaged.

"Do you think they'll let us stay there?" Martha asked, hopeful. "No telling," Cal replied quietly as they stumbled across the yard in the flickering firelight. "Oh, look...now we can see a little better," he quipped with irony. Their former home suddenly lit up the compound, as it became fully engulfed in flames. "Oh, Cal..." was all Martha could manage.

Hal was virtually mute with fear. He clutched his mother's dress and kept his eyes focused on the ground looking down so that he didn't stumble and fall as they moved across the compound. The crashes, explosions and screams all about him felt like some kind of horror movie or being caught up in a vivid nightmare that just wouldn't end. He'd never known such terror. His mind went blank. Smoke burned his lungs and tears streaked his face. He sobbed without being aware of doing so.

As Hal ascended the steps to the porch at Elsie's house, he glanced up briefly just in time to catch sight of a group of the bare-chested raiders running by, torches in hand. A sudden recognition brought him back to reality. "Papa, look! That's Biungu, Nsuka's big brother."

"I'm afraid you're right, son. I guess we now know where he's been, don't we?" was Papa's astute reply.

The same dark rebel figure reappeared before the missionary group still bearing a torch and machete, this time completely surrounded by his company of wildly excited, young raiders. With a loud voice he addressed his audience on the porch.

"*Mindeles*, you have done a very bad thing in harming our beautiful country by joining hand-in-hand with the evil thieves and liars who lead our government. Because of your cooperation with them it is plain for all to see where your loyalties lie. It was necessary to destroy your station so that we can start over. All will be better in the new Congo. We are done here now. Note, *mindeles, toyoteli bino mawa,* (white people, we have pity on you) it is only due to our kindness and generosity that we leave you unharmed and do not put a torch to this final dwelling."

With that, the leader and his group turned and headed off into the night.

It was not until the last retreating figure disappeared from view that Hal finally released his grip on his mother's dress and took a deep breath. It seemed like he had been holding his breath the whole time. Could the nightmare be over, he wondered? Maybe now it was safe to relax a little. He stepped over to the low stone porch wall and plopped down hard.

Behind him was the low murmur of the adults who had begun to discuss what they should do next and to identify what was left in Elsie Buller's house that could be used. The diesel generator continued its chug-a-chug in the background though all the station's electric lights were out. None of the raiders had figured out how to turn it off. The porch was dark. After all the chaos it seemed quiet, almost peaceful there, though across the way flames still crackled and popped and now and then timbers crashed as they fell in the buildings that had burned.

But then, across the darkened station grounds came the sound of low murmuring voices and the shuffling of many bare feet. Hal jumped up and moved to his father's side. Out of the dark shadows emerged yet another band of *Jeunesse* raiders, arrows notched in bows, spears held at shoulder height.

"*Basi boni?* (How many women are there?) *Wapi basi a bino?* (Where are they?)" The demands came from a tall, bushy-haired figure dressed in shorts and a sleeveless army jersey. His red-rimmed eyes suggested he was well fortified with palm wine, hemp or both. An army rifle was slung over one shoulder. His initial queries brought a chill to the assembled missionaries. This was not a good sign. Hal looked at his mother's face. Her lips were trembling. He could tell she was praying.

Cal and Larry tried using *Gipende*, the language of the area to discern the reason for the scraggy leader's inquiry. Their exchanges went back and forth for several minutes before his bony arm was finally raised and promises made that no harm would come to the women and children. "Now, move over to that tree and watch. We are going to burn this house." With that, torches were lit and thrown through the windows and the final missionary dwelling burst into flame, taking with it the hopes of the former Kisambo station residents for an easy end to their nightmare.

"You will follow us to our forest camp. You are going to go on trial before our president for your crimes against our country. *Toke!* (Let's go!)" No further protests by Calvin or Larry were allowed. With arrows and spears at their backs, the five adults and two children were herded across the station grounds toward the dark forest.

"Are they going to hurt us, Mama?" came Barbara's little voice. Beth did not answer but hugged her daughter closely as they walked.

They had to watch their step in the dim torchlight since the ground was littered with broken glass, torn clothes, smashed pottery, ripped furniture pads and other debris taken from the missionary residences earlier in the raid. Elsie Buller's former dwelling popped and crackled as the fire consumed it behind the line of raiders and captives.

The column came to an abrupt halt at the edge of the forest. Blocking the pathway were two figures clad in white, arms folded across their chests. They were male nurses, well known to the missionaries. What they didn't know, however, was that the two had secretly joined the rebel movement, believing it to be a legitimate political protest. Horrified at the violence and destruction they had just witnessed in the burning and sacking of the station, the two men now bravely drew the line at the abduction of their missionary colleagues and their families. "*Bakolala na zamba te!* You will not take these good people into the forest this night. *Bakolala epai na biso!* They will stay with us in the dispensary."

The raiders met this proposal with loud and agitated protests. Hal watched with open mouth and big eyes as the debate raged. The nurses were obviously taking a big chance in challenging the wishes of so many armed rebels. At long last, the bushy-haired leader shook his head, spat to the side and stomped off into the night with his entourage trailing behind.

One of the male nurses then turned to the group, and in a soft voice said, "We came to an agreement. You may all sleep in the dispensary." With words of gratitude and considerable relief, the Schroeders, Clausens and nurse Elsie thanked their rescuers and made their way to the dispensary. They were supplied with water and cloths to wash off the smoke and grime and given split bamboo mats for a restless but unmolested night of sleep.

Before they settled down, however, tearful prayers of thanks were offered to their heavenly Father for their deliverance from harm; ardent petitions were made for the safety of their missing and unaccounted-for colleagues, Marvin Elrich and Philip Bartel.

#11 Kisambo Station

January 1964

Hal woke with a start and sat up rubbing the sleep from his eyes. He could barely make out the slumbering figures of his parents and the other missionaries in the dim light. He wondered what time it might be, but since all watches had been removed, he just guessed it must be about a half hour or so before sunrise, probably about 5:20 or 5:30.

He rose as quietly as he could but the bamboo mat he had slept on made a scratching noise on the cement floor. His mother's head popped up. "What's wrong? What are you doing, Hal?"

"I need to go to the bathroom."

"Can you just step out by the door and go?" his mother asked. "It's too dangerous to find the outhouse. I'll stand just inside to make sure you're okay." Mother and son rose and moved quietly to the open, unguarded dispensary door.

Hal accomplished his mission with great relief and as he did so, surveyed the compound in the faint pre-dawn light. Wispy columns of smoke still rose from the charred skeletons of former buildings. Equipment, supplies and clutter was strewn everywhere about the grounds. He could make out small clusters of *Jeunesse* squatting or huddled around warming fires here and there in the yard. He caught a whiff of an acrid scent: charred timber mixed with diesel fumes and burned leaves. It brought tears to his eyes. *"Well, maybe the tears are not all from the smoke,"* he thought to himself as he wiped them away. Even in the dim early morning light the shadowy images clearly revealed that his former world was shattered, destroyed. *"What's going to happen to us?"* This thought was as jumbled in his mind as the debris he viewed all about him.

Frowning, Hal stepped back into the dispensary. His mother whispered, "I'm next," exchanging places with him. He moved to the side of the room and sat down on a chair, head in hands, elbows on knees. Shortly, his mother returned to join him, carefully pulling up another chair alongside his. As they sat, knees touching and heads together, Hal quietly voiced his anxious

61

thoughts.

"What do you think the *Jeunesse* bush council will decide, Mama? Are there other rebel groups that want to harm us? They burned down our station. Do you think they are still mad at us? Will they do more?"

Mama put her arm around Hal. "The two nurses who arranged for our stay here told your father they were going to try to find answers to those very questions. We may know a lot more sometime later today. Our best response right now is prayer. Would you like to pray with me?"

"You pray, Mama. All I can think of is...'Help!'"

Martha chuckled and gave him a squeeze. "That'll do," she replied. "That'll do just fine."

He smiled.

***

By the time the first beams of morning sunlight streamed a window pattern on the dispensary floor, all in the missionary group were up and moving about. Several had negotiated with nearby *Jeunesse* to visit the latrines behind the building. There was much discussion and speculation among the adults regarding their fate. It all led to the same frustrating conclusion, however...wait and see, time will tell.

By mid-morning the first visitors arrived at the dispensary. Alongi, the Clausen's house worker entered the dispensary cautiously, bearing a worried and fearful expression as he scanned the room. He also brought along a welcome but undersized loaf of bread wrapped in a palm leaf. Breakfast that morning for the missionaries turned out to be more nearly a communion event than a meal.

Kintuntu, the nurse's aide and Rosine, the receptionist arrived shortly after Alongi's departure. They each brought small gifts of food items as well: papayas and mangos. They came with tears in their eyes and deep emotion in their voices as they inquired about the health of their missionary friends. "We never expected anything like this. We're so sorry," they repeated over and over. Warm embraces were shared.

Close to midday Pastor Kinbumba appeared at the door. He looked like he had aged a decade overnight. His red eyes bore dark bags beneath, his forehead was deeply creased with worry lines, and his shuffling, sloped-shouldered bearing looked like he bore the weight of the world. Trailing behind him were his son Tika, and Ilunga, Hal's two friends.

Calvin rushed forward to greet fellow clergyman and friend, Kinbumba as soon as he passed through the doorway. He reached out to extend an embrace, but his arms closed on empty space; his colleague had flung himself at his feet, grasping Cal's ankles, sobbing out grief and despair. "Forgive me, brother. We never imagined it would come to this. We have all lost much, but our silence has put you and your dear family in danger. It was never supposed to happen. Please..." And then his words dissolved into deep sobs.

Calvin dropped to his knees and grasped Kinbumba by the shoulders, raising him up to look him in the eyes. "I do *not* blame you, brother for all the violence and destruction that has descended upon us. Such wickedness was never in your heart or in that of the elders, I am certain. None of us saw the *Jeunesse* for who they really are, for their depth of evil and threat to our community. We must find a way to get past this...as friends, as brothers."

While these somber exchanges were taking place, a greeting of a very different kind was happening across the room. Hal's two friends rushed to him and the three of them grasped hands, clenching together in a tight knot. They released their grips at the same time as if on cue, and launched into their special hand-slapping, hip-banging greeting ritual, ending in nervous laughter that briefly lit the far corner of the room. The seriousness of the recent events quickly brought it to an end, however.

"I'm sooo glad to see you," Hal gushed, "but where is Nsukula? Has something happened to him?"

"No, he is well, but Tata Muzeka is not letting him out of his sight. He is fearful that Biungu might recruit him to join his *quipe*. He's determined to prevent that."

"Are you well, *Lumwenu?*" Tika inquired. "We saw your burned house on the way here and feared the worse...that you might have been caught inside."

"I'm okay, but everything is gone now. We don't know if the *Jeunesse* are going to return and take us to their forest camp to be punished. Truly? I'm afraid," Hal admitted simply, looking down.

He hated to disclose his fear even to these close friends. He winced at the thought, "I hope they still *are* my friends." Though he promptly dismissed this flicker of doubt, Hal found he still could not look up.

Tika volunteered, "Ilunga's house was burned to the ground but our place and Nsuka's escaped the torches. Ilunga's Mama got burned trying to remove her cooking bowls from the flames. She will heal, but there are others from the village that will not. They were killed or badly wounded. It was awful. Everyone is angry at the *Jeunesse*, but we are also afraid."

Ilunga continued, "Tata Muzeka told us we must thank you. Your predictions allowed him to protect his dwelling and family. He told us you were exactly right in reading the bones. He is very grateful."

Hal managed a nod and slight smile. He wasn't so sure his predictions were a blessing; they felt more like a curse.

Near midday Kinbumba reluctantly departed with the two boys, offering assurances that someone from the church would remain nearby -- as close as the *Jeunesse* would permit -- to keep alert for any new developments and to be available if help was needed.

Shortly afterwards, the two male nurses returned from their overnight foray into the forest. They bore good news, reporting that the rebels' "tribunal" had met during the night. It was determined that the Kisambo *mindeles* had suffered enough. They were now free to make plans to evacuate.

The nurses' message was received with mixed emotions. It became readily apparent to the missionaries that they were not going to just walk out of there. A quick inventory revealed that they were barefoot, lightly attired with no provisions and it would take days to trek to the nearest source of help. Marauding bands of *Jeunesse* and miles of rough, exposed country made any such plan dangerous, even deadly. They would have to stay put and wait for help to arrive.

Calvin addressed the others, in a more positive tone than he actually felt inside. "The sudden and complete absence of Kisambo from the daily phonie net should surely prompt a check by our colleagues. I'd guess it'll happen within the next day or so. We need to plan how we can signal if that check is a fly-over."

Barbara had wandered over by the dispensary door while the adults were talking. Suddenly she called out, "Hey, there are the Bible school students, over by the chapel." She began waving in the doorway.

Beth rose from her chair and stepped behind her daughter, raising a hand to wave as well. She turned to her spouse. "Larry, could you ask our captors if we can go over there and meet with the students?"

Permission granted from the young rebels lounging in the shade of the dispensary and the entire missionary group exited the building, picking its way, barefoot across the debris-strewn yard to the front of the still-intact chapel. A cluster of Bible students occupied the open doorway with their wives and young children huddled closely by. Each had in hand a small bundle of salvaged possessions.

Warm greetings were exchanged between the two groups and inquiries made regarding each other's well-being. Muteba Fabrice, one of the senior students, spoke for the others. "We managed to grab just a few things from our huts before they were torched. We all escaped, but we didn't know where to go. Someone noticed the chapel was not burned so we came here. Though we are Congolese, as Baluba, we are not safe here." Motioning with his arm, "These rebels are mostly Bapende."

Calvin ran a nervous hand through his hair, frowning. "The *Jeunesse* have told us to plan to evacuate but that seems impossible. We don't know what to do. If we were to travel together with you our presence as *mindeles* could make things even more dangerous for you and your families."

Larry chimed in, a hint of a smile on his face. "I know the next suggestion that's coming...prayer, right?"

Calvin knelt as he replied. "Well, the Apostle James teaches in Chapter 5, 'Is anyone in trouble? Let them pray.' We're clearly in trouble, here, so I say let's take his advice." The others joined him, kneeling in a circle of prayer, their petitions offered up with urgency and emotion to *Nzambi ya Mpungu* (Almighty God).

12 Kisambo Station

January 1964

The former teachers and students, Americans and Congolese, took refuge from the still, blazing heat of the tropical afternoon on the benches of the station's chapel. They found themselves sharing not only common space but also a common threat. For the next several hours they sat together talking quietly, exchanging ideas for escape and offering encouragement to one another. The circular discussions came to the same conclusion: walking out from there could only be attempted as a last resort. The distance, hazards and very present threats were simply too great. What remained was to wait...and pray.

Hal found the adult talk disconcerting, not reassuring. It made him nervous. It seemed that no one could come up with a good escape plan. He looked down at his bare calloused feet and thought, "I could probably do a long barefoot march, but there's no way Mama or Papa could...they're hobbling as it is right now. And then there's always the *Jeunesse* lurking about..." It was boring just hanging around in the dim chapel, but on the other hand he didn't want to leave and miss out on anything.

As Hal turned to wipe a drop of sweat from his forehead, a movement caught the corner of his eye. He gazed across the room to one of the small open widows at the back. Peaking over the sill was a pair of eyes in a dark head. A small hand tentatively waved beside it. His head snapped around sharply as he checked the room to see if anyone else had noticed the figure at the window. Everyone seemed occupied; no one else had spotted it.

Hal rose slowly and stretched, faking a yawn. He leaned down to speak softly to his mother. "I need to pee." She nodded without comment and returned her attention to the exchanges taking place before her. Hal sauntered to the chapel door rubbing the small of his back, as if bored and stiff from sitting. Once he cleared the doorway he dashed behind the building. There sat Ilunga, squatting in wait with a big smile on his face.

"*Mbote, Lumwenu. Ngolo ikele?*" (Greetings) "I brought you something to eat." Ilunga held out a small burlap sack filled with peanuts and offered a banana in the other hand. "Here is some water as well." He then passed along a water-filled gourd.

"*Merci mingi, nduku.* (Thanks a lot, friend) I am starving!" Hal pealed the banana and gobbled it down in one motion. He took a long drink and then grabbed a handful of shelled peanuts. "What are you doing here, Ilunga?" he asked through a mouthful of food.

"I snuck away from the village. My parents are in the forest gathering materials to rebuild our home. I brought you the food, but also came with a special message from Muzeka. He said to tell you, "*Kuwa ve boma. Widikila ba lemba na ndoshi*" (Don't fear, but dream and listen to the ancestors) He wants me to check back with you tomorrow. He thinks there is very likely more trouble ahead and that you can find out what it is."

Hal frowned. He hadn't had any of *those* kinds of dreams recently and certainly did not relish the prospect of figuring out what was going to happen to his friends. He sighed and reached out, resting his hand on his friend's arm. "Thanks for coming, Ilunga, and for the food," motioning with the sack in his other hand. "I doubt I'll have anything to report by tomorrow. Who knows what's going to happen...or if we'll even sleep tonight?"

The two friends visited quietly for a few more minutes before Ilunga rose, announcing "I'd better get back home before Mama returns and finds me gone. Stay well. See you tomorrow." And off he dashed back toward the village.

***

As the shadows lengthened, the Kisambo missionaries said their goodbyes to the students and made their way back to the dispensary from the chapel. They were mostly silent as they found chairs and settled into their quarters for the evening. Beth attempted to smooth Barbara's hair with her fingers and remake her ponytail, while her daughter whined about being hungry.

Beth was about to respond to her daughter when she stopped in mid-sentence. A small female figure appeared in the doorway balancing two ceramic pans on her head while carrying a little teapot wrapped with cloth. It was Cécile, the wiry maternity ward cleaning lady, bringing food. She had prepared warm fufu mush and manioc greens seasoned with palm oil and also a bit of hot tea to drink. Her toothless grin was met with hugs and exclamations of gratitude by the hungry *mindeles*, who offered a quick prayer of thanks before their eager fingers dipped into the mush and greens.

In between bites, Beth made sure her daughter received the message of this kindness. "Barbara, Mama Cécile made a special effort to show love to us with this food. She took a big risk coming here. The *Jeunesse* could very well punish her for helping us. It's brave acts like this that let us know God is aware of our needs, and that in spite of enemies all about we also have Congolese brothers and sisters looking out for us."

Barbara just responded with "Mmmm..." but when she had finished eating, she rose and placed both arms around Mama Cécile in a big hug, as her approving parents looked on. *"Merci mingi, mama."*

Hal was mostly correct in his assessment of the uncertainties of the evening ahead. As one of the few remaining structures in the station, the dispensary became a central gathering spot for various marauding rebel groups throughout the night. Loud denouncements were made toward the missionaries, shouted epithets echoing across the room and down the hallway. Arguments erupted between the leaders of different bands and periodically the occupants of the dispensary could hear the sounds of beatings taking place just outside the door.

At one point in the evening a band of expressionless teen-aged girls filed in the shadowy, lantern-lit room, lining up on all four walls with sharpened machetes and bush knives at the ready. Their male leader announced that they had brought the spirit of Gizenga Antoine to visit the missionaries. He then propped a blurred photo of the rebel leader on the table and, sitting next to it, leaned his ear close to the photo. Straightening up, he declared that "The elder is saying this..." as he denounced the European population for all their failures in the Congo and justified the burning of the mission station. This listening, reporting and denouncing routine continued for some time before the group finally departed.

Around midnight the beleaguered missionaries heard a loud commotion going on outside. Their heads swiveled toward the doorway just in time to see their two colleagues, Marvin Elrich and Philip Bartel come staggering into the room, propelled by unseen hands. Matted disheveled hair, dirt streaked faces, red rimmed eyes, and drooping shoulders attested to some sort of grim ordeal they had endured in the preceding twenty-four hours. They were immediately surrounded by their missionary friends and with warm, tearful embraces ushered to chairs, as the group hovered about them, rejoicing at their unexpected appearance.

At the prompting of their colleagues, the two men recounted in weary tones their harrowing ordeal beginning with their initial interception by the rebel squad on the road back from Gungu two days earlier. After an arms-bound, forced march through the jungle and a nighttime pirogue crossing of the Kwilu River they had been taken to the rebel headquarters hidden deep in the forest "to be tried." On the way there they had observed flames from over the hill at the Kisambo Station making them aware that the terrorists had overrun it. They had feared the worst for their friends, both Congolese and missionaries.

The men's story took a dangerous turn at that point. They recounted that throughout the night they had been subject to repeated interrogation sessions by various members of the *Jeunesse* hierarchy. Notched arrows were pointed at their faces and knives were pressed to the back of their necks. Threats and shouts of "kill them!" were heard all about. Marvin observed, "The faces of no less than 800 angry "youth" from 12 to 40 + years of age, were turned to us, gloating over our capture and urging our death. It was terrifying!"

They were informed that the only thing that had kept them from being killed on the spot was that they had not tried to flee when stopped but had greeted the rebel unit in a friendly manner. Completely exhausted by the grilling as well as parched and famished, the two were finally taken to a nearby village, given some food and placed in a hut under guard for the night.

The next day, the men were roused at dawn and again forced to march for three hours to yet another *Jeunesse* camp, an even larger one. There they remained for several hours in the shade of a mango tree, waiting in dread to learn of their fate. Later that afternoon word finally came from the rebel president: they were to rejoin their missionary colleagues at Kisambo Station, or at what was left of it. Their papers were returned but their rings and watches were removed. A final exhausting trek brought them to the dispensary at the midnight hour.

As the men concluded their recounting, the group fell silent for what seemed like minutes. Calvin finally broke the silence. "I'm sure all of us can agree that what you two brothers have just shared of your last two days is nothing short of divine deliverance. What a miracle that your lives were spared! We were so relieved to see the two of you stumble through the door. We're not out of the fire yet, but let's not fail to express our gratitude to the Lord for keeping us all safe so far."

And so, they did.

The kerosene lamps were finally extinguished and the group at last settled onto their mats for a few hours of restless slumber. For most, it was a dreamless sleep of physical and emotional exhaustion fueled by the tensions and trauma of the past two days.

For one of their number, however, sleep was accompanied by very vivid images and a message that woke him in alarm at first light. Hal had heard from the ancestors.

#13 Kisambo Station

January 1964

"Whooah...no, no!" The cry – more of a loud moan – shattered the still, pre-dawn darkness of the dispensary awaking all of its occupants. Hal staggered upright still in a half-conscious state. Martha leapt to her feet, surrounding her sweaty, trembling son in a comforting motherly hug.

"Shhhh, Hal. It's okay now...you just had a nightmare. It'll be okay," she repeated in a soothing tongue as she smoothed his tousled hair. Others nearby croaked in sleepy tones, "Is everything all right? What's happening? Is that Hal?"

Martha responded, "Hal just had a bad dream. No alarm."

Hal hugged his mother tightly, shuddering in irregular spasms. "It was awful, Mama. Scary." He began to sob. "My friends...Nsuka, Tika. The *Jeunesse*...they tried to kill us. Arrows, beating, bush knives..." His convulsive sobbing then took over, drowning further words. Martha continued her soothing stroking of Hal's hair. "That's okay, son. You don't have to retell it. Let it go. Only a bad dream..." she crooned. Hal burst back in reply. "But it was so vivid, so real, Mama!" His sobs gradually lessened but he maintained his tight grip.

At last she released her arms and, taking Hal's hands in hers, bent down to kiss him on the cheek and look directly into his eyes. "After all we've been through in the last couple of days, it's no wonder you have bad dreams. Don't take them too seriously, Hal. God is with us and we're still safe and together. We're going to get through this. Okay, honey?"

Hal nodded to acknowledge his mother's attempt at comfort and reassurance, but his thoughts were far from those she had expressed. He silently reflected, *"Mama has no clue about my dreams. I take them seriously. That's what's so awful...they're likely to come true."*

***

It was mid-morning when the buzz of an aircraft overhead brought the little missionary group out of the dispensary and onto the soccer field across from the building. Circling the station was the familiar sight of George Kimble's MAF plane. Not having heard from Kisambo Station for several days, the mission's legal rep, Paul Gingrich, had flown to Kinshasa and contacted the U. S. Embassy, the UN military headquarters and MAF for assistance. Kimble had been dispatched to fly from Kikwit where he was stationed to survey the situation at Kisambo and Mukedi and assess what might be needed.

The group of nine – missionaries and family members – stood motionless in a small circle in the center of the field, faces turned upward as the plane passed overhead. Clusters of rebels hid beneath palm trees surrounding the field. The plane dipped low and a message was dropped to the group. It asked if it was possible to level an emergency landing strip in the road that ran in front of the station. Lacking tools to accomplish the task and concerned about the rebels' reaction to such an action, the missionaries remained motionless. A second pass and note was dropped. Did they want evacuation by helicopter? If so, they were to sit down. The group abruptly sat. Acknowledging their signal with a wiggle of its wings, the MAF plane headed off toward Mukedi to check out the situation there.

The sound of the departing plane could still be heard when the rebels burst out from their various hiding places, shouting threats and heading in from all directions toward the seated circle of *mindeles.*

"You have tricked us. You called the airplane. Search them!"

Calvin, Larry and the other men were pressed to the ground and many hands pulled and probed the clothing of the entire group, including the children. The *Jeunesse* were keenly aware of the function of the short-wave phonies in linking the mission station with outside resources. They had been careful to locate and destroy the communication equipment prior to burning the missionary residences. To be on the safe side, they even crushed the mimeograph machine from the Schroeder residence, and machete-chopped Beth's curlers before torching the houses.

The shouts and agitation continued for some time with Calvin and Larry attempting to reason with the rebel leaders over the din. Finally, they were able to convince them that it was in fact the *absence* of regular phonie contact that had prompted the visit of a plane to check on the well-being of the missionaries. Further, if they were to be evacuated, a plane would have to return. But where could it land? Cuing from the first dropped note, Calvin proposed that they level a portion of the road that ran past the station. This suggestion immediately prompted renewed debate and agitation among the rebels. In the end, the outcome was to grant permission to clear a landing site but with several key stipulations.

First, only the missionaries would be allowed to do the leveling. They would be supplied with short hoes and shovels. Even the Bible students were forbidden to help them. Second, no government officials would be allowed to set foot on the station. If any were to accompany a future flight, they would be killed and decapitated on the spot in full view of the missionaries. Finally, the mission's legal representative, Paul Gingrich, was declared persona non grata. Were he to arrive, it was announced that he would be arrested and tried at the rebels' forest headquarters.

As the sun rose and the day wore on, knots of young wannabe soldiers could be seen lounging in the shade finding great amusement watching the tiny group of sweating white folk, hacking away at the rutted road, attempting to create a level landing site for hoped-for rescuers. Bare headed and bare footed, the *mindeles* toiled in the hot sun, completely exposed. By midafternoon the sideline laughing and jeering faded and most of the bored rebels wandered away, allowing the station's Bible students to take up tools and labor on behalf of their exhausted and sunburned missionary friends.

The landing zone preparation came to a natural end with the arrival of dark afternoon thunderheads. One moment the dry grass across the soccer field shimmered in the still, intense sunlight. The heat and humidity of the tropical afternoon baked any exposed flora or fauna like some kind of giant celestial oven. Then, without warning a cool blast of wind invaded the laborers, tumbling leaves and lifting dust to twice the height of the work crew. For any who raised squinted eyes in the midst of the swirling grit they witnessed tumbling clouds rising and curling into dramatic anvil-like shapes. Soon, the first huge drops of rain fell, lifting little poofs in the sand as they hit. They were the signal to stop work and run for the tree line and that's just what happened. As one, the Bible student work crew dashed for cover. Boosted by a series of huge wind gusts, the rain first arrived in sheets, and then in a torrent, almost as if an unseen hand turned on a giant faucet.

Back in the dispensary, the weary Kisambo Station missionaries listened to the roar of the afternoon deluge as they tended to their blisters and wiped down their dirty sweat and dust caked limbs with wet cloths. Larry summed it up for the group. "I sure hope all that effort will prove to be worth it. I'm praying for a rescue aircraft in the morning!"

Mama Cécile made another meal delivery shortly before dark. The exhausted missionaries ate their meager fare with gratitude and prepared to spend another evening in their dispensary refuge. They all hoped for a quieter night this time. Beth wrapped some gauze around Martha's hand, badly blistered from their day's labor. "Surely George will return to check on us tomorrow, don't you think? Perhaps even send a UN helicopter? I'm sure not feeling any safer as time goes on."

Martha winced as the bandage was applied. "Yes, the uncertainty is wearing on me, too. But I'm most concerned about our children and their reaction to all of this."

Loud voices were heard just outside the door, drawing the attention of the group. After several minutes of clamor, Pastor Kinbumba appeared in the doorway with his son, Tika. He greeted the group warmly but with a somber demeanor, explained that the *Jeunesse* guarding the building did not want to allow him to meet with them. They confiscated the foodstuffs and clothing he had intended to share with the group that evening. He shook his head in frustration and disgust. "This is not how we treat people in the "new Congo.""

Tika and Hal stepped off to the side of the room. "Ilunga told me he was supposed to meet with you again today, but when he tried to come here his Mama stopped him. I sneaked up to the hut where they took him and spoke with him. He urged me to find a way to see you, and so I convinced Tata to bring me along on his visit. *Lumwenu*... have you heard from the ancestors?"

Hal motioned for Tika to step further away from where his father and the adults were talking. He pulled two chairs together and they sat, head to head, knees touching. Hal took a deep breath. "Yes, last night I had a dream." He paused, gathering his thoughts.

"Well, what was it? Don't stop now," Tika exclaimed. It was loud enough that Hal sat up and looked around to see if anyone could hear them.

Hal continued in a low voice. "Here is the message you must give to Tata Muzeka Adoko: Stay away from Kisambo Station. Neither you nor any member of your family are to set foot on the station as long as any *mindeles* are present. If you do, great harm will result. The ancestors are displeased with Biungu and his rebel friends."

Tika sat very still, taking in the seriousness of the message. "I will tell him. Did they reveal what will happen if the family don't stay away?" Hal's eyes were filled, tears streaked down his cheeks.

After a long pause He nodded.

#14 Kisambo Station

January 1964

The early morning light that filtered through the barred windows of the dispensary arrived with a sense of promise and hope for the Kisambo missionaries; hope that their rescue would somehow take place during the course of the new day and that their perilous trials would soon be over.

Pastor Kinbumba was true to his word about the church looking after their needs. Claudine, the wife of one of the elders arrived carrying a pot of steaming tea, some fruit and two whole loaves of bread. It was a welcome breakfast. They took encouragement not only from the provision of food, but also from Claudine's inquiries about their well-being and her tender smiles at their replies. She repeated a familiar theme, "We are so sorry, friends. We never imagined anything like this could happen here. Not at Kisambo!"

As the group was together sipping their tea and savoring small chunks of bread, Philip Bartel spoke up. "You know, last evening some of us had a chance to visit at length with our rebel guards. There are several former students among them who seem sympathetic with our plight. They were candid, almost friendly. One of them told me that the loud arguing we heard our first night here was in part because the two local rebel bands who attacked Kisambo had exceeded the orders given by their superiors."

"What?" Elsie Buller jumped to her feet. "You mean, all this destruction and chaos was *not* supposed to happen?" She held her head with both hands, as if to keep it from exploding. "What folly! I can't believe it...so much self-inflicted suffering in this land." She paced back and forth and finally headed for the door with one final exclamation of disgust, hands raised, and head thrown back, "Aggghh!"

Elsie's reaction prompted the hint of a smile on the part of her audience along with rolled eyes and several heads nodding in agreement. After a pause, Beth looked at Philip. "I'm sure those of us who have lost everything we own, including some of the Bible students and villagers will find *small comfort* in that little piece of information."

Calvin brought the conversation back to their present circumstances. "I've been thinking about how we might communicate in the event of further fly-overs today. I've got an idea I'd like to share. What if we used the gauze bandage strips that fill those two barrels over there to spell out some words on the soccer field?"

The others immediately sat up and voiced agreement with this idea. Lively conversation followed about what message should be scripted on the field and what words could best be used to succinctly spell it out.

Next, negotiations took place with the group's *Jeunesse* guards. They needed some convincing that the *mindeles* had to somehow signal arriving aircraft if they were indeed to be evacuated as their top leaders had directed. After lengthy discussion, the rebels agreed to allow a soccer field message to be placed. They concluded that since there was much work yet to do to conquer all the government posts and mission stations before attacking the region's cities, they needed the missionaries out of the way and the sooner the better.

By mid-morning the two-inch wide strips of cloth had been unrolled and in two-foot-high block letters the following message was created on the playing field:

OK TO LAND   350 YDS   BRING NO SOLDIERS GUNS OR PG SAFETY ASSURED

Contact was made with the Bible students and it was agreed that the missionary and Congolese wives and children would be the first to leave. The men – both students and missionaries – would wait for later flights.

In the capital, Leopoldville, Paul Gingrich's advocacy and urgent appeals to both the U. S. Embassy and the United Nations peacekeeping headquarters brought about a hopeful response. The head of the UN Congo Operations (ONUC), Canadian Brigadier-General Jacques Dextraze had just appointed and dispatched a fellow Canadian, Lt. Col. P. A. Mayer to head a small force of two 10-men sections to the troubled Kwilu region with orders to "rescue as many missionaries as possible who want to be rescued." Mayer was based in the diamond-mining center of Tshikapa, 100 miles to the east of Kisambo. After the surveillance report by MAF pilot, George Kimball confirmed the crisis, a rescue/evacuation task force was quickly organized.

It was nearly noon when the sound of a single-engine aircraft caught the attention of the Kisambo missionaries. They were seated in the shade of palm trees that bordered the soccer field, waiting and hoping. The Canadian de Havilland DHC-3 Otter, one of four used by the UN forces for surveillance in their Congo operations, began to circle over the station. They found out later that Lt. Col. Mayer, himself was the spotter. Shortly, the sound of additional aircraft could be heard. This time it was a pair of helicopters approaching.

The old Sikorsky S-55s, also known as Chickasaw H-19s, were square shaped workhorses, 40 feet long with an unobstructed cabin just below the main rotor that could hold 7 – 10 occupants. Their bulky shape and four-wheeled landing gear earned them the French nickname, *"éléphants joyeau"* (joyous elephants). The cabin had a large, accessible sliding door and two small windows on each side.

The loud Pratt & Whitney 800 hp engines roared, rotor blades kicking up sand and dust from the field as both craft settled down right in front of the missionaries. They had by then scrambled to their feet. Just to one side of them the Bible students and their families crouched with eyes squinted and arms raised to ward off the eruption of sand and dust.

Calvin dashed to the side of one of the helicopters. The pilot, whose perch was located some distance off the ground, held his door partially open and beaconed Cal to approach. He climbed up the built-on rungs and held on tight, straining to get close to the cracked door. The rotors were deafening, and their downward force threatened to blow him off the side of the helicopter. He yelled as loudly as he could to the pilot first in English and then in French. "Take the women and children first. Then come back for the men." The Swedish pilot removed his earphones in an effort to hear Cal's shouts, but he barely understood either language under ideal conditions. After several attempts at communication he shook his head and raised both palms in defeat.

In the meantime, trouble was escalating. Lt. Col. Mayer, circling in the Otter, was able to observe from his aerial perch that a large force of *Jeunesse* was closing in on the evacuees from three sides. He radioed to both helicopter pilots, *"Load the missionaries, by force if necessary and lift off. Immediately! You are about to be attacked by sizeable group of hostiles."*

Each helicopter had two UN soldiers/crew with automatic weapons. They slid the doors of the cabins open and motioned to the missionaries to come, gesturing in a rapid manner to communicate urgency. As the Kisambo group started toward the aircraft the rebels burst from surrounding vegetation that had hidden their approach. War cries mingled with terrified screams of the missionary women and the deafening roar of the rotor blades. In an instant the orderly boarding of evacuation aircraft morphed into a chaotic melee.

Hal stumbled after his mother, struggling to keep ahold of her hand. Someone grabbed his arm and he stumbled and fell, releasing his grip. One of the UN soldiers grasped Martha by the waist, lifting and propelling her into the cabin before turning to do the same with Beth. As Hal scrambled to his feet, the "Brrrritt" of automatic gunfire caught his attention. He looked in the direction of the second helicopter just in time to see two of the rebels who had attempted to breach the cabin door, fall mortally wounded. He recognized one of them. Hal shook off grasping hands and wrenched away from the grip of swarming rebels attempting to stop him from entering the helicopter. He heard several more short bursts of gunfire but did not dare look to check them out.

As he neared the door, reaching for an extended hand, a sharp pain shot through his arm. He collapsed to the ground once again. A rebel arrow had penetrated his forearm. Agonizing pain...he couldn't breathe. Grimacing, Hal looked up, in time to see a grinning attacker rushing at him, bush knife drawn back to strike. Then, in a sudden crash, down he came with a blurry figure on top of him, pummeling the assailant with both fists. Hal watched on in pain and shock as if it were a movie, the blur of action before him seeming like slow motion.

The recognition came in a flash...*Nsuka!* He had come out of nowhere and was pounding Hal's would-be assailant with all his might. Hal tried to shout something, but the earsplitting roar of the rotors continued to drown out any utterance. A UN crewman grasped Hal beneath his arms and lifting him, unceremoniously cast him through the cabin doorway. This action made him moan and wince with pain, the arrow still fully lodged in his arm, but Mama was immediately present to surround him with comforting arms. The cabin door slid shut with a bang, the pitch and whine of the engines increased, and the helicopter lifted off.

Both helicopters rose simultaneously, but the drama on the ground had not yet concluded. All of the missionaries were now in the custody of the rescue team. All that is, except one...Calvin. In the confusion no one had noticed that he remained in the center of the soccer field held firmly in the grasp of the same wiry little man with the wisp of a goatee and flecks of gray at his temples...the *President* of the rebel band who took Philip and Marvin into custody on their return from Gungu. Calvin tried repeatedly to wrench free, but his captor refused to let go of his wrist.

"You must stay, *mundele*. If you do not remain the soldiers will not return for your Bible students." Calvin was unsure whether this was a ruse to gain a ransom or to inflict further harm, or a genuine concern for the welfare of fellow Congolese.

He did not have time to reflect on this point since one of the helicopters, realizing there was still a missionary left on the ground, returned and rapidly descended near where Calvin and the *President* were struggling. Nearby rebels scattered as the S-55's landing gear touched down. The doors slid open and a Swedish crewman motioned for Calvin to come. With one last effort that left bloody scratches down his forearm, Cal broke away and dashed for the open door.

Hal lay cradled in his mother's arms watching through the open cabin door, the struggle between his father and the rebel leader. He managed a weak smile of relief seeing his father break free and approach their location. His smile turned to cold horror, however, as his father stepped around two still figures lying on the ground near the cabin door. One of them lay face down, but the other was sprawled out, face up. He had two rebel arrows just like the one in Hal's arm sticking out from his chest. It was *Nsuka*.

The heart-wrenching moan that reverberated through the noisy cabin came from some deep place that Hal could not begin to imagine. It penetrated the roar of the rotors, startling even the others in the cabin. *"Nooooo! Not Nsuka, not Biungu! Nooooo! I told them to stay away. Nooooo!"*

Martha, both baffled and startled, managed to gasp, "What has happened, Hal? What did you see, honey?"

Through deep sobs Hal blurted out, "I saw my friend dead. I

saw his brother shot. I warned them but they came anyway. *Nsukula* saved my life but it cost him his. I saw it all. I saw it in my dream and now I saw it happen." And then, mercifully, Hal collapsed into a dead faint and saw nothing further.

Part II:

Protection

#15 Rancho Palos Verdes

January 2009

Hal sat at his home office desk, gazing out the broad expanse of windows that offered a spectacular view of Los Angeles from the edge of the Palos Verdes hills. Though it was early, LA's brown haze had already formed in the distance blurring the downtown high-rise structures. His computer screensaver had been cycling images for some time already. Hal was supposed to be putting the final touches on his anthropology lecture on ethno-photography, but the sharp creases between his eyebrows and his glazed, unfocused stare signaled that his mind was far from the task at hand. The only "photo essay" his mind would process at present encompassed vivid images from the previous night's dreams. Actually, he would characterize them as more of a nightmare than simply bad dreams, or so he reasoned, leaning back in his office chair. He reached for the half full coffee cup before him, but as he took a sip, he nearly spit out the cold liquid. *Ugh! I waited too long*, he thought.

It had happened again – the vivid nightmare-like dreams. It was always distressing to him when they suddenly invaded his life. It was mostly because he had learned time and again over the years that just as he could not control or predict their arrival, neither could he ignore their message. They were often personal in nature, these special dreams with their technicolor reality. Last nights was. It had been nearly a year since the last one. Each time he hoped and prayed it would be the last. Well, not prayed, he corrected the thought. It had been a long time since he last participated in *that* childhood practice. But still he wished...

"Papa, Papa, Papa!"

Hal spun around just in time to catch a little blonde blur of motion and squeals that signaled the appearance of his four-year old granddaughter, Emily.

"Hey, Emmie, good morning!" he called out, a smile erupting on his face. He swept her up on his lap and continued to spin his chair. Emily gigged and snuggled her pony-tailed head into her grandpa's chest, relishing the whirl. This greeting had become a morning ritual for the two over the past six months that she and her mom had been living there.

"Morning, Dad. Have you had breakfast already?" Hal glanced up, his smile broadening.

The chipper greeting belonged to his daughter as she swept into the room. A strikingly beautiful, shapely brunette with long, thick hair, Tricia was the youngest of his three children. She had managed to pack a lot of living into her 28 years. "Entirely too much," Hal would have contended, if asked. The combination of her physical attributes and a winsome but addictive personality had given Tricia ready access to a partying lifestyle. Lack of restraint in general and with drugs in particular had propelled her in and out of both jail and multiple rehab facilities since her late teens. Her arrival at her father's doorstep with daughter Emily was occasioned by Tricia's most recent relapse event. She had lost her job, been evicted from her apartment and arrested for passing a bad check. Once again, Dad had come through to save the day and extract her from the clutches of disaster.

"Just coffee so far, Trish."

"Here, let me have that cup. It looks cold. I'll get some fresh from the kitchen." Tricia leaned down to kiss his cheek and with Hal's cup in hand turned to head back to the kitchen.

"Wait, Trish. There's something I want to ask you."

She paused in the doorway, as Emily climbed off Hal's lap and headed for the dog curled up on his pillow bed by the wall. "Something serious?" she asked.

"No, just a small favor to ask. I'd like to trade cars today. I'd like for you to use my CRV to drive to your NA meeting, and I'll take your old Corolla to the university. Just for today."

Tricia got a puzzled look on her face. "You'd rather drive my old clunker to work? It's a lot further to USC than to my meeting in Torrance, and your Honda is new. Why the trade?"

"I have my reasons. You won't object if I bring your car back with a full tank, will you?"

Frowning, she tilted her head to one side in thought. After a brief pause she shrugged. Turning and heading for the kitchen once again, Tricia called over her shoulder, "OK, fine. The keys are on the table by the door." She had learned by now not to demand explanations from her father. He seemed to have a mysterious side to him sometimes.

***

Hal exited Parking Lot 6 on the USC campus and turned the corner past the four-story collegiate gothic edifice of Irani Hall, home to the university's College of Letters, Arts and Sciences. It faced Kaprielian Hall, a brick building similar in size and architecture that housed his department and faculty offices. As he approached the side entrance, his cell phone buzzed. A chill went down his spine. *"I just hope she was able to drop Emmie off at preschool before it happened,"* Hal thought to himself.

Taking a deep breath, he lifted the phone to his ear. "Yes?"

"Dr. Schroeder? This is the Torrence Police calling. I'm afraid we have some bad news to report. Your daughter, Tricia has been in a serious accident. She has been injured but the good news is that apart from a concussion and broken bones, she will recover. She's a very fortunate young woman. It appears that the side airbags on her CRV may have saved her life. She's been taken to the Harbor-UCLA Medical Center. I'm afraid her vehicle is totaled. It was T-boned by an SUV that blew a red light. That driver, unfortunately, did not survive."

"Was she alone in the car? She was taking my granddaughter to preschool." Hal stopped breathing.

"She was alone, Dr. Schroeder," came the reply. "She must have completed the drop off prior to the accident." Hal exhaled and looked for a place to steady his wobbly legs.

Finishing the call, He made his way to a nearby bench and collapsed, shaken by this latest development. He ran a hand through his hair and stared up at the sky, thoughts swirling in his head: *"Why couldn't it have just been a dream and only a dream? As if Trish doesn't have enough troubles! She's going to be out of commission for some time. Emmie is going to be really scared. That was the right decision to trade cars. I'm going to need new wheels."*

That phone call ended the official workday for Hal. As he headed down the 110 freeway toward the Harbor Med Center, he thought further about next steps he would have to take to manage this latest "Trish crisis" as they had come to be known in the family.

He'd first have to call Phyllis. That'd be the most difficult one. They'd come a long way in the nine years since their 24-year marriage broke up, but there was still a strong element of blame and guilt that clouded any contacts. She had opposed his allowing

Tricia and Emily to move in, favoring a "tough love" stance instead. He would have to brace himself for an "I warned you..." response when he reported this latest event. *"I suppose I'm just going to have to take it if I want to persuade her to come down and watch Emmie until Tricia gets out of the hospital,"* he reflected.

The other difficult call would be to Mama. She would be concerned and offer to pray for them all, but she would also want to know if he had seen it coming. He'd have to tell her the truth. His father, God rest his soul, when alive was always skeptical about any examples of clairvoyance that had been shared with him. Papa feared they were signs of demonic possession or the like, expressing strong disapproval and alarm. Mama had always been more empathetic, even helping him conceal certain things from Papa at different times over the years, but to Hal she privately expressed a good deal of confusion and discomfort with the whole thing. At least he had never told her about the bones instruction he received as a youth from Kisambo shaman Museka. Her questions would stir up those painful old memories; that was the main reason he didn't want to hear them.

Tricia was bandaged and medicated by the time Hal was finally able to see her. She managed a weak smile and returned a kiss on his cheek when he bent over the bed to greet her. "Hi Daddy. I'm sorry I wrecked your new car. It wasn't my fault, though."

"Don't worry about that, honey. I'm just so relieved you're going to be okay. I haven't been home yet and I didn't call the preschool. I thought I'd better tell Emmie in person. She's going to be upset. I'm thinking I'll ask Phyllis to come down and stay with her for a few days until you get out of here."

Speaking slowly and slurring her words, Tricia replied, "Do you think Mom will agree? If she comes it will be great for Emily, but don't you think Greg might object to his wife staying under the same roof with her ex-spouse?" Tricia groaned as she shifted in her bed. One arm was in a cast as was one of her legs, elevated on pillows.

"We'll find out shortly. I'll call her when I leave here. I'll let you know the outcome."

"Dad, it's kind of weird that you traded cars with me today. It probably saved my life, but what made you do that?" Tricia raised herself on her good elbow from her pillow as she posed the question.

Hal brushed her query away with a wave of his hand and a change of subject. "Just a hunch, Trish. A lucky one, it appears. I'm heading out now to give your Mother a call and see what she says. Assume that she's coming unless I tell you otherwise." And with that, he rose, gave her a peck on the cheek and strode out of the room.

#16 Rancho Palos Verdes

January 2009

An all too familiar sense of dread and anxiety gripped Hal as he turned into the driveway of his home. He was anxious about Tricia and her latest brush with disaster. He was apprehensive about the task of informing the family, especially Phyllis and his mother, albeit for different reasons. But the bone-deep tension that made it difficult to swallow and knotted his shoulders and arms came from the unfolding of his dream into the physical reality of Tricia's accident. The knowledge of impending disaster had once again left him feeling helpless, depressed, angry. *"Why did I have to be cursed with this?"*

As Hal decoded his security alarm and unlocked the front door, his thoughts returned to the task before him. He had decided to make his phone calls at home before he picked up Emily from preschool. She would surely be upset with the news that her mommy was injured. It would seem best to have completed any phone calls that included descriptions of Tricia's accident before Emmie's anxious little ears came into range.

He poured a glass of his best Merlot and settled back into his favorite recliner in the living room. "I might as well get comfortable before my uncomfortable calls," he said out loud as if to reassure himself.

Hal dialed his ex-wife's cell phone in Portland and as expected, she picked up on the first ring. His caller ID appearing on her phone did not signal an invitation to a friendly chat; it seldom meant anything to her but trouble. Of that fact he was painfully aware.

Sure enough, Phyllis answered alarmed. Her response to his crisis report was a rapid series of queries that put Hal on the defensive. "Was Tricia driving too fast? Under the influence again? How do you know she's sober...it's only been six months and she's fooled us before. Was Emily in the car? Is that rattletrap car of hers even safe to drive? Was the accident her fault? How badly was Tricia hurt?"

When the barrage of questions paused so she could take a

breath, Hal interjected with measured cynicism, "I was hoping you'd finally get around to asking how our daughter was doing after her near-death experience." Phyllis' silence let him know that he'd scored with that reflection. He proceeded to answer her questions one by one, offering a positive report on Tricia. Then, he made his request.

"I realize that it's asking a lot but I was wondering if there was any way you'd consider coming down here for a few days to watch Emily while I'm at work and Tricia is in the hospital; maybe help out for her first few days home as well? My teaching load is especially heavy this semester, and we have tenure reviews for our junior faculty all of this month. Both responsibilities require me to spend extra time on campus. It would be so helpful if you could come. Besides, Emily adores you. She is always excited to show us the little gifts and pictures you send her each month."

Phyllis started several sentences without completing them. "Oh Hal, I don't see how... You know, I'm a board member of several non-profits and my schedule... Greg may not be pleased..." Her voice trailed off and she sighed deeply, continuing after a pause. "Okay, I realize that you're in a bind, Hal. Tricia needs a mother's care at present as well. It *is* something positive I can do for her at this juncture in her life...something besides just being critical. I don't like being that way. I love her. It's just that we've been hurt and disappointed so many times."

Her tone of voice then changed, taking on a clear resolve. "Well...I will talk it over with Greg and unless he has strong objections I'll be there. I'll be there in the next day or so. I'll call you with my flight schedule as soon as I know it."

Hal couldn't help feeling relieved as he hung up. *"That went better than expected,"* he thought. He took a couple of big swallows of Merlot. *"It'll be good for the two of them – Trish and Phyllis – to spend time together, but I'm less sure having her around here will be good for me,"* he mused to himself.

Hal's next call was to Martha, his mother. At age 85 she was still plenty alert and responsive. Her home at present was in an assisted living facility in San Jose, very near Hal's older sister, Patty. She was able to look in on her mother on a daily basis. Mother and son, however, shared a special bond that traced back to their mission station days in the Congo. They spoke by phone every week without fail. Martha insisted on being informed not only about Hal's personal life but also about his professional activities. Anthropology field studies had taken him to many exotic spots on the planet and his mother derived a great deal of vicarious satisfaction from reports of his travels and adventures.

Hal's account of Tricia's accident brought immediate expressions of empathy from Martha. "Oh, how awful. Your poor dear Tricia! She's had to face so much misfortune in her young life. I pray for her daily. I certainly won't let up now."

"Thanks, Mama. I'll be sure to let her know. The accident wasn't her fault, by the way; the other driver blew through a red light and hit her broadside. The police said that she was saved by the side airbags."

"Her old car has side airbags?" Martha queried.

"Um, no. She was driving my CRV." *"Here it comes,"* thought Hal. *"I can't get anything past her radar."*

There was a break in the conversation as Martha gathered her thoughts. "Okay, son...you must level with me here. You saw it coming and traded cars, didn't you!" Her words were presented as more of a declaration than a question.

Hal's eyes suddenly pooled. He couldn't speak. Mama's statement shook him to the core. He felt suddenly exposed, vulnerable. How could she discern that so quickly? What should he say?

He struggled to regain his composure and searched about for a response, but nothing came to mind.

Martha resumed in a gentle tone. "Oh sweetie, I'll just bet this touches a tender spot." These insightful words prompted more tears in her listener.

"It sounds like once again you came up with the right decision, Hal. It may indeed have saved Tricia's life. We've talked about this in the past. You can't prevent events from happening with your foreknowledge, but you can influence the outcome...and once again you did. Now, this is your mother speaking: stop taking responsibility for the trials of life that come your way. Stop it!"

It took Hal some time to regain enough composure to reply. "You're right, Mama. It's gotten to me. I guess it was a bit too close to home this time. I appreciate your understanding. I do. But, when you update Patty and Rhonda about this, please don't tell them about my part."

"Hal, you should really talk this premonition business through with someone, a counselor or therapist or pastor. This facility of yours has a high price tag. I just hate to see you struggle with it again and again."

"I've tried counseling in the past, Mama. Don't you remember...during college? It didn't do any good. But I'll be fine. This just alarmed me since I'm pulling so hard for Trish's recovery, and I guess it stirred up some unpleasant memories as well. That's all."

"Well, I'll be praying for you, sweetheart. It only makes sense to do so when things happen that are beyond our understanding or control. Perhaps you should give some thought to prayer as well."

Hal let that one slide past without comment.

Once they had said their goodbyes and disconnected, Hal sat back in his recliner and finished off his wine. He remained in that position for several minutes staring out the windows, pondering Mama's words. Her recognition and acceptance of his foreknowledge of disaster was both comforting and disconcerting. It was comforting to know she didn't judge or blame him. It was disconcerting, however, that she could so clearly recognize his pain and vulnerability and expose the rawness of his feelings in response to this latest premonition. *Should I heed her advice and try therapy once again?*

He stood, pushed these thoughts away and pacing the living room, phone in hand, made quick calls to each of his other children. He was only able to reach Cal's voice mail. *"He's probably in court today,"* Hal reasoned regarding his attorney-son's failure to pick up. He left a brief message about Tricia's accident, ending with "I think your mother will be flying down to help out for a few days. Don't worry. Everything is okay for now. Call only if you have questions."

He reached his daughter Judy's cell phone in the midst of a math lesson in her fifth-grade classroom. She made a quick assignment, then stepped out into the hall for a brief chat. He reported the basics of Tricia's accident. Judy's questions ended with her inquiring what she might be able to do. "Thanks for your concern, sweetheart, but I think we've got things covered. Perhaps the best thing you could do is to give your sister a call in the next couple of days to let her know you're thinking of her."

"Of course! I just wish I could stop by and see her or help out more directly. At times like this it's frustrating to be so far away here in Portland with you guys in LA." Hal didn't know what else to say so he excused himself and hung up.

And then he headed for preschool to pick up Emily and complete his notifications.

#17 Rancho Palos Verdes

January 2009

In spite of rainy skies and blustery winds, Phyllis's United flight from Portland arrived at LAX on time. Hal and Emily waited just outside of security watching for the familiar stride that would identify her arrival even before they could see her face. It was a loud and confusing wait. A cacophony of noise: loudspeaker announcements, calls and loud exchanges in multiple languages echoed in the broad hallway. Businessmen raced by, computer cases over one shoulder, carry-ons wheeling behind. Mothers pushing strollers, elders escorted in wheelchairs, college kids in school colors all burst through the double doors seemingly at the same time. A parade of multiple shapes, sizes and complexions of travelers emerged from the "Arrivals" doorway anxiously looking for family and friends.

"There she is!" Emmie squealed, jumping up and down pointing with one hand as she grasped Papa's with the other. As Phyllis drew closer, Emily let go and ran to her Nana who had crouched down to greet her with open arms. "How's my Sweet Patootie?" Phyllis managed to somehow ask, voicing Emmie's pet name between her chuckles and a barrage of the four-year-old's squeezes and kisses.

Hal stood by smiling. "Welcome to LA, Nana."

Phyllis stood with Emmie in her arms as Hal retrieved her computer bag and reached for the handle of her carry-on. "No checked bags?"

"You know me," Phyllis replied still smiling. "I prefer to travel light."

***

Hal turned off the 405 and headed down Highway 1 toward his home, driving a newly acquired rental car. His nearly new CRV was totaled and he really didn't intend to use Tricia's old Corolla unless he absolutely had to. It was less than 20 miles from LAX to his home, but the rainy weather added travel time stretching it into an hour's drive.

"So how is our daughter doing by now?" Phyllis asked

pleasantly after occupying much of the drive with attention to Emily. The latter was now cheerfully singing in her car seat behind the adults.

"She's pretty sore, but generally in good spirits. The hospital staff are being very careful with the administration of pain meds since Tricia is a recovering addict. The doctor had some very specific instructions for when she is discharged this week. Until she gets weaned off the prescription stuff and back to Tylenol and over the counter meds, all pain pills stay in our control – yours and mine – to administer. And we are to keep careful account of the supply."

"How are you doing with your alcohol consumption these days, Hal?" Phyllis asked rather pointedly as she glanced over at him. "You have had some pretty bad days yourself in the past. Like around the time our marriage broke up," she added.

"And thus it begins, within the first hour of her arrival," Hal thought to himself.

"I'm doing just fine, thanks for asking," he replied in a detectably sarcastic tone. "Alcohol is a very minor part of my life these days."

"Well, I ask because it played such a big part in killing our 25-year marriage," Phyllis continued, lowering her voice so Emily wouldn't hear. "That, and your little tryst with that grad student while on field studies in the South Pacific." Now, her voice had taken on a definite edge.

Hal sighed deeply and his eyes narrowed. His hands gripped the steering wheel so tightly that his knuckles turned white. "You're not going to spend this visit rehashing history, are you Phyllis? I'm just not going there again. It's too painful and we've both moved on from there."

Not willing to abandon the subject quite yet, Phyllis crossed her arms and looked down as she spoke. "Again? Ha! I've never yet been able to get you to talk through those miserable days, Hal. It's so frustrating to me. I think you should get some therapy. You'd benefit from shining a little light into the dark corners of your life."

"Of course, you'd think that's best," Hal snapped. "As a life-long social worker you're all about expressing feelings and the like, as if that's the panacea for past pain. For some of us, life works best if we leave well enough alone and don't rehash the past." With that response, he made it clear that he was done with this topic.

Turning his face, he called back to Emily in her car seat behind them. "How're you doing back there, Emmie? We're almost home."

***

Later that same day, after dropping Emily off at a friend's place for a play date, Hal and Phyllis drove to Harbor Medical Center to visit Tricia. She was sitting up in her hospital bed reading a magazine, arm and leg in casts with her lower limb elevated on pillows. She glanced up as her parents appeared in the doorway.

"Well, look at the two of you!" she exclaimed as they came into view. "Together again. I guess that's my calling in life...to bring the two of you together to respond to my latest disaster." She was smiling, pleased at her clever greeting. Her parents were not amused at the comment, however. Both rolled their eyes on cue.

"Hi sweetheart," Phyllis offered as she bent down to give Tricia a hearty hug that made her wince. "It's good to see you, though I am sorry it has to be from some personal calamity." She sat on the bed and took Tricia's free hand in hers. "I suppose it must seem like that...I mean, seeing your parents together because of some trouble of yours. It has happened that way in the past, perhaps a few too many times. Well, in all our imperfections we do love you, Trish, and we genuinely care what happens to you."

Hal bent in to give Tricia a peck on the cheek. "That goes for me too."

"How's Greg?" Tricia asked with a slight upturn of her mouth and a twinkle in her eye. Hal smiled, recognizing his daughter's not-so-subtle attempt at bating her mother.

"He's just fine, thank you for asking," was the even reply.

That wasn't nearly satisfying enough, so Tricia tossed out another line. "I'll just bet he was thrilled to see you head off for your ex's place for the next week or so."

Phyllis' face flushed, whether from embarrassment or anger, Hal couldn't be sure. "I'm here to look after you and Emily, not to talk about Greg, Tricia. So, tell me more about your accident. Your Dad said that the other party ran a red light. Is that how it happened?"

"Yes, Mom, it was completely her fault and it ended up being a fatal mistake...for her, and almost for me." Tricia shifted her position in bed. "Let me anticipate the question that I know is simmering in your brain. I *am* maintaining my sobriety and I *was* driving responsibly. In fact, I was headed for my NA meeting in Torrence when it happened."

Phyllis did not question her daughter's assumptions, but with a forced smile, patted her on the cast-covered forearm. "I wondered at first, it's true. It has not been all that long since your last relapse, you know, and I'm afraid nothing that happens to you surprises me anymore."

With that, Tricia's face fell, and her eyes became liquid pools. "I just want to get this out now, mother, before any more time passes." The first tear coursed down her cheek and she sat upright to look Phyllis in the eyes.

"Mom, I know you've been through a lot with me and I've failed you many times. But the truth of the matter is that I'm an adult. I'm my own person. I'm not your responsibility to worry about. And neither is Emily! I've made my own choices in life, some of them pretty bad ones I'll admit, but I'm on the right track now and I'm determined to make a good life for Emily...and for me. I don't yet know all of what that means but here's the deal: my life is *my* responsibility and I'm finally *being* responsible. Any well-intentioned probing and advice-giving you may be tempted to offer does not help me maintain my sobriety, my serenity."

Phyllis sat back, speechless, her face white as a sheet. Then, she slowly reached across the bed and wrapped both arms around her daughter, tears streaming down her cheeks. After a long embrace Phyllis sat up and fished for a tissue from her purse. Hal watched on, touched by the exchanges before him, an expression of pride on his face at his daughter's honesty and courage.

Phyllis blew her nose on a tissue, wiped her moist eyes and smiled. "I'll try to respect your wishes, honey. Thank you for saying that. But I warn you...old habits aren't easily broken."

Tricia's eyes crinkled, her teeth shining through a warm smile as she reached out her one free arm to invite another embrace.

#18 USC Campus, Los Angeles

January 2009

The excited grad student continued her monologue without interruption oblivious to the fact that her professor was nowhere in the vicinity. Well, his attention was clearly elsewhere though to be perfectly correct, his body was seated directly in front of her at his office desk in USC's Kaprielian Hall.

"Ever since I saw Barbara Meyerhoff's *Number Our Days* I just knew anthropology was my calling," she rattled on. "I have this passion to explore aging in other cultures. And now, I get to go to Maumu..."

"It's Makatea, Jennifer. The island in French Polynesia is called Makatea. The main town is Maumu," Hal corrected, half listening to the enthusiastic soliloquy droning on before him. He had a splitting headache and the last thing he wanted to think about right now was his upcoming research field trip to the South Pacific. These were his regularly scheduled office hours, however, and this student had every right to make use of them.

"In your lecture you said there are only sixty-one inhabitants on the island...on Makatea. How many of those residents are seniors, Dr. Schroeder and will I have to use a translator to interview them?" The student sat on the edge of her chair, eyes sparkling, hands poised above an iPad placed on the front corner of his desk.

Hal slowly stood to his feet and ran a hand through his hair. "Jennifer, I'm sending a memo at the first of the week to our whole research team. It will have a lot of details and answer most of your questions. Rather than continuing on now and repeating things, why don't you just plan to stop by after you review the memo. We can clarify anything you need to know that it doesn't address. I'm not feeling very well this afternoon and I need to excuse myself."

Jennifer scrambled to her feet, iPad in hand, her expression a mixture of confusion and disappointment. "Um, okay Dr. Schroeder. Sorry you aren't feeling good," she mumbled in reply, reaching for her backpack on the floor. "I'll look for your memo.

Have a good weekend." She glanced back over her shoulder as she exited the room, obviously troubled at the abrupt termination to her office hour appointment. Hal remained standing behind his desk, gazing out the window.

The events of the past week kept replaying in his mind. Ever since he first awoke from the dream that held a premonition of Tricia's accident, a deep inexplicable sense of dread and fear had settled on him. These feelings that he hated so much had once again returned, churning his guts. They just would not leave. In the past whenever they haunted him, he would reach for the nearest bottle of booze to calm his spirits. It helped for a time, dulling pain and distracting troubled thoughts, but he had learned the hard way that all too soon alcohol becomes a cunning, cruel master. Most distressing, however, was the disabling anxiety that filled every corner of his mind. Waves of angst made it difficult to concentrate on anything. This awareness of impending disaster triggered a return of lifelong fears: that he should be doing something to prevent it; that it was his responsibility to act on this knowledge, to rescue the situation, to save the day. He felt powerless, caught in an emotional riptide that threatened to pull him under.

"Ko-Ko!" The office door cracked open and the familiar face of Brad Waterhouse appeared. His background – growing up as the child of missionaries in Ghana – made him not just a valued department colleague but one of the few persons on the planet that Hal trusted. In most things Brad was very much a kindred spirit. Even his typical African greeting, a verbal "doorbell" from a place that had none, was unique, always a welcome announcement of his arrival.

Hal jumped, his exaggerated reaction sending a stack of papers flying off his desk as he groped for the edge to steady himself.

"Oh, Brad! Hey." He bent down to collect the papers. "You startled me. Guess I was deep in thought."

"Sorry about that, buddy. Just checking...are you still on for Indian food at Tutor Hall? My stomach is growling...it's almost lunch time." Brad knelt down and collected scattered papers, handing them to Hal. "You seem pretty jumpy today, Hal," he said lightly.

Hal stood, lining the papers up and restacking them on the desk. He was quiet for several beats before he turned to look directly at his friend. "I'm actually feeling pretty distracted. I'd like to talk with you about it, Brad, if you can stomach a little of my crap along with the fine fast-food Indian cuisine." His intense expression and somber tone were clear clues that this was going to be a serious conversation in spite of the quip.

"Hey, I like zesty food. It's okay with me if you want to add some spice of your own to our lunch, but let's head out *now* if we want to avoid the noontime rush. If we hurry, we can get a good table...so we can conspire in private."

During the two-block walk to the Viterbi Engineering building that housed the Tutor Hall Café, Brad inquired about Tricia's recovery. "All I've heard about the accident was what Norman announced at faculty meeting on Tuesday. Is the accident what you want to talk about? How is the lovely Tricia doing by now, incidently?"

Hal offered a short summary of the facts related to Tricia's accident adding that he had invited his ex, Phyllis, to come help out with extra care for Emily and her mother during the first part of the latter's recovery. The corners of Brad's mouth turned up slightly. "I believe I'm starting to get a hint of what this conversation may be about."

Shortly, they arrived at their destination. The two professors made their meal choices, paid and found a private table near one wall. Brad immediately dug into his Tandoori chicken, but Hal sat staring at the Panini sandwich before him. He didn't have much of an appetite.

He finally broke the silence. "I'm having trouble sorting all of this out, Brad. It began with another one of those unusual dreams. In this one, I saw Tricia getting into an accident. It was so vivid I knew it was going to happen. As a result, the next morning I traded cars with her thinking that she'd have a better chance if she crashed in my vehicle rather than hers. And it *did* happen, just as in the dream."

At that, Brad stopped eating and placed his fork on the plate listening intently. "Amazing. So how did it impact you...what did you do, Hal?"

"I was plenty alarmed but not surprised. I quickly clicked into "fix-it" mode. I checked on Tricia, dealt with the officials, called Phyllis to see if she'd help out, and informed my other kids and my mom. But that's when things went south for me. Ever since I spoke with Mama, I have been in some kind of emotional state. It's hard to describe." Hal stopped to take a sip of iced tea and gather his thoughts. Brad sat back remaining quiet to give his friend plenty of space to sort things out.

"I sometimes wonder if I'm going crazy. I can't concentrate. I have these waves of dread and anxiety...and guilt, like there's something I should have done to prevent this. But I can't think of anything I realistically *could* have done other than what I did. And then there are the dreams. Ever since the accident I've had recurrent nightmares that take me back to my childhood, to our evacuation from the mission station. I've had them almost every night. I end up staying up until late, not wanting to go to bed for fear of what sleep will bring. Mama's picking up on my premonition in my call and her sympathetic response seemed to flick on some kind of internal switch."

Hal fiddled with the straw in his drink. "I don't think I've told you, Brad, but a lot of these things I've experienced before at different periods in my life. This time, however, it seems different. I'm not shaking it off as easily as I have on other occasions." He kept his eyes on the drink, not looking up.

Brad listened carefully, shaking his head slowly, baffled. A look of kindness and concern slowly spread across his face. "So, you called Phyllis to come. Has her presence been a help to you?" He picked up his napkin to absentmindedly dab his lips, as if to signal that he was done eating.

"Yes and no," was Hal's reply. "You'll recall from past conversations, she and Tricia have always had a difficult relationship, a contentious one. Well, this time the two of them actually seem to be trying to make it work. And Phyllis has genuinely been helpful preparing meals, offering nursing care and babysitting Emmie. But...she keeps wanting to process our breakup." Hal's hand went through his hair once again.

"I'm loathe to go anywhere near there, much to her great disappointment. Brad, if this other stuff isn't bad enough, having to revisit that god-awful time of pain and failure is a real minefield for me. So...when I'm here on campus I can't think worth a damn and when I head for home, I'm an emotional mess. I close down completely. I can't keep going like this..." He held his head with both hands, elbows on the table.

Brad reached across to place a hand on Hal's arm. "I'm very

sorry, my friend, for your distress. I wish I could offer you some great advice or counsel that would lift the weight, but as a wise man once said, *'one does not teach the paths of the forest to an old gorilla.'* Since we share an African heart, challenges like yours stir in me the village wisdom of my youth. Sayings like: 'Smooth seas do not make skillful sailors,' 'Every misfortune is a blessing,' and 'However long the night, the dawn will break.'"

Hal looked up with smile cracks at his eyes, one corner of his mouth turned up ever so slightly. "Nice try, Brad. I'm afraid your ever-present African clichés won't do it for me this time. I do appreciate your listening ear, though and I get your genuine concern."

"Seriously, Hal, some of my proverbs are worth pondering. For example, *'Unless you call out, who will open the door?'* Or how about this one? *'Ears that do not listen to advice, accompany the head when it is chopped off.'* I know you are opposed to therapy, but perhaps you should revisit that notion. I felt that way for years but really benefitted when Shari and I divorced. I know a therapist who specializes in former MKs and Third Culture Kids, TCKs we're called now...those of us who grew up outside our passport country. She's good: insightful, kind and helpful."

"Let me think about it," was Hal's last word on the subject as they rose to head back to their offices.

#19 USC Campus, Los Angeles

March 2009

Hal sat back in his office chair, took off his glasses and rubbed his eyes. He looked up at the clock on the wall, surprised to see that it was almost 8 PM. His late afternoon of video editing had somehow gotten away from him. Man, there didn't seem to be enough hours in the day to complete everything he had to do. He'd been scrambling ever since his return from the Makatea field research trip. He still had a long way to go in editing the interviews they had recorded before even beginning any analysis of their substance. Meanwhile, still awaiting his attention for the coming week were undergrad lectures to review and reading to catch up on for his grad seminar.

Hal reached for his coffee cup and took a sip, grimacing at the bitter brew that bit back. "Ugh! That end-of-the-day drink is more put-me-down than pick-me-up. Hmm...I wonder if Tricia made supper. Guess I'd better give her a call...or pick something up on the way home," he said thinking out loud to himself. He switched off his desk lamp, but before shutting down the computer, brought up his email account for one last scan of the inbox contents. There, between a long list of university announcements, student inquiries and research-related postings a subject line popped out: *"TASOK Class of '70 Reunion."*

"What's this?" Hal said to himself, his hand automatically going to his hair. He sat back down to open up the message. The computer screen illuminated the dimly lit office as he leaned forward to read.

> *"SAVE THE DATE.*
> *Class of 1970 is planning a 40th reunion in Kinshasa July 13 – 17, 2010 (Tuesday – Saturday). Because of the challenges of travel to the DRC (costs, time away from work, visas, plans to link to other destinations, etc.) we are asking class members and their accompanying spouse/partner to circle the dates and begin planning NOW for a*

return to your African roots. Reunion headquarters & lodging will be at the MPH guesthouse across from the TASOK campus.

We anticipate this to be a highlight experience of our adult lifetimes, a revisit to a magical place and time that significantly shaped all of our lives. The reunion committee has some awesome experiences already lined up: meals, tours, picnic outings, TASOK updates, and reminiscence sessions. More updates & details will arrive in coming months. This is your FIRST NOTICE.

Please check the attachment for a current list of known names and addresses. If you can help locate any of the missing persons reply asap to the email address given. We are asking you to let us know of your intent to attend the celebration by July 17, 2009. Look for monthly email updates.

Oyé, Class of '70!
Reunion Planning Committee"

Hal sat back in his chair, staring at the message before him for several minutes. A flood of pleasant memories and sensations unexpectedly gathered, transporting him to another time and place. Hot humid Kinshasa afternoons, the familiar odor of garbage and diesel fumes, sweaty soccer matches, storytelling in upstairs dorm rooms, picnics along the Congo River, African meals – *mwamba, saka-saka* and *pili-pili,* swimming at the *Petit Chutes.* But then, the image of an earlier time emerged, interrupting his musings. Kisambo Station. A jolt of alarm accompanied it, tightening his guts and bringing a quick end to his reverie.

"Enough of that!" he voiced out loud, dismissing any further ponderings of the past...and the invitation before him. Hal reached over to shut down his computer, then sent a quick text to Tricia to let her know he was on his way home. He took a deep breath and as he closed the door on a darkened room, the knot in his stomach relaxed.

***

Hal did not think further about the reunion email for some time. He had plenty of distractions both at work and at home.

Tricia was working on moving out, "getting on with my life," is how she framed it. Emily, however, was presenting a serious impediment to her plans. She was not happy with the prospect of leaving grandpa's safe and familiar home and threw a fit every time her mommy brought up the subject. No way was *she* ready to move on with *her* life!

Happily, Tricia's injuries were nearly healed. She landed a barrister's job at a nearby Starbucks. Further, she arranged to move in with a friend she met through her Narcotics Anonymous group. Her prospective roommate was also an employed single mother with a young daughter. They planned to share both expenses and childcare duties. That seemed like a good solution to Hal, but the "Emmie resistance" would likely take some work. "I'm staying out of that one," he told himself.

Tricia's two weeks under Phyllis' well-intentioned but smothering care had only heightened her motivation to move out on her own as soon as possible. Thinking about it now, as he sat in his favorite chair staring out the window, Hal concluded that progress had been made. There had only been two incidents – shouting-tearful blow-ups – during Phyllis' stay and this time the two female firebrands had managed to re-engage after only a few hours, rather than enduring months of silence as in the past. He had kept his distance in spite of Phyllis' urgings: "Are you going to let her talk to me like that, Hal? Say something to her." Dodging rather than engaging such emotional minefields still seemed to be the best strategy.

It actually hadn't been difficult to stay away from home with so much going on at the university. The busy tenure review process took many extra hours of reading and reference checking over and above usual class prep and advising duties. This year's process had become even more intense with the discovery that one of the untenured faculty had plagiarized from other's research, including some of Hal's. Meetings with the university counsel, faculty union reps and the faculty member and his attorney added to the spring workload.

The analysis of interviews taken on the February Makatea field research trip had also proved to be far more complicated than anticipated. It was seriously behind schedule. Chief translator, Mme. Simone, unexpectedly died. An elderly woman who had grown up in French Polynesia, Simone knew the island language and its nuances well. Several key interviews required translation, so her demise brought the project to a halt. An extensive search for a substitute only produced a young person who did not have a good grasp of the native tongue, complicating efforts to classify comments and deepen insights on their research goal: to study the influence of modernization on aging in the islands.

Hal smiled as he sat back, crossing his feet up on the desk. It was good to be able to retreat to the home office. Here one could think. With Emmie in preschool and Tricia at work it was quiet, peaceful in the house.

The cell phone rang, and Hal jumped. Feet flying off the desk, he lurched fully upright answering the call with a startled, shaky voice. "Yes? Dr. Schroeder here."

"*Mbote, ndecko. Sango nini?*" (Greetings brother. What's new?) came the voice on the line. Hal recognized the Lingala greeting but not the speaker. "*Mbote na yo. Nani wana?*" (Greetings. Who's there?) He answered in-kind as he sat back down at his desk, attempting to regain his wits.

"It's me, Carl, your buddy from Congo days. Long time no speak. It's been ages since we were last in contact. In fact, the last time we spoke I think you and Phyllis had just parted ways. That was probably seven or eight years ago, right?"

"Hey, Carl!" Hal responded with some enthusiasm as his mind finally focused on the caller. "What a surprise. I'd lost track of you. Are you here in LA? What prompts this call?"

"Yeah, I'm at LAX headed back to Chicago shortly. Still living there. I've been at a conference all week and thought I'd try reaching you while waiting for my flight. Your former hostel roommate, Paul Bannon, is on the TASOK class' 40th reunion committee. He gave me your number and asked me to call you. I'm to make sure you sign up for the event in Kinshasa. You *are* planning to attend, right?"

Hal paused before replying in a subdued tone. "You know, I just got that first announcement a few days ago and haven't really given it much thought. I've got a pretty full plate these days with my university work. Summers often involve field research trips in my discipline. I don't know that I can fit in the class reunion."

"Come on, Hal. You were always the cornerstone of our adventures. Native speaker, half-Congolese at heart, talking us out of trouble, arranging pirogue escapes, bartering food, you name it.

All our best stories involve you. No *way* will the gang let you bypass this event!"

"There are plenty of stories to be told without my being there, Carl," Hal responded with a chuckle, then shifted to a thoughtful tone. "Besides, I'm not exactly excited to return. I last visited Kinshasa during college when my folks were still working in the city. After dad passed away, I told myself I was done with Congo. Too many painful goodbyes associated with that place. Not sure I've changed my mind."

"Yeah, I hear you on the goodbyes thing," Carl replied softly. "Still," his voice reanimated, "I'd sure like to see you again, to catch up on our lives, find out what's happened to everyone. I'm sure the others feel that way too. By-the-way, have you remarried or partnered up again by now?"

Before Hal could reply, a loud departure announcement blared in the background, bringing a quick end to Carl's call. "Oops, last call on my flight. I've got to head out fast. Give it serious thought, okay buddy? *Tikala malamu.*" (Stay well) The call abruptly ended but the thoughts of Africa lingered.

#20 USC Campus, Los Angeles

May 2009

It was the final lecture of the semester in Anthro 200, "The Human Animal." Kaprielian Hall 319 was full as might be expected, since even the course's sporadic attenders were hedging their bets that some hint of next week's final exam might slip out. Hal waxed eloquent, presenting an elegant defense of the importance of psychology in human identity, in one last major attempt to push back the walls of ignorance in his popular undergrad class.

His cell phone buzzed on the podium, distracting him momentarily but as he was nearing the lecture's end, he disregarded it to launch into a final story. It was only as the students filed out that he noticed he had received not just one but three missed calls from the same number. Caller ID revealed the origin to be his sister Patty's phone.

"This is not good news," he thought to himself as he quickly redialed and placed the phone to his ear.

"Oh Hal, it's finally you! I've been trying to reach you," came the anxious voice of his older sister. "Something very bad has happened. Mama has fallen. They think she broke her hip and may have hit her head when she fell. The housekeeper at her assisted living residence found her unconscious in her room. I'm at the hospital now...Good Samaritan Hospital."

A cold shiver coursed down Hal's spine. All week he had felt a puzzling heaviness that kept him tense, a sense of dread as if something bad was about to happen. There had been no technicolor dream signaling a distinct premonition, so he had dismissed the sensations as just typical end-of-semester regrets and pending pressures of final grading. But now he wondered if it weren't something more all along. He sat down hard on one of the lecture room chairs, his mind filling with questions.

"How long ago, Patty? When did it happen?"

Patty was sobbing. "I don't know. They just found her and brought her here an hour or so ago. They told me that she has gone into shock. Oh Hal, it's just awful. Poor Mama, lying there in pain..."

Hal felt numb, as if his inner emotions had seized up, frozen solid. "Have you spoken to the doctor yet?" His mind was spinning. *I'd better get a flight to San Jose immediately. This just can't be happening to Mama. She's indestructible, the one rock-solid constant I can count on in my life. My lifeline, my anchor time after time. If I can be there with her, maybe there is something I can do, something I can fix...*

"Not yet, Hal. I've only spoken to the EMTs and the admitting nurse. They said the doctor would come out to talk with me as soon as he could. I need to call Rhonda yet, but I thought I should reach you first. Pray for Mama, Hal. She'd want you to."

That comment paused the exchange. Hal sighed and frowned, mumbling, "I'm afraid I'm not much good at prayer, Patty. I'll leave that to you and Rhonda." Changing subjects, he continued, "I'm going to see if I can catch a flight to San Jose yet today. I'll rent a car and come straight to the hospital. Be sure to call me back as soon as you talk to the doc, OK? Hopefully, I'll see you later today."

By the time Hal arrived at the hospital in San Jose all of the Bay Area family members were there. Patty and Arnie sat close together with the latter's arms around his grieving wife. All three of their adult children were seated nearby, casting anxious glances toward their parents and speaking to one another in low tones. Marty, the oldest, had brought her two-year old with her. His wiggling antics provided a distraction for the somber waiting room gathering.

Patty's phone call report from the doctor as Hal traveled had not been encouraging. Mama was still unconscious, with low blood pressure and kidney failure, signs of Stage III Shock. She had been declared too weak to go into surgery for the broken hip. It would be a waiting game to see if she survived.

Hal greeted each family member with a hug before making a beeline for the nursing station to request a direct report from the doctor. The only new information he received, however, was that the doctor intended to keep his mother sedated until morning. The family was advised to return home for the night, with the assurance that hospital staff would call if there was any change in their mother's condition.

Hal refused to leave, insisting that he would rather stay at the hospital in spite of the family's repeated appeals for him to join them at Patty's place. In the end, they relented from their persuasion efforts. As Patty and her family filed out, she offered a quiet aside to her spouse, "You know I'm not surprised, Arnie. It's just like Hal to imagine his presence might somehow help keep Mama safe."

Hal was sprawled out in a waiting room chair. Head back and arms crossed, his breathing was deep and regular; tension and fatigue had finally taken their toll. A hand on his shoulder propelled him suddenly awake. He jumped and cried out, sending the startled aide back several paces. "Sorry to bother you, sir. It's just that your mother is asking for you."

That comment brought Hal fully awake. "Um, no...that's just fine. What? You mean Mama, er...my mother is conscious? What time is it anyway?"

"It's a little after 5:30 am, sir. And yes. Your mother is weak but conscious. She asked if her son was nearby and if so, could she speak with him, so they sent me to get you."

Mama's eyes were closed when Hal entered the room. She had pillows on one side supporting her hip and an IV line was attached to one arm. Her forehead and cheek bore the purple color that documented her disastrous fall on the previous day. A deep wave of sadness swept over him as he stood quietly surveying the scene. *This is not how life is supposed to end,* he thought. *She deserves far better.*

As if sensing his arrival, Mama's eyes flickered open. Through vision clouded by pain and medication, a clear spark of recognition spread across her face ending in a weak smile and a low murmur of acknowledgment. "Harold...son. You are here!" The words came out in a whisper.

At Mama's greeting Hal's legs failed him. He half knelt, half collapsed on the bed next to her. Placing one hand gently on her cheek he bent down to kiss her bruised forehead. "Oh, Mama...I'm so sorry this has happened to you. I...I wish..." and then a sob overtook him.

With glassy eyes, Mama raised a trembling hand to signal for his silence. She strained to speak, obviously in a good deal of distress. Her comments rasped out at just above a whisper. "We have been through a lot, you and I, haven't we, son? I think, though, you are going to have to continue the journey from here without me."

At that comment, in spite of his attempt to keep his composure, fear crept into Hal's eyes and he visibly shuddered. He shook his head, "No, Mama...please don't talk like that."

His protests were interrupted with another raised hand. She continued in a familiar, soft voice. "It's okay, honey. I have Jesus to accompany me. I always have...and so have you, though you haven't recognized him. Harold, I am convinced those wonderful special gifts of yours are from him. Others may have misunderstood them, but they are gifts. I believe in you, son."

"You always have, Mama. I knew I had one person on the planet that always loved and understood me, who wouldn't let me go. Don't *you* leave me now!" Hal put his head down and wept as his mother slowly petted his hair. Finally, she reached a weak hand to cover his. "It's time to go, now son. I need to rest. Thank you for coming. I'm so glad I could talk with you." A weak smile touched the corner of her mouth. "It is my prayer that the eyes of your heart will be opened."

Martha's eyelids closed. Her chest rose in a shallow sigh and then assumed a quiet rhythm. Hal remained sitting there absolutely still for some time, searching his mother's face intently, as if memorizing every line and wrinkle. Finally, he shifted to stand and as he straightened up, glanced down one last time. The rhythm had ceased; Mama had left.

#21 Rancho Palos Verdes

June 2009

Hal whacked at the dense vines that grew wild on the slope beneath his house with a fury and resolve that were uncharacteristic of his typical even-tempered demeanor. He wasn't a great fan of yard work in the first place, but his present attack on the vegetation was clearly driven by emotion, not reason. It couldn't quite be described as "demented ferocity," but an outside observer might suggest it was moving in that direction. Rivulets of sweat coursed irregular lines down his dust covered neck and arms. It was, after all, a warm June afternoon in LA and his warrior-like assault was generating more heat than order on that particular hillside.

Finally standing up straight, Hal discovered he was gasping for air. Whew, so much exertion! He wiped a sweaty wrist across his forehead, took a quick glance up at the sun and sat down to catch his breath. "What am I doing?" he said out loud. He knew the answer, of course. He was distracting himself, keeping his body tired and mind blank so he didn't have to think about things. Not all that long ago he would have reached for a Modelo twelve-pack rather than a machete to dull his senses, but the hard lessons that had descended on him in his drinking days had registered their mark. Hal described them as "permanent scars" to his AA group. No way did he care to repeat any part of that personal history.

He sat gazing out at the hazy urban jungle that stretched before him in all directions, eyes unfocused, mind far away from the present locale, mulling over the events of the last few weeks. Mama's sudden passing created shock waves that immobilized the entire family. Had the legendary San Andreas Fault gone active it couldn't have been more disruptive to their lives, or so it seemed to Hal.

Patty fell into a deep depression, blaming herself for not having checked more closely on her mother and for not insisting she wear a medical alert pendant. Arnie and the kids made valiant attempts to rally her spirits, but their best efforts melted in exposure to the intense grief and sadness that had overtaken their wife and mother. Rhonda and family flew in from their home in Dallas. Hal's children, Calvin and Judy and their families arrived from Portland. Phyllis accompanied them. Tricia and Emmie flew up from LA.

The gathering of loved ones is often a source of comfort and encouragement when a family member dies. Unfortunately, in this case the presence of the extended family only seemed to deepen the mourning, adding to the total of distressed and grieving souls.

It was Hal who stepped up to guide the mourners through those dark days, suppressing his own profound loss and rising to the occasion. Hospital and funeral home arrangements, death certificates, probate and legal issues, disposal of personal effects, announcements and memorial service planning – he took the lead on it all, making decisions and delegating responsibilities to the few family members functional enough to assist. It was even Hal's hand that scripted most of his mother's obituary. Cal was the reader at the service, however. Everyone has his limits.

As he sat on the hillside thinking about it now, a gentle breeze lifting his hair, Hal found his mother's impact on her community to be...remarkable. The memorial service at her home church was a standing-room-only affair. Her pastor finally had to cut off the open mike sharing at the post-memorial reception since after two straight hours of participation there was still a long line of mourners waiting to speak and the family was exhausted from the emotional strain of the day. "It wasn't just me she loved and affirmed," he thought, eyes filling with tears.

The longer he reflected, the more distressed Hal became. A knot formed in the pit of his stomach shortly accompanied by nausea. He shivered as an intense wave of sadness and dread hit him, discovering that his heart was racing, and his breathing was rapid and shallow. Cold, perceptible fear suddenly possessed him with a horrifying grip and he audibly moaned. "I must be dying!" he thought as he fell back and curled into a ball. He lay, panicked, shivering and terrified for several long minutes before the feelings slowly lifted, leaving him gasping deep lungsful of air. Knees still shaking, Hal slowly regained his feet and stumbled toward the house.

An hour later Hal entered his sunny, spacious living room in the company of best friend and colleague, Brad Waterhouse. The smell of freshly brewed coffee filled the room. "Thanks for coming over on short notice, Brad," Hal offered handing him a steaming cup of java. The two men settled down, coffee cups in hand.

"Sure buddy. Who's to delay coming when told it's an urgent matter?" Brad took a sip from his mug, privately relieved to find his friend in a composed state. It had seemed very much out of character for Hal to make that urgent request for his presence, so he did not know what to expect, driving over. "So, what's going on?" he queried, concern creasing his forehead.

The words came tumbling out. "I must be having a nervous breakdown or something, Brad. I seem to be falling apart. Ever since Mama, er my mother...left, and I got back from San Jose it's like I've been in a daze. I've had trouble focusing on things, trouble even wanting to think about work. I've been distracting myself with stupid, mindless tasks. Today I attacked the weeds on the hillside. In the middle of the afternoon, no less! When I finally sat down and started thinking about stuff, I couldn't breathe. I thought I was having a heart attack or something. It really shook me up."

Hal was sitting upright on the edge of his chair, arms gesturing and eyes wide. He ran a nervous hand ran through his hair as he finished his comments.

"Whoa, slow down there, pal." Brad held up a hand up. "Just think what you've been through in recent days. You and your Mama were close. She was a very special person. Her death is a huge loss. Also, from what you and Tricia reported, it was you who carried a lot of the emotional weight for your family through the deep waters of those first days. No wonder it's finally catching up to you."

Hal was not consoled. "I just can't believe I'm such a wreck. I'm having nightmares – flashbacks to Congo days, really – and not sleeping well at all. I feel weird. I'm fighting myself to keep from drinking. I haven't had to battle that demon for some time, but now it's daily...hourly at times. What should I do?" Hal was on his feet, pacing by that time, hands clenched and eyebrows down, angst written across his face.

Brad sat forward, elbows on his knees, silently watching his agitated friend pace the room. Finally, he spoke up in a quiet, even voice. "Do you really want to know what I think?"

Hal stopped and turned toward Brad, the simple question

catching him up short. "Well, yeah. That's why I called you."

"I recall the village elders from my youth in Ghana, telling us repeatedly, *'There can be no peace without understanding.'* Perhaps that wisdom-gem applies to *you* at present, Hal. Hasn't the time finally arrived to increase your self-understanding, to consult with a therapist? Like I told you before, I know just the person you should see."

Hal slowly lowered himself back down on one of his big chairs, a thoughtful expression on his face. He voiced a weak protest, mostly to himself. "I've lived a lot of productive years stuffing my feelings rather than talking about them. Changing my ways at this stage of life? I'm pretty skeptical it will produce much peace."

Brad's eyes twinkled as his mouth spread in a grin. "Ha! So much for your damn resistance. I have another African proverb for you: *'In a moment of crisis the wise build bridges but the foolish build dams.'* So what's your next construction project gonna be, friend...a bridge or a dam?"

#22 Huntington Beach

June 2009

Lyndsey Franklin pulled her silver Lexus SC 430 convertible into the office parking lot and pushed the button to activate the retractable top, returning her special chariot once again to a mere luxury coup. Driving through the ocean-side streets of Southern California with the top down was a dream-turned-daily-indulgence for the otherwise no-nonsense psychotherapist. It left her feeling energized, refreshed and mellow, a perfect preparation for long days of intense interaction with troubled clients.

Lyndsey's counseling practice was pretty much her whole life these days. She had retired early after twenty years of teaching Psychology at Claremont McKenna College. Her primary interests there had centered on the development of the Cultural Influences on Mental Health Center. Having grown up as the child of missionaries in Papua New Guinea, her personal experience, professional education, and clients' issues all added up to a lifetime of expertise making her a much sought-after expert in matters of culture and mental health.

In Lyndsey's personal life, a disastrous early marriage had ended badly. Her young husband's alcohol abuse had rapidly morphed into domestic violence destroying the relationship and nearly so, the two individuals. That painful experience left her content to share her life with a series of bright, well-trained Golden Retrievers rather than a spouse. She enjoyed regular contact with a wide network of friends and acquaintances, fruits of her professional activities and extensive international travels, another lifelong interest. Lyndsey could claim few close friends, however, and always considered herself more of a participant observer of mainstream American culture than a card-carrying member.

On this particular June morning Lyndsey rose at the knock on the door by Julie, her receptionist. As she stepped from behind her desk to greet a new client, she braced herself internally, remembering that beginnings and endings were usually the most difficult parts of relationships. Opening the door, she extended her hand with a smile to the person standing before her: a solidly built middle-aged man, six feet tall, in his mid-fifties, thick hair graying at the temples. "Good morning, I'm Dr. Franklin and you must be Dr. Schroeder. Welcome."

The man flashed a nervous smile. His palm was damp, but he offered a firm handshake, returning her greeting with, "Hello Dr. Franklin. Yes, I'm Hal Schroeder. You have been referred to me by my colleague, Brad Waterhouse. He said you were very helpful to him in the past."

"Yes, how is Brad these days? He's still at USC, isn't he? Come on in and take a seat." Lyndsey pointed to one of two comfortable chairs placed at 10 and 3 O'clock positions around a circular lamp table.

Hal settled down into the chair and crossed his legs, trying to look relaxed and not to betray the anxiety he felt, anxiety that had fired up his adrenal glands and accelerated his heart rate. He decided to jump into the moment with both feet. "I'm going to tell you up front, Dr. Franklin, that I'm not a fan of therapy, not convinced that this is even a good idea. I'm pretty skeptical that you can help me."

Lyndsey's eyes crinkled into a soft smile. "That's quite a set of untested assumptions for a USC Professor." She spoke easily without a hint of defensiveness. "Have you had any personal experience with therapy that would lead you to that conclusion?"

Hal crossed his arms and frowned. "Well, I had some issues years ago when I was in college. I spoke to a counselor back then. It wasn't particularly helpful. He wanted me to swat an inflatable doll with a bat to get out my anger. Dumb stuff. You don't do that sort of thing, do you?"

Lyndsey had put on her reading glasses, balancing them on the bridge of her nose and was studying a piece of paper. She looked up over the lenses and replied dismissively, "No, of course not!" Glancing down again she asked, "It says here on the intake form you filled out that you were born in the Congo. Does that mean your parents were missionaries?"

Hal's face clouded. *Where is she going with this?* "Yeah, they were missionaries. I was born there. Other than three years of what we called "deputation" spent in California, I grew up in Africa. I graduated from high school there."

"Interesting." Lyndsey removed her glasses and set them on the table. "So, Dr. Schroeder...or would you prefer me to call you Hal? What brings you to see me today, in the light of your pre-formed conclusion that it's probably not going to be helpful?"

"Hal is fine," he replied meeting her gaze evenly. "I...um, had a kind of breakdown recently and it shook me up. Brad thought I should talk it over with someone, with you. So here I am." Hal had uncrossed his arms and was gripping the arms of the chair with his hands.

Lyndsey took notice that her new patient had a white-knuckle grip on his chair. She shifted her weight and leaned forward with interest. "Why don't we begin with you telling me in detail what happened? What did you consider to be a breakdown and when and where did it occur?"

Hal recounted an abbreviated version of his hillside episode, conceding that he had been under a lot of pressure and stress lately with work pressures, his daughter moving out and his mother's recent death. The fact that he felt out of control, couldn't breathe and had collapsed made the incident much more significant in his thinking. "I thought I was having a heart attack or something. Later, I wondered if I was just losing it." Hal released his grip on the arms of the chair, crossed his legs and grasped one knee with clasped hands. "So, what's the verdict, doc?"

Lyndsey replied in an even, matter-of-fact tone. "Racing heart, sweating, shaking, breathing difficulties, feeling faint or dizzy, loss of control...you are describing classic panic attack symptoms, Hal. The short answer to your implied 'why' question is that panic attacks are triggered by heightened anxiety. How does that 'verdict' fit your fancy?"

Hal sat back in his chair. "Humph." After a pause to reflect he continued, "Yeah, all the pressure has been pretty intense in recent days. I suppose it's possible..." He scratched his jaw. "But do you think just worries can do all that to a person?" he inquired, a puzzled look narrowing his eyes.

Lyndsey did not answer his question but responded by offering perspectives of her own. "To figure it out, I suspect you might well benefit from a journey into the mysterious world of feelings and meanings." Her eyes and the slight upturn of her mouth conveyed a hint of cynical humor.

"You mentioned several sources of pressure: work responsibilities, your mother's recent death, your daughter's departure. Perhaps there are others. It could be helpful to know more about these issues if they are indeed creating enough anxiety to trigger a panic attack."

Hal's forehead creased in a frown. "I don't like the sound of that...a panic attack. It sounds so...so helpless, vulnerable. That's not me. Are you sure that's what I had?" He ran a hand through his hair.

Again, the counselor did not directly address his query but added her own. "One more question, Hal. Have you ever had such an experience before?"

Hal sat very still looking at his feet. He did not respond for some time. Finally, he looked up at Lyndsey to reply. "Yes. When I was younger, once in high school and once in college. It's what made me seek counseling the last time, er...the first time. What made you ask that?"

"Sometimes, Hal, wounds that have never fully healed are carried unnoticed in life, making us vulnerable to anxiety. They only make their appearance when things build up in a major way or if some significant loss occurs compromising our usual defenses. I suspect that if you and I work together we can identify those factors and diminish their power to disrupt your life." She paused to allow her words to sink in.

"You seem like a bright lady," Hal replied slowly, selecting his words with care, "but I'm not sure you can understand my world. I'm not your average American, never have been. Besides, this whole prospect of talking about what you called "wounds" makes me feel more nervous, not less so."

Lyndsey smiled. "You are certainly a TCK, all right. But then so am I. We no doubt share many commonalities not the least of which is an aversion to analyzing our past."

She stood to end the session. "Why don't you just take some time to think about it, Hal? If you decide you are ready to move out of your comfort zone and begin a new adventure, a healing journey, I'll help you."

#23 Rancho Palos Verdes

June-July 2009

"You didn't tell me she'd be a matronly middle-aged shrink." These words of greeting met Brad Waterhouse as Hal opened the door to usher his friend in. He had driven straight home from his therapy session with Dr. Franklin and on the way, phoned Brad to meet him at his place. He was anxious to debrief the past hour's conversation. He had questions that needed answers now that he had actually met face-to-face with Brad's former counselor.

"You didn't ask! Besides, what difference does it make what she looks like?" Brad removed his shoes, placing them in line with others as Hal closed the door and motioned him into the living room. "If anything, Dr. Franklin's – shall we say – additional life experience is an asset. Hey, I never intended an eHarmony moment when I recommended her to you." He smirked at the cynical humor in his retort.

"Ha, eHarmony my aching clavicle! You know what I mean. After your big build-up I expected someone with a more professional demeanor. Maybe someone more classy or elite or something." Hal settled down in his favorite chair and raised his feet onto the coffee table, crossing his ankles. "She's like a regular person, dresses and looks like a faculty colleague. Comes across as plenty bright but more approachable, less slick than I expected."

"Jeez Hal, what do you want...an elitist? In real life Lyndsey Franklin is an expert, in-demand mental health professional. She grew up in the South Pacific, in Papua New Guinea. I think she once told me her parents were missionaries, like ours. I believe they were with Wycliffe, the Bible translator outfit. She was the head honcho at the Cultural Influences on Mental Health Center at Claremont McKenna College before she retired and went into full time practice. You've heard of it, right?"

"Yeah, I've heard of it." Hal stroked his chin staring out the window. "Hmm, maybe the MK thing is what she meant when she said something about sharing many things in common." He shifted his focus back to Brad. "But she also quipped about me being a typical TCK who didn't want to analyze my past. What is *that* about? I've heard those letters bantered about but I'm not familiar with what they refer to."

"You don't know about TCKs? That surprises me. The whole Third Culture Kids thing has been around since it was coined in the 1950s." Brad mimed a smiling shock reaction. "Basically, it refers to children who accompany their parents into another culture. As they – or *we*, since both of us are TCKs – grow up we assemble an identity from both our home and host countries, creating a so-called "third culture." It ends up being a unique style of living, thinking and being that we share with our peers." Brad laced his hands behind his head and leaned back in his chair before continuing.

"Supposedly it's the reason we relate more easily with other international folks and why we don't ever feel like we belong, don't identify with our passport country. A new book just came out on the TCK phenomena. I have a copy in my office."

A half smile on his face, Hal sat forward leaning his chin on folded hands, feet on the floor once again. "It sounds like you're working up to that 'no peace without understanding' quote again, Brad. Seriously, though, you've got me curious about what Dr. Franklin might have to offer. I think I may just walk a little further down the therapy path and see for myself."

***

The light from the office window suddenly flashed directly into Hal's eyes signaling the afternoon sun's movement and that his therapy hour was nearly over. The time had gone by so rapidly. It was hard to imagine he had gotten so absorbed in his reflections. This was now his fourth session with Dr. Franklin. Much of his early resistance had melted away in response to her low-key questions and genuine interest. She had begun by asking him about his work and professional life. Then followed inquiry into his family life, identifying persons and relationships, past and present. Dr. Franklin was curious but to his great relief, decidedly non-judgmental when he got to the part about Phyllis and the divorce. In today's session she had asked about Hal's experience of growing up in Congo.

Lyndsey stood and adjusted the levelers at the window. "Sorry about the sun in your eyes, Hal. Is this any better? We need to wrap things up shortly."

Hal had come to expect some sort of summary at the end of each session. Those wrap-ups helped him to know what Dr. Franklin took away from his rambling narratives. They also frequently contained insightful suggestions for him to consider going forward.

Lyndsey looked down at her jottings from today's session to gather her thoughts before continuing. She took notes only sparingly during her therapy sessions. She found that taking them was distracting to her clients. The exceptions included jotting down names and dates as part of her social history interviews, like today's and sometimes recording medications or other details that might otherwise be forgotten.

"I want to remind you that these first meetings are necessary fact gathering sessions. They also allow me to get a picture of your life from your point of view. It will help us to identify what produces stress and anxiety in your life and to understand how it operates, how you respond to it. Our goal is to develop insight and strategies to better manage these factors that interfere with your well-being. Does that make sense?"

Hal nodded, clasping his hands on one crossed knee.

Lyndsey continued. "Today I asked you to tell me a little about your experiences growing up in Congo. It sounds like you enjoyed a wonderful childhood on a small mission station in the bush. That idyllic period ended abruptly and dramatically in the mid-1960s when rebels burned down your station and the UN evacuated you and your family. You were pretty sketchy about that, Hal. I'm thinking there are likely a lot of memories and emotions that you have packed away pretty securely. I'd like to have you spend some time unpacking them. Why don't you take a stab at writing down your memories in some detail to share with me next time?"

Hal's face had tightened, and his knuckles turned white. In a monotone voice he replied, "I'm going to be pretty busy this week, doc. Not sure I'll have the time for that."

"I'd like you to do it anyway, Hal, to make yourself and your life a priority." She bore a pleasant expression, but her direct eye contact said she was unlikely to take no for an answer. Hal swallowed hard.

"Oh, yes...to continue my summary, it sounded to me like your high school years at TASOK were very active and meaningful. You have some great stories that tell me you and your former classmates continue to value that season of life to this very day. However, like many if not most TCKs, your adolescent years also contained frequent losses: friends, teachers, places and experiences. Some researchers believe that unresolved grief is the chief legacy and principal liability of growing up overseas. Think about whether that observation in any way fits your situation. We can talk more about it next time."

As Hal left Dr. Franklin's office and headed to the parking lot, this time he did so with a heavy heart. On previous occasions he had ended his sessions feeling quite positive. Lyndsey's questions and attentive listening actually lifted his spirits. It seemed good to share these private parts of his life in a safe setting, to shine light on dark corners long hidden from illumination. This time, however, the prospect of revisiting his last days at Kisambo Station filled him with dread.

"No peace without understanding," Hal repeated to himself out loud.

#24 Rancho Palos Verdes

July 2009

Hal stood at the desk in his home office and wadded up the paper before him, sending it to join the pile of others in and around the wastebasket in the corner. "Damn it!" he exclaimed, emitting a rare expletive. "I can't do this. I don't want to do this," he declared out loud. He kicked his desk chair across the room on its rollers, and leaned down on his desk, elbows locked, resting on the heels of his hands. Eyebrows nearly touching in a frown, he pondered, *Maybe I'll just call and cancel my session, be sick this week. No, she'd see through that and make an even bigger deal out of it than it is. But maybe it is a bigger deal than I imagined if I'm having this much trouble just thinking about it.*

Hal had been troubled ever since Dr. Franklin gave him the dreadful assignment. Waves of nausea had swept over him every time her challenge came to mind. *Or is that just anxiety I'm feeling?* he had wondered. Hal had not slept well all week. Several nights he had awakened, sweaty and trembling from nightmares that were undoubtedly scenes from his final days at Kisambo. Screams and shrieks, fire crackling in the night, stumbling in the dark holding his mother's hand, scary shadowy figures chanting and racing about, and most distressing of all, bloody forms lying deathly still, arrow shafts protruding from their bodies. Not the stuff of pleasant dreams, that's for sure.

"How am I supposed to put words to all that happened?" he asked Dr. Franklin when finally facing her in his weekly therapy session. "That was such a long time ago. I have not even tried to remember it over the years. The only times I've even spoken about it in the last twenty years were a couple of short exchanges with my mother, reminiscing. None of my other siblings were there at the time so they can't really relate. It is part of my distant past. So why is this so hard for me, doc? Does it mean that I am losing it?"

Lyndsey let Hal's question settle between them before finally responding carefully. "What I think is that your reaction to my request simply confirms my suspicions. You have most certainly

123

buried the facts and the emotional impact of those difficult days, deeply and securely. It is an entirely natural defense, Hal. Especially so for a twelve-year-old who did not have the opportunity to make sense of it all at the time."

Hal's eyes had flooded. The overflow created wet lines down his cheeks. He sat very still, staring. His mind was focused at a great distance, on another time and place, on a different continent a lifetime away.

After a long pause, he finally rasped, "It was so scary. I lost my best friend. He tried to save me." His last words ended in a sob.

Lyndsey reached across and rested her hand on his arm, leaving it there for some time while the spasms from his silent sobs continued. When they had gradually subsided, she sat up and in a quiet voice continued.

"I'm sorry for your discomfort, Hal. But this is the hard work of therapy, uncovering the wounds and shedding light on hidden infections. Healing requires that we move toward the pain not away from it. So, now I'm going to ask you to put words to those toxic memories that just surfaced and describe to me in detail what happened."

Hal nodded, took a shaky deep breath and began his narrative of the last days leading up to the evacuation of Kisambo Station. His internal resolve to recount the story without further tears proved abysmally futile. The final scene, escaping into the helicopter with Nsukula's intervention and later viewing his young lifeless body left Hal choking, unable to continue, elbows on knees, hands covering his face.

Lyndsey patiently waited for him to regain a measure of composure. "That was good, Hal, perhaps excruciating for you but very well stated. I wonder, do you remember talking with your parents about what happened? I mean, did you sort it out with them some time after you were rescued?"

Hal got that far-away look in his eyes once again. "I remember Mama comforting me about Nsukula. He wasn't supposed to be there. He'd been warned, but he came anyhow. I always wished he had stayed away." He glanced back at Lyndsey. "But, to answer your question, I think my folks wanted to protect me or something, so they avoided discussing it with me directly. They always changed the subject if I was around whenever others would ask for details about the evacuation and what led up to it."

"What about your parents' reactions to all those life-changing events? You said that they continued working in Congo through your high school years and beyond. Did they ever return to Kisambo?"

Hal shook his head. "No, I don't think they ever went back there. From time to time over the years different ones from the Kisambo community visited them in Kinshasa and expressed regret and remorse for all the folks had been through, but I think Momma and Dad considered it a closed chapter. Dad, at least, always expressed sadness and disappointment that his Congolese friends and colleagues had misled him and had withheld knowledge of how much they knew of the rebellion. I think that experience permanently damaged his trust."

"And what about you? Didn't you ever miss your childhood friends who remained at Kisambo, ever want to see them again?"

Hal ran a hand through his hair, eyes narrowing as he reflected on Lyndsey's question at some length. "That's a complicated question to answer. I certainly did miss them, but in my twelve-year old way I felt partially responsible for the bad things that happened. It's hard to explain. I didn't want to face them. I still don't."

Lyndsey's face bore a puzzled expression. "I'm not sure I follow you there, Hal, but perhaps we can explore that another time. You look pretty thrashed by now and I see our time is almost up. Do you have any questions for me before I attempt to summarize?"

Hal uncrossed his legs, glanced down and then lifted his head looking Lyndsey directly in the eyes. "Well, just the obvious one. So, am I losing it, doc? What do you make of this? Why all the emotion from something that happened forty-five years ago?"

Lyndsey's eyes crinkled at the sides and the corners of her mouth turned up slightly. "I'll bet it felt like you were losing it today. But rest assured you're not. What I suspect we may be uncovering are some indicators of PTSD, Post Traumatic Stress Disorder, that has plagued you for a long time, for most of your lifetime. You can look it up at home. I think you'll agree. "

"PTSD? I thought that's what Vietnam vets have. I'm not a vet. Say more."

"Yes, in short...PTSD occurs when people are exposed to some sort of significant trauma. It's usually something that shakes them to the core, life-and-death sorts of things. They end up with a heightened sensitivity to stress, plus they automatically avoid any reminders of the trauma, also known as "triggers." Starting to sound familiar?"

Without waiting for a reply, Lyndsey stood to her feet. Hal took the hint, rising out of his chair with a slight smile. "OK, OK, time is up...I intend to look up PTSD. My follow up question that you're clearly not going to answer today is 'So what?' I *do* expect to hear more from you on that!"

#25 USC Campus, Los Angeles

August 2009

It was Banh Mi sandwich day at the Tudor Hill Café and the two anthropology profs had settled down at their usual side table to enjoy conversation over lunch without interruptions. Student traffic through the cafeteria was light during USC's summer session so the sound volume surrounding them was decibels lower than during the school year. Both Hal and Brad had come on campus for a graduate admissions committee meeting. Their interaction was light and amiable, covering grad student prospects, new faculty hires and preparation for the fall semester that was rapidly approaching.

Brad took a savory bite of BBQ beef and Hal used the pause in their conversation to change the subject. He leaned forward, one elbow on the table; a serious expression clouding his face. First glancing to each side, with a lowered voice he divulged. "So, Dr. Franklin thinks I have PTSD from the trauma I experienced as a child. Do you know what that is?"

Eyebrows lifting in surprise Brad managed to swallow his mouthful without choking and took a big gulp of iced tea. He had not expected that disclosure, but he quickly recovered. "As a matter-of-fact I do. Jerry Bradshaw over in Physics has wrestled with that for a bunch of years after his army stint in Iraq. We used to carpool and so I heard a lot about it from him. Unpleasant stuff. How does Dr. Franklin think it's affected you?"

"She thinks it triggered my panic attack. You know...the thing that drove me to see her in the first place. That, and my Momma's death. According to her, flashbacks, nightmares, avoidance, a strong startle response and even depression and guilt are all PTSD symptoms." Hal did another quick scan back and forth to make sure he was not being overheard. "Those are all things I have experienced at different times over the years, Brad. Kinda spooky, eh?"

Brad continued his attack on the sandwich, reflecting between bites, "Doc Franklin knows her stuff, Hal. Sounds like she's spot on. What does she think you should do about it?" He smiled.

"Personally, I'm hoping she'll recommend electric shock therapy. You could use a little mellowing out."

That prompted a chuckle. Hal quickly returned to serious mode once more. "Shock therapy might be easier than having to sit in a counseling office each week and relive all that crap. Franklin thinks my PTSD is tangled up with the whole MK experience, what she calls 'TCK issues.' According to her, healing will come as I revisit and resolve those tangles. So that's what we're attempting to do."

"According to *her* maybe but what do *you* think by now, Hal?" Brad cast an expectant gaze across the table as he finished off his iced tea.

Hal looked down at his uneaten sandwich, gathering his thoughts before proceeding in a careful tone of voice. "Well, I'm starting to think she might be onto something. Therapy puts me out of my comfort zone for sure but for the first time in a long while I'm beginning to feel hopeful...hopeful that I can understand things that have troubled me about my life. Restlessness, alcohol abuse, my divorce, relationships... all are puzzles, shadows on my life that doc Franklin considers TCK imprints."

Brad scooted his chair back and stood. "TCK imprints, huh? Heady stuff, my friend. I hope you'll keep me informed. Some of that shit may apply to me. I apologize for dashing off, but I need to head back to the office. I've got a student waiting."

Hal waved him off with a cordial smile but remained seated for long minutes, replaying his words to Brad. With thoughts spinning and his gut in a knot, he discovered he no longer had an appetite.

***

Loud voices, screams of "No, no..." the scuffle of feet and grunts of a struggle, dark images moved rapidly, a scent of fear surrounded the figures, the clap of a gunshot abruptly ended the scene. Hal woke with a start, sitting upright in bed, sweaty, shaken and breathing rapidly. A mugging...it was a violent mugging! And one of the victims was very familiar. It was...Lyndsey Franklin. That much was clear in his mind. Entirely too clear! How many others were in the scene? There seemed to be several. It was confusing, alarming. He shuttered at the realization that this was one of "those" nightmares. Hal glanced at the clock beside his bed: 4:30 AM. He reached for his phone.

Voicemail came on. His words tumbled out in a voice thick with sleep. "Dr. Franklin, this is Hal Schroeder calling. I need to speak with you about an urgent matter. Please return my call as soon as you retrieve this message."

Hal was now wide-awake, pacing the room. Having given up on further sleep he headed for the kitchen to brew a quick Keurig cup of coffee. By 6 AM, anxiety got the best of him and he called once again leaving the same message. Abandoning the bedroom, Hal shaved, showered and dressed all within earshot of his iPhone. Finally, by 8 AM he could stand it no longer. He had to do something! Dashing out the front door, he jumped into his car and headed south on the Pacific Coast Highway toward Huntington Beach. At this hour of the day the 40 miles distance would take him well over an hour to complete. Surely, she would be at the office by 9 AM, he reasoned.

His cell phone rang through the car's audio system as Hal approached Sunset Beach heading south in the rush-hour traffic on highway 1. "Good morning, Hal," came a familiar voice. "You sound alarmed. Has something happened?"

Hal pulled off the main road and entered the drive through lane of Starbucks. The three cars ahead of him would give him time to talk with a head clearing cappuccino bonus at the end. "Yes, something has happened, and I need to tell you about it face-to-face. Otherwise, you'll be sure I've flipped out. Maybe you'll conclude that anyhow. Do you have time to see me before you start your day?"

"It sounds like you're driving. Are you headed this direction?"

"Yes, I'm in Sunset Beach. I can be at your office in about fifteen minutes, by 9 o'clock."

"That will be fine. My first appointment is at 9:30, so we can take a few minutes to chat. You've got me curious about what's going on with you."

Hal screeched into the counseling center parking lot ten, not fifteen minutes later, swinging his car door shut behind him as he dashed to the office. Lyndsey jumped to her feet as she heard the office door bang open. Her receptionist was standing in alarm mode as a breathless Hal stood before her.

Once ushered into the office with the door closed, Hal launched into his hastily rehearsed monologue. "You will think I'm really crazy for my comments, but you have plans to go into downtown LA to attend a theater event in the next couple of nights, don't you?"

Lyndsey's eyebrows rose in surprise. "Why yes, as a matter of fact. I have tickets for tonight's performance of "9 to 5: The Musical" playing at the Ahmanson Theatre in the Music Center. How did you know?"

Hal sat on the edge of his usual stuffed chair, face creased with worry. "That's what I need to share. I haven't disclosed this to you before now but since it concerns *you,* I figured I've gotta say something." His hand went through his hair as he took a deep breath. "I have dreams, this...ability to see things that are going to happen. They're nightmares, really, but they are very vivid. Many times over the years what I have dreamed has turned out to come true. Last night I had one of those...vision-like nightmares and you were in it. So, I'm warning you here-and-now that if you go to that production, don't go alone and don't take anything of value with you."

Lyndsey sat silent, thinking as Hal dabbed at the perspiration on his forehead with his forearm. "What exactly did you see that alarmed you enough to drive all the way here in such distress, Hal?"

Relieved that she didn't question his sanity, he blurted out. "It was a mugging that ended badly. I awakened to the sound of a gunshot. I recognized you but didn't see who else was there or who might have been injured. Given what has happened in my past, I couldn't dismiss it. I had to say something. If it actually transpires and I believe it will, I couldn't live with myself if I hadn't said something, if someone were injured or worse." Hal's eyes were swimming.

"I can see this is very upsetting to you, Hal. And I will exercise caution, but this may just turn out to be some kind of PTSD flashback that has incorporated new data. I'd like to explore your history with this in our next session. If it's any consolation, my theater attendance tonight *will* be with a couple of good friends. We'll use caution. I know what...I'll give you a call tomorrow morning to report about our experience. Does that help any as a measure of reassurance?"

Hal sat back in his chair, silently looking down. Finally, he looked up as if forcing his words. "I'd frankly feel better if you cancelled altogether, but thanks for taking me seriously. And if you go, do use extra caution." He stood and turned partway to the door. "I'll breathe easier when I get your call in the morning saying you had a grand *uneventful* evening."

Lyndsey smiled as she rose. "You timed your visit well. It's now 9:30. Thank you for being concerned and for acting on it. We'll talk tomorrow."

Lyndsey stood, deep in thought, staring out the window as Hal crossed the parking lot to his car. *"What a strange development. What if…"*

#26 Huntington Beach

August 2009

Hal picked the phone up on the first ring. The kitchen clock read 7:00 A. M. and his toast had just popped up. He had not slept much at all. So far, he had checked the daily weather forecast, endured silly human-interest stories and stared at ads for Flex Seal tape and Granite Rock cookware on TV. He had scanned the entire *LA Times*, pausing only briefly to focus on the sports and comics sections. He was now on his second cup of coffee and in the process of preparing breakfast. "Hello, Dr. Franklin, is that you?" he asked in a hurried, anxious greeting.

The familiar even-toned voice on the other end sounded strained in reply. "Yes, Lyndsey Franklin here." There was a pause as if the caller were contemplating how to proceed. "Um, Hal I'd...I'd like you to tell me *exactly* what you saw in your dream, the dream that prompted yesterday's surprise office visit."

Hal's voice was filled with alarm, "Something happened, didn't it? I knew it! Was anyone injured? Are you okay?"

Lyndsey repeated her request. "I'll get to all that but first I want to hear from you. Please describe that dream of yours once again, your premonition. Then, I'll fill you in on last night's experience."

Without delay Hal recounted the content of his dream in as much detail as he could recall, beginning with the setting, a dark alley adjacent to a parking lot behind a concert venue. He described loud voices, struggling figures, the surrounding fear and his alarm at recognizing his therapist on the ground. Finally, he referenced the sound of a gunshot that had brought his dream to an abrupt end.

There was silence on the other end of the line. "Dr. Franklin? Are you there?"

"Remarkable. Truly remarkable." Lyndsey appeared to mostly be talking to herself, her soft words filled with incredulity. "It's like he was an eyewitness. Er, I mean, it's like *you* were an eyewitness, Hal. What you just described is exactly what happened last night." That comment brought Hal to his feet, fumbling and almost dropping the phone.

She continued, "After enjoying the performance last night my friends and I headed for our vehicle. Two young men suddenly dashed out from the shadows and accosted us, knocking me and one of my friends to the ground. There was a struggle as we both resisted surrendering our purses. That's what they were after, a slam and snatch, a quick score. Our friend who was still on her feet began screaming. Her cries summoned a nearby security guard who came running. He fired his gun into the air and the two muggers took off at full speed. It was frightening! Thankfully, no one was seriously injured. Just skinned knees and elbows."

Hal sighed deeply and sat back down hard, his knees giving way. "Whew, I am greatly relieved to hear that," was all he could manage to utter.

"You and I have some interesting things to discuss when you come in next week." Lyndsey reiterated the time and day of their next appointment, ending her comments with, "Finally, I'd just like to say that my friends and I believe we owe you a word of thanks for alerting us to potential trouble. Your warning no doubt helped us be more alert, to react much faster, perhaps avoiding further injury or loss. So, thanks."

Hal mumbled something in reply. He didn't really know what to say. After goodbyes were exchanged and he had hung up, Hal sat with his elbows on the table and his head in his hands staring down at the cold toast on his plate. On one hand, he felt relieved that no great harm had occurred and that his warning had proved credible, that Dr. Franklin had believed him. On the other hand, he felt curiously vulnerable now that his secret was out. *"I'm not sure I feel like talking about this even with a shrink. Maybe...especially with a shrink!"*

***

"Let's begin with you telling me about the history of those premonitions of yours, Hal." Dr. Franklin's pointed question opened the therapy session. Hal's stomach was in a knot. It appeared he was not going to be able to sidestep discussing his secret any longer. Hal had thought a lot about what he might say in the days since Lyndsey's phone call. He had finally concluded that he would talk about the dreams dating back to his childhood but was determined not share anything about Muzeka Adoko who had recognized the gift, or that he had been given training in tossing bones. He reasoned Dr. Franklin would never approve of that.

Hal began his reflections by reciting several tales of childhood premonitions from his days at Kisango Station. The young girl who had fallen in the river, the cobra in his friend's hut, the switched medications in the station pharmacy and finally the *Jeunesse* threat and torching of the station. Lyndsey listened carefully, nodding and jotting notes, only occasionally posing a clarifying question or expression of concern. Hal's agitation grew as he proceeded in his story telling. By the time he began to describe his dream about the day of evacuation, wet streaks ran down his cheeks and his voice was trembling.

"I told Tika to tell Nsuka that neither he nor any of his family should show up at Kisango Station as long as any of us missionaries were present. I sent the word through Tika to Nsuka and his father, Muzeka." His voice broke. "Only...Nsuka and his brother Biungu showed up anyway. Both of them were killed." Hal's shoulders shook with sobbing as he covered his face with his hands.

Lyndsey reached out and rested a comforting hand on his arm, remaining silent for some time. Finally, in a soft voice she asked, "Do you feel somehow responsible for what happened to your friends?" Hal nodded without looking up.

"Tell me more about that, Hal. Help me understand. You had a dream, you passed on a warning that your friends ignored, but *you* still feel responsible for the outcome? Why is that?"

Hal sat back in his chair, ran a hand through his hair and stared at the floor, reflecting deeply on the question posed to him. "I...I suppose it doesn't make sense, does it? But that's how I feel. Responsible. I've always felt that way." His eyes pooled once again.

Lyndsey shifted slightly forward as she spoke. "Is that how you felt when I told you earlier about my experience with the wanna-be muggers?" Hal rested his chin on his folded hands. "Hmmm" was his response, as he remained deep in thought.

"Hal, I'd like you to know that in my opinion, this responsibility thing is a dysfunctional pattern of thinking you have carried with you for many years. It likely dates back to those childhood experiences of seeing trouble in your dreams and then having the visions replayed in reality. Children often carry guilt for things that are outside their control. Yours was certainly compounded by your experiencing PTSD-level adversity. Can you see how this might apply? The fact that you felt similarly when faced with your most recent premonition suggests this is a well-traveled emotional pathway."

Hal looked up, a half-smile spreading across his face. "That's a pretty amazing piece of insight, doc. But I *do* feel somehow responsible and *guilty* for not preventing the outcome, having known about it ahead of time. I hate that. It's a curse. How can I keep it from happening? I can't control my dreams."

"We'll talk some more about that later. You've taken a good first step in recognizing the process, the connections. Our goal moving forward will be to prevent aversion from dictating what you do and how you feel when premonitions occur." Lyndsey stood to signal an end to their session.

Hal stood slowly; his brows wrinkled in quizzical reflection. "And by aversion you mean...?"

"I mean fearful avoidance of whatever is associated with your premonitions, or in the case of your PTSD, with your history. But we'll explore all that next time."

#27 Rancho Palos Verdes

October 2009

"Hey Carl. Good to hear from you again." Hal opened the sliding door to take the call on his patio. From its hilltop location he had a panoramic view of the LA basin. It was a typical balmy 75-degree October day in LA. The light blue sky was streaked with high wispy clouds. In the distant north the San Gabriel Mountains shimmered with a familiar murky smog haze that made him glad for his hilly Palos Verdes residence. Its proximity to the ocean with its air-cleansing breezes made all the difference. After a few pleasantries were exchanged, the caller – former TASOK classmate Carl Cooper – got to the point.

"Hal, the TASOK 40th Reunion Committee has asked me to make follow up calls to recruit those who haven't yet signed up. Shirley Bond – you'll remember her as Sexy Shirley Hansen – specifically asked me to give you a call. The committee wants to extend its strongest possible encouragement to you to attend. Quoting her, 'Tell Hal it just wouldn't be the same without him. He's *got to* come!'"

"Sexy Shirley, huh?" Hal smiled at the reference. "Thanks, Carl, for passing along that encouragement. You do realize that some of us still have careers to pursue, right? I've been busy. Frankly I haven't given the reunion much thought." Hal's gaze drifted to the southeast toward the hazy San Bernardino Mountains. Mentally, his view extended far beyond their distant, light brown profile to another continent on the far side of the globe.

Carl continued. "Well, then let this call be a reminder to give it your full attention. Now is the time to lock in good airfares before they go up at the first of the year. Besides, Shirley indicated that she and the others on the committee want to recruit you to lead a tour of present-day Kinshasa during the reunion. Everyone remembers your ability to communicate and relate to Congolese nationals. Most of us have totally forgotten what little French or Lingala we ever managed to learn in our youth."

"I appreciate the call, Carl. I will give it some thought. I want you to know, however, I've got some personal business to attend to that complicates any decision to attend the reunion. But I'll let you know either way in the next couple of weeks, OK?"

Hal continued standing, staring off in the distance, phone in hand after he had signed off. He did have a couple of work conflicts with the July 2010 reunion, but he was more concerned about leaving Trish and Emmie now that things seemed to be going well for them. Would his absence, the lack of his positive influence open the door to another relapse? And what of his usual July plans to visit his kids in Portland: Judy and her brood plus Cal and his family? Some renegotiation with them would also be necessary if he were to miss his annual visit.

But in truth, Hal had to admit the biggest issue wasn't actually work or family obligations; it was his struggle with the whole idea of returning to DR Congo. On one hand he felt strongly drawn to his roots, at least to the people, places and things that had positively shaped his adolescence. On the other hand, his guts tightened, and his jaw clenched whenever he contemplated going back to the setting where he had lost so much: friends, his faith and his peace of mind.

Hal turned to the phone in his hand and speed dialed best friend Brad Waterhouse. "Hey Brad, how's it going? Can I test something out with you? I just received another call from my 40th high school class reunion committee urging me to attend the event in Congo next summer. I told you about it earlier, right? It's happening in July and I'd have to miss the American Anthropological Association subcommittee meetings in advance of our annual conference. I have mixed thoughts about attending the reunion. What's your counsel?"

Brad was quick with a reply. "I think you can well afford to miss the AAA prep meetings so that's not a problem. But I'm not entirely clear as to why you're resisting a return visit to Kinshasa. Why *wouldn't* you want to join in celebrating your 40th with former classmates?"

"I'm not entirely sure myself, Brad. I just feel...well, apprehensive. That's why I called, to get an outside perspective."

"You've got *that* part right...I'm definitely an outsider when it comes to understanding how your mind works. So, what does Dr. Franklin have to say about it?"

"I haven't actually asked for her opinion. Perhaps I will at our next session. Actually, that's a good idea, come to think of it."

Brad ended the conversation in a familiar manner. "You know, Hal, your question reminds me of an old African proverb: *'Return to old watering holes for more than water; friends and dreams are there to meet you.'* Perhaps that saying contains a gem of inspiration for you."

Hal signed off but for several minutes remained standing on his patio facing the southeast, motionless, a faraway look in his eyes.

***

"So, you feel apprehensive about attending your class reunion in Kinshasa next summer? What's that all about, Hal...have you come to any conclusions for yourself?" Lyndsey turned Hal's report right back to him at their next therapy session.

"No, that's my question for *you*, doc." *Stupid me, I should have expected she'd do that,* he thought. Hal reached for his glasses and removing them, rubbed the bridge of his nose absent-mindedly. Since his therapist made no reply, he sighed and continued. "I suppose the idea of returning to Congo just puts me closer to the people and places that are identified with my PTSD. I don't know...it doesn't seem very logical to me. I liked my TASOK classmates. It would be good to see them again."

"Might one surmise that this is another example of avoidance behavior?" Lyndsey asked in a quiet but even-toned reflection. She paused for a response but when Hal did not answer she reminded him, "One of the therapy goals we've agreed upon is not to let old emotions rule present day decisions and relationships. Does your reunion attendance question fall in that category?"

Hal mulled over her question for some time before he replied. He crossed his legs, scratched his shoulder and rubbed his temples, deep in thought. At last, he looked up gazing directly at his questioner. His next words spilled out with a confident new tone of conviction...and relief.

"Yes. That's it. It's high time for me to open the shutters and let the refreshing breezes blow out all the cobwebs. I'm going to attend my reunion!"

Lyndsey smiled. "Good for you, Hal. That move may well provide you with results you simply cannot attain in talk therapy."

Hal returned home and promptly dialed up his travel agent.

#28 Los Angeles, LAX

July 2010

"I don't want you to go, Papa." Emmie hugged her kneeling grandpa tightly around the neck. The security line at LAX was long and those behind Hal were impatient to move forward. Trish stood close by with glassy eyes, waiting her turn to say her goodbyes. The trio stood in the midst of a cacophony of sounds, movement and colors, distractions typical to the busy international departures area.

"I'll see you both soon," Hal gave Emmie an extra squeeze and a tweak on her cheek. "I love you, Punkin,' and I'm going to miss *you* a lot." He rose to receive Trish's tight embrace. "You two are doing so well, honey. Stick with it. I will be thinking of you the whole time I'm away. Perhaps we can Skype. That is, if the Kinshasa guest house Wifi is working." He swung his backpack over one shoulder, picked up his computer bag and stepped back into the TSA Pre-Check line, waving one last time to his tearful escorts.

As he turned to go, Trish blurted out, "Miss you too, Dad. We'll be fine. Really. I know how you worry but I'm in a good place now. Expect no more emotional train wrecks from your youngest child." Her remark drew a hesitant smile from the departing father, who started to reply and then chose not to.

Hal had accumulated many frequent flyer miles in countless anthropology voyages so on this trip he had upgraded to business class. The extra comfort of more space and services – especially the excellent food and drink – alleviated much of the stress from the long flight ahead. The stewardess welcomed him aboard. After directing Hal to his seat, she handed him a mimosa cocktail. *Ah,* he thought, *this reunion adventure is off to a good start.*

As he settled down into his seat sipping his drink Hal thought back over the last nine months since he decided to make this trip. All things considered, he felt good about what he had accomplished in therapy. With Dr. Franklin's able help, he had a pretty decent grasp on the whole PTSD thing by now. It still seemed remarkable as he thought about it now, to have lived so many years unaware of what drove his determined avoidance of any reminders of childhood. The PTSD diagnosis certainly explained his recurrent nightmares. But it also accounted for a life-long tendency to place guilt and blame on himself for the troubles that afflicted others close to him, especially if they were preceded by a premonition. How did Dr. Franklin term it... "a distorted sense of blame and negativism?" That was *her* interpretation, however, rather than any personal epiphany of his own. Accepting it as true was a reluctant concession.

A smiling stewardess stopped by with a warm scented washcloth interrupting his musings. Hal refreshed hands and face and then reached down to slip the iPad out of the computer bag at his feet. He had some time. The general boarding process was still in its early stages. He turned the device on and opened a Word document to a new page. Since he was headed for a gathering of former TASOK classmates, he reasoned that it might be helpful to list some of the TCK qualities Dr. Franklin had identified; characteristics common to people who, like him had grown up overseas. As classmates shared their stories in coming days, he'd thus have specific patterns to look for. Hal was still not entirely convinced this TCK phenomenon was a real thing. The anthropologist in him needed more "cultural data" to resolve the question to his satisfaction.

He began to type a list of TCK patterns he remembered Dr. Franklin identifying as key TCK characteristics, the "Three R's": Relationships, Restlessness and Resilience.

> *Relationships - include an ease with forming friendships along with a tendency to release them and move on, thereby avoiding the pain of deeper commitments with successive losses. It may explain late marriages, guarded intimacy and higher divorce rates among TCK ranks.*
>
> *Restlessness - according to Dr. Franklin, is born of the widespread tendency for TCKs to feel "out of sinc" with their U. S. peers. It manifests in multiple campus transfers in college, frequent relocations in adulthood, careers that feature ample amounts of change or challenge, and a life-long interest in travel.*

Resilience - is a TCK quality demonstrated in an ease with multilingual, multicultural adaptation to change, travel, and friendships, along with an expanded world view in general.

In addition to the Three Rs, Dr. Franklin contends that TCKs frequently express a kind of nostalgic longing for something or someone that has disappeared from their life. This unique form of homesickness, she termed "saudade," a Portuguese term. It often motivates TCKs to return to their childhood locales overseas, drawn back as if by some unseen force.

Saudade reminds me of the migrating Mabamba butterflies of my youth, thought Hal with a cynical shake of his head. *And here I am winging my way back to Congo!*

Hal smiled to himself, satisfied that his list would guide informal conversations with former classmates. *It will be interesting to see how much we have in common after all these years,* he thought, *and even more, interesting to see if Dr. Franklin is correct.*

***

The TASOK reunion began with Hal's Kinshasa arrival. Former classmates Shirley Hansen Bond and Tyrone Williams rushed to meet him as he cleared customs. The three of them quickly moved to a waiting van for the 20-mile drive from Njili Airport to the MPH guesthouse near the TASOK school compound. As a member of the reunion organizing committee, Shirley had arrived in town several days earlier. She had accompanied the driver to welcome the two new arrivals at the airport and was full of bubbly non-stop questions and enthusiasm, excited to meet up with her former classmates once again after forty years.

Shirley was a slender, deeply tanned woman with long bleached blonde hair. Her blue eyes sparkled as she spoke in rapid animated speech, hands constantly in motion. Hal smiled to himself, noting that the years had treated "Sexy Shirley" pretty well. Her curves were still very much in place – well, maybe they'd slipped just a little – but she seemed quite the spark plug that attracted attention and animated group conversation with her presence.

Tyrone was still recognizable as Tyrone, though he appeared a good deal heavier than when the two of them last met. His '70s Afro had disappeared, replaced by a closely shaved head. He remained a tall, handsome black man, whose bright white teeth lit up his face whenever he smiled. He possessed a thoughtful, reflective demeanor tending to let others take the initiative in conversations and observations. Hal observed that he still moved with the confidence and smooth grace of an athlete.

Tyrone had been on the same Paris-Kinshasa flight with Hal, but they only recognized one another upon disembarking from the aircraft. Hal had been seated in business class and Tyrone, in economy so neither had glimpsed the other during the long eight-hour flight. Shirley's incessant chatter was barely noticed by either of them as they looked intently out the van's windows, soaking up the colors, chaos and clutter of urban Africa once again, scanning streets and intersections for familiar landmarks.

As the van whizzed along the crowded streets, Hal and Tyrone could hardly pull their eyes off of the sights flashing by. To Hal, it seemed like they were driving through the aftermath of an atom bomb. Piles of smoldering, gray garbage lay on both sides of the road, wisps of smoke drifting fog-like over the rubble. Ghostly gray figures moved about here and there poking through the debris scrounging for anything of value: cloth, bottles, cans, discarded cutlery, pieces of wire, even an occasional edible morsel. Roadside figures in colorful mismatched prints strolled along carrying large woven bags packed with food or merchandise in their arms; others proceeded on their way balancing heavy water jugs or piles of firewood on their heads. The familiar aroma blend of rotting garbage, smoke and diesel fuel penetrated even the closed windows of the visitors' transport.

Hal finally addressed his talkative classmate in the front seat. She was half turned, twisting to face the new arrivals in the back. "Thanks, Shirley, for arranging that airport facilitator to usher us through customs so quickly. My memories of past arrivals at Njili are mostly colored by tension... subject to hassles and multiple shakedown attempts. I was bracing myself for major aggravation. Happily, it turned out to be an easy entry. Things have changed!"

"Yes, in some ways things *have* changed, Hal, but in other ways things are just the same. Well, on second thought...more subtle or complex, perhaps." Shirley flicked a quick glance in the direction of their Congolese driver and shifted her position to face the fellows more squarely, lowering her voice slightly.

"Human rights abuses, the war in the east and north, civilian casualties, and exploding inflation dominate the present reality here. On a local level people still struggle to survive...in spite of tons of new buildings and business expansion, unemployment continues to be astronomical. It seems like nearly everyone on the street has a side hustle of some kind just to stay alive. That part hasn't changed much since you guys were last here. Also, politically things are tense at present. Gendarmes and secret police are everywhere...and they're not friendly."

"Wow, that sounds grim." Tyrone reflected while continuing to stare out the window. "Apart from the huge garbage piles, everything looks so...so built up compared to what I remember back in the day. Too bad life is still so hard, post-Mobutu."

"When *were* you last here, Tyrone?" Shirley inquired.

"I returned here after my sophomore year in college, in the summer of 1972, just before my father was reassigned to Italy by the Marines. You will recall, he was a U.S. military advisor to the newly renamed 'Zairian' army."

"I remember that summer visit *well* since that was also the last time I was here." Hal smiled in recall. "I think you were just in the process of transferring from Oklahoma U to Kansas State...on a basketball scholarship, right Ty?"

Tyrone chuckled. "Yeah, that didn't work out so well. I couldn't ever get along with the coach. I finally ended up graduating from Sacramento State of all places, near where my folks settled after Dad retired." He swatted at a fly buzzing around his face. "But what I remember *best* of the summer of '72 was our little coastal camping trip to Muanda with Muhammed and Tim who were also back in town from college. Your Lingala, Hal, bailed us out of deep shit at the roadblocks, especially the one where we got hauled off to an army camp."

Shirley blurted, "Hey, I haven't heard about that one yet. What happened?"

Hal and Tyrone looked at each other and laughed. "Maybe later, Shirley," Hal replied. "There will be lots of time for story telling this week. Some of it, however, may require a bit of editing. We were pretty naïve and adventurous in our youth."

"You mean *stupid*, don't you? Just plain stupid," chimed in Tyrone with a snort.

After another half hour of stop and go traffic they finally arrived at the MPH guesthouse. A worker, waiting for their arrival honk swung open the dark brown iron gate. Simultaneously, out of the doorway emerged a dozen or more smiling faces, cheering the latest arrivals. Hugs and whoops welcomed Hal and Tyrone as they stepped out of the van. The reunion had begun in earnest.

#29 Kinshasa DRC

July 2010

"Man, am I glad to see you!" Paul Bannon, dressed in a flashback MK uniform of cutoffs, tee shirt and flip-flops, had Hal in a vice grip, his muscled arm wrapped firmly around his former roommate's shoulders. "You're rooming with me, just like old times. C'mon upstairs. Hey," he called back over his shoulder "...someone bring Hal's bags!"

The crowd of former classmates swept up the stairs as a single moving organism, escorting the newest arrivals to their rooms. The cement block construction amplified the sounds of the excited voices and laughter creating a deafening din. *Ah,* thought Hal, *just like hostel life at the end of the school day forty years ago.* He couldn't hide the smile from spreading across his face. The recall sent a shiver down his spine, though he was in fact sweating from the warm afternoon humidity.

"You, me and Ty are sharing this room," Paul explained, as Hal looked around at the Spartan accommodations. The room contained a bunk bed and a single bed, with three small desks and chairs placed at separate walls. A single large armoire, doors ajar stood to one side. "We three are the only ones at the reunion who are unaccompanied, so they put us together. I get the top bunk. Ty can take the bed over there. He'll need to hang over the end. I think it's too short for him; I *know* the bunk beds are."

Hal opened his suitcase on the bed and removed several items to hang in the armoire. As he shook the wrinkles from a shirt, he turned to Paul who was straddled backwards on a desk chair, arms folded across the top. "So, tell me, roomie, didn't you ever marry? When we graduated, I thought you and Tonya – she was a year younger, right – were headed in a serious direction. Someone told me you two broke up and that you never married."

"Yeah, you heard it right. The short version is that the tropical heat of our high school romance faded fast when I got back to the States, to Indiana where my folks were from. College was a total disaster. I was miserable, eventually dropped out, found my footing in mechanics, got into Indie car racing as a team mechanic and traveled the circuit for over a decade. I loved it. Was good at it. I moved around a lot, met interesting people and places, made good money. Unfortunately, there wasn't much room in that lifestyle for relationships. I guess I kinda got out of practice doing relationships. I finally determined I actually like the solo life, value my independence."

"I'm surprised," Hal straightened up to look Paul in the eye. "I wouldn't have ever guessed you'd do the single thing. Were there no 'just-abouts' along the way?"

Paul took off his glasses, rubbed his eyes and pinched the bridge of his nose. He hesitated before continuing. "Well, there was this one. I did a little racecar driving myself and ended up getting into a major accident in my late 40's. One of the rehab nurses – Annette was her name – she and I developed a friendship. She was a beautiful gal, a sweet thing but way too conservative, kind of sheltered. In the end I just couldn't see us making a life together. So, we didn't and here I am."

At that point, Tyrone appeared at the door. He was concluding a conversation with someone in the noisy hallway and turned to enter the room. Setting his bags down, with one foot he shoved the larger one sending it rolling across the tile floor in the direction of the single bed. "Still segregating the black boy, I see," he said to his two roommates with a chuckle.

"No, no...it's just," sputtered Paul, turning beet red.

Hal laughed out loud. "You've still got it, Ty. You can hook Paul every time with that line. Now, are you going to be able to hang your feet over the end or will you have to pull the mattress onto the floor?"

"Ha, me down with the cockroaches all night? I don't think so! I'll make it work...up on a bed frame, thank you very much," Tyrone quipped, smiling as he opened up his suitcase and began pulling out items for the armoire. "So, what were the two of you talking about? You look serious."

By that time Paul had regained his composure. "I was just explaining to Hal why I'm here unaccompanied. Never married. What about you two?"

Tyrone continued his unpacking and with a wry smile that appeared with a glance over his shoulder, he quipped. "I'm one for two on the marriage score but if I'm not mistaken that still beats our bro Hal here who is 0 for one. My current squeeze is home caring for our two preschoolers. I also have two adult children by wife number one. Does that catch us up?"

Hal chimed in, "Yeah, my marriage survived for nearly 25 years, but to be candid I stumbled. The fall was mine, not my wife's. Alcohol played a nasty role in the disaster. The good part is that our union still produced three great kids and six grandkids. Only one daughter lives near me, however."

Hal finished his duties and settled down on his bunk. "To change the subject, Paul, have you returned to Congo since high school or is this the first time? Ty and I were back here for one summer a couple of years after graduation, but I haven't returned since. Have you?"

Paul stood up and slowly returned his chair to the nearest desk. Still reflecting on Hal's question, he leaned back on the desktop with straight arms behind him, the heels of both hands resting on its surface. "I wanted to come back. Really badly at first, especially when I felt so lost at college. But there was no money. No way. Our mission didn't pay for kids to return to the field and my folks had zero savings. So, life simply filled up the empty places. I haven't talked or even thought about Africa for a long time. I guess my friends didn't know what to ask. Silly questions have come, at best: Tarzan, lions, snakes, naked natives...that sort of thing. Still, in my private moments I've missed Congo. That's why I volunteered to be on the organizing committee for the reunion. I'm really psyched to be here...at last!"

Smiling broadly, Tyrone quickly stepped over and with a familiarity that spanned forty years, clapped Paul on the back with a blow that sent him staggering toward Hal on the bunk bed. Using his best John Wayne imitation, he declared, "Well, little fella, a hearty *Mbote mingi* to you! We're glad you're here, too."

As Paul rubbed his shoulder, not sure whether to be mad or pleased at the cuffing, Tyrone continued. "I've actually thought a lot about returning here over the years...even traveled to South Africa and Kenya on business a few years ago, but I never found enough incentive to make it here. Until now, that is. Thanks, buddy, for helping make it happen."

The dinner bell announced mealtime and the entire TASOK reunion crowd made their way to the MPH dining room for a first meal together. The combination of high spirits, laughter, good-natured teasing and general banter created a wall of noise that made communication nearly impossible. Lawanda Jones, a tall, heavy-set black woman finally climbed up on a chair and repeatedly clanged a spoon against a drinking glass. She appeared completely comfortable requesting the group's attention, suggesting her own self confidence and leadership skills evident in high school were still very much intact.

"Quiet everyone!" she repeated a half dozen times before the noise level finally dropped. "As chair of the organizing committee, I want to welcome you all to the 40th reunion of the TASOK class of 1970." The cheers and whooping erupted immediately and went on for a full minute or more. When it subsided, she continued. "I want to also welcome you back to your roots, to Kinshasa and to the MPH guest house that is hosting our event."

After the cheering in response to her second set of declarations died down Lawanda changed tone. "I have asked committee member Carl Cooper, or "Chicken Coop" as he was once known, to say grace for our meal." Her reference to Carl's high school nickname brought titters of laughter and several cries of "Coop!" from his former classmates. Carl's frown and blush as he rose in response to Lawanda suggested he was not particularly pleased to have that moniker resurrected.

"My thanks to our very own *mwasi mundele moyindo* for remembering what I've tried for forty years to forget," Carl managed in a sarcastic retort. However, few in the group recognized or remembered enough Lingala to appreciate his derogatory Congolese reference to a "black white woman." As a result, the comment only solicited a couple of appreciative "Humpfs" from his listeners. Lawanda showed no sign of recognizing his return jab.

Carl somehow managed to retrieve enough dignity to salvage a blessing for the food and for the reunion event ahead. The group responded in unison with a loud "Amen!" and dug into their meal and into their visiting with gusto. The crescendo of noise and spirited chatter quickly filled the dining hall.

At the end of the dinner hour, Lawanda once again banged spoon against glass to solicit the group's attention. "At 7:30 we will all gather in the meeting room for some announcements regarding our activities this week and for a round of introductions. Some of us may not remember each other's names; indeed, some have acquired new ones. We may also not recognize the (ahem), transformations that have taken place since we graduated." That remark stirred scattered laughter. "We also have a number of guests with us – spouses, children and partners – whom we'd like to meet as well, so let's take a short break and then head for the conference room." With that, the meal was ended.

#30 Kinshasa DRC

July 2010

The reunion attendees meandered in twos and fours from the dining room to the conference room slowly making their way to chairs set up in a large circle. The center of the room had been cleared of tables and once again the group's animated chatter echoed against the cement block walls creating a virtual wall of sound. Lawanda stood waving both arms and called out a loud "*Mbote!*" greeting to attract the group's attention. Hal glanced around the circle making a quick head count...twenty-four altogether, fourteen classmates total. *Hmm,* he thought. *Not bad...nearly half the class made it to the reunion.*

"Welcome everyone to TASOK Class of 1970's Fortieth Reunion. I'm Lawanda Jones, reunion coordinator and daughter of former US AID Director, Nick Jones, for classmates with long memories." That comment stirred smiles and a low murmur from the group.

"I'm currently a manager with Etna Insurance, living in Seattle. My youngest daughter, Olive, is here with me. I'm no longer married, have two other kids both grown and on their own."

Without further elaboration Lawanda launched directly into a description of the week's schedule. "This is Congo, everyone, so I must caution you that *everything* is subject to change. Never-the-less, here's what the organizing committee has come up with for planned activities during the next five days we're together."

Her list included a tour of the TASOK grounds led by the current school board superintendent; a bus tour of the city, led by a TASOK alumnus from a later class who currently lives and works in Kinshasa; picnic/swimming outings to les Petites Chutes de la Lukaya nearby and to Ngombi Beach on the Congo River; an afternoon visit to Lac de Ma Vallee; a tour of the Academie des Beaux-Arts; a visit to Lola ya Bonobo apes and finally, a formal reception at the American embassy. She identified other optional outings both in and around Kinshasa that were available for people to explore on their own. Several of the attendees spoke up acknowledging plans to travel to other locations outside the city after the reunion ended.

"Tonight is 'get acquainted night'...or rather, get re-acquainted night for classmates." Lawanda's white teeth flashed a big smile. "I propose that we go around the circle and ask each one to clearly state your name – for the sake of our travel partners – and share three things: 1) where you are living, 2) your family status – married, divorced, single and kids, if any – and 3) your primary occupation or profession since high school. We'll have plenty of time for Q & A later. Since most of us are jet lagged, we don't want to make tonight a super late evening."

The introductions began in a straightforward manner. Muhammed Kakazai, currently living in Sidney, Australia, reminded his classmates with a wry smile that "back in the day" his father was most likely their family's main source of money, since he operated a back door black market currency exchange through his successful import-export business. Muhammed had continued in the family business that by now had expanded to another continent. His travels brought him back to DRC on many occasions over the years, so he was well oriented to being in Congo at present. His three grown children were reportedly all settled in successful professions. His cousin, Ali, accompanied him on this journey since his wife did not share his passion for travel. Ali just sat quietly by Muhammed's side, no discernable expression on his face. *Cousin Ali is clearly the beneficiary of that disinterest*, thought Hal as he took this all in.

Kasandra Taylor's soft voice was heard next. A daughter of Assemblies of God missionary parents, Hal remembered her as a somber and pessimistic classmate during their TASOK years, one with intense spiritual convictions. She informed the group that after graduation she had returned to the States, attended nursing school and married a pastor. She was now, however, divorced and living in Tulsa, Oklahoma.

Hal made a mental note that contrary to his expectations, Kasandra reported this information in a matter-of-fact manner with no hint of apology or embarrassment. "*She seems to have found some peace of mind*," he thought to himself. Her 20-year-old son, Ryan, accompanied her to the reunion. He had already discovered Tiffany, the attractive teenage daughter of classmate Joanna Brubaker. The two were sitting together across the circle from their mothers, whispering side comments to each other and snickering.

Tyrone's description of his life in St. Louis was typically short and to the point. He was a partner in a busy law practice, had survived two marriages, two children from each and was a frequent international traveler. That completed his statement. Paul Bannon's similarly succinct report began with his disclosure that he was a never-married single man. The major post-TASOK discovery he reported was that mechanical aptitude rather than academic prowess had held the key to success in life for him. He cited several exciting years of indie car racing that had come to an unwelcome and abrupt end with a life-threatening accident. Finally, Paul indicated he was presently well settled as the owner of a high-end foreign auto repair shop in Indiana.

Mona Conrad next rose to her feet to speak. She was dressed in a stylish safari suit, accented with expensive shoes, a leopard skin handbag and a huge sparkling diamond on her ring finger. She appeared to have stepped out of the centerfold of Vogue magazine. Her monologue came across more as a campaign speech than a simple self-introduction. Mona began by informing the group that she was a proud board member of the prestigious World Wildlife Fund. She launched into lively detail describing the dire condition of wildlife in Africa and the need for all to help preserve vanishing species.

Paul leaned over to Hal and whispered, "Still the high-flying Ambassador's daughter, it would seem." Hal did not reply but managed a quick roll of the eyes.

Lawanda finally intervened. "Mona, a reminder...tonight is for *intros*. Back on track, please!" Mona flashed an annoyed glance at the interruption, cleared her throat and resumed her comments with a long introduction of her suave, gray-templed banker husband, Bradford. He sat next to her, legs crossed, hands clasped on one knee, chair slightly pushed back and a practiced smile on his tanned face. She noted that they have two beautiful and brilliant stepdaughters from Brad's first marriage, currently attending Ivy League colleges. She concluded her speech with a reference to the pair's many international junkets and an invitation for her classmates to "look us up the next time you go skiing in Aspen, Colorado, where we presently live...when we're not travelling abroad."

Alice Broadbent, Mona's best friend during their TASOK years, bounced up clapping as Mona moved to resume her seat. She burst out in an excited voice. "Oh, Monie that was wonderful. What a life you lead! Hello everyone. I'm Alice and as you may recall my father was with the UN Mission. Some of you remember coming to our place in Djelo-Binza to watch movies on Friday nights. Rodney, here, and I live in Manchester, UK." She motioned to the thin man next to her smiling with yellowed, irregular teeth. "I'm the HR Manager of a textile firm and Roddie is a CPA there. I've got two grown kids – a boy and a girl – from a previous relationship, er...I mean, from my former marriage. My daughter has a two-year-old, so that also makes me a Nana. Oh...Rodney and I haven't yet tied the knot, but we're still together after three years and I guess that says it all." She giggled, nervously. "Well, that's about it for now."

Alice sat back in her chair as Rodney continuing his uninterrupted smile, gave her a hug. There was an awkward delay before the next person in the circle shared. Finally, Lawanda chimed in, "Okay, Oscar, your turn."

A short, stocky, well-tattooed man was leaning forward, staring at the floor. Oscar Peters voice was shaking when at last he began to speak. Rivulets of sweat coursed down ruddy cheeks from his bald head. "I...I don't know where to begin," he stammered. "My life has not been a success. I probably get the prize for being this class's biggest disaster. Oh, I've got my own welding shop now, in Round Rock – that's near Austin, Texas – and my girlfriend, Patty, here is great, but most of my life after Congo has been a disaster."

Those words stilled the room. Previously a low buzz of whispered side comments had provided an undercurrent of sound but now the room became silent. Paul once again leaned over to whisper in Hal's ear. "This ought to be good: Hemp Man's confessions." Hal did not respond; his attention remained riveted on the speaker.

"Like Paul, college wasn't for me. That's no surprise to some of you. So, I flunked out and joined the Marines. Did two tours of Vietnam. I actually returned to Congo afterwards for a ten-month construction stint with Inga-Shaba. I don't remember much of any of that, however, since I was pretty drugged up at the time. I have six kids from three marriages, none of which lasted more than a few years. Alcohol and drugs took me down hard. At one point I ended up on the streets in Austin. I finally got into rehab and cleaned up my life. That's where I met Patty."

Oscar's companion reached over to put her arms around her tearful partner. "I almost didn't come to this reunion, but in AA they tell us to face our fears, not avoid them so here I am."

The circle spontaneously stood as one and burst into applause though Oscar remained seated, face in his hands. Hal stood and clapped along as well but unlike his cheering classmates, he was deep in thought. *"That's what I'm doing here as well...facing my fears. Not that it helps much to know I'm not alone...it still sucks!"*

Lawanda finally brought things back to order. "Thanks, Oscar, for being real with us. We're not here to compare lives, just to enjoy one another's company. We're glad you found your way out of the darkness and glad that you're here."

No sooner were Lawanda's words spoken than the door at the back of the room banged open and the evening's sharing came to an end.

#31 Kinshasa DRC

July 2010

All eyes turned toward the loud noise at the rear of the room. A large Congolese soldier appeared in the open doorway, followed quickly by two companions. All three were dressed in green khaki fatigues and each bore the distinctive red beret of the venerable Republican Guard on their heads. Each escort carried a rifle; their heavily muscled leader bore an officer's sidearm on his hip. The reunion crowd was in shock. The sudden appearance of the President's elite security forces always meant trouble.

In a deep bass voice that rang across the conference room the leader declared, *"Nous sommes ici pour Monsieur Muhammed Kakazai. Où est-il?"* At first no one moved a muscle. Then, Darrel Baylor, the MPH host, rose from where he was sitting at the rear of the room and moved toward the soldiers, asking in French "What is the problem here, officers? Why are you disturbing our peaceful social gathering?" He stopped short as one of the invaders swung his rifle around leveling it at his midsection.

The burly officer simply ignored Darrel's question. Looking around the circle, he stepped over to the first Asian figure that came into view, Abdul Malik, and stepped in front of him. "Monsieur Kakazai?" he demanded with a scowl. "No," came the shaky reply. "Je m'appelle Malik, *Docteur* Malik." The soldier's thick neck then turned in the direction of the real Muhammed, who slowly rose to his feet in response. With a puzzled expression on his face he asked in French, "Why am I being sought by the Republican Guard?"

"I have orders to take you to Makala," was the terse reply. "You can ask your questions there." Showing no further interest in conversation the officer grasped Muhammed by both arms, whipped them behind him, slapped handcuffs on his wrists and shoved his wide-eyed captive toward the door.

A second attempt by Darrel Baylor to intervene was accompanied by a growing chorus of protests from the conference room's roused occupants. It was met with a similar response to the first attempt: a frowning beret-clad soldier leveled his rifle barrel at the group as he slowly backed toward the door.

Darrel followed the foursome as they swept out of the room, down the hallway and out into the yard. He watched from the doorway as they climbed into a jeep parked near the building. The engine roared to life and they sped out the open gate in a cloud of dust and exhaust. Darrel's wife, Bonnie, rushed up to his side. Wrapping her arms about his waist she looked up, forehead creased and eyes full of fear. "What's going on, Darrel? Why are they taking Muhammed?"

"I have no idea, Honey, but we need to get help right away. Makala Prison is a nasty place. Last I heard over 8,000 prisoners are housed in a facility built for 1,500. No one wants to even visit there let alone inhabit the place as a prisoner. All I can imagine is that Muhammed's family that still does business here in Kinshasa, has somehow crossed the President. What other reason could there be?"

Agitation and alarm now reigned in the conference room as noisy clusters of former classmates and guests milled about, rehashing the events that had just occurred, asking each other, "What just happened? Why did they take Muhammed? What should we do? How can we help him?"

Hal was every bit as distressed and confused as any of his classmates. He followed Muhammed's cousin, Ali, who had moved toward the door, as Darrel and Bonnie reappeared there.

"Are they gone?" Ali inquired gesturing with both palms up.

"Yes, just one jeep," Darrel reached out to wrap a comforting arm around Ali's shoulder.

"I must go in search of my uncle," Ali declared in an even voice, pulling away from the well-meaning embrace. "He's in charge of business here in Kinshasa. We were told yesterday when they met us at the airport that the family expected trouble from the President's security forces. For that reason, they are not staying at their residence these days. I suspect that when the record of our arrival was reported an order was issued to arrest Muhammed." Not waiting for a reaction, he continued. "So...can I borrow your van and driver?"

"Absolutely. Let me call him right now." Darrel turned abruptly and headed back toward the yard.

"What's this all about, Ali?" Hal inquired, reaching for the man's arm to delay his exit. He was surprised at Ali's coolness and calm demeanor, given the seriousness of the situation.

"Probably money," was the quiet reply. Ali looked Hal directly in the eyes and offered a matter-of-fact explanation. "We were told numerous abductions have occurred in recent days; abductions of successful merchants or family members. It's always the same: arrest, accusation of anti-government activity and finally, release after payment of a large ransom. I'm guessing the Republican Guard got lucky this evening in their dragnet."

Ali headed off into the night with the MPH chauffer and Hal returned to the conference room to report what he had just learned. No one slept well that night. The reunion's celebratory mood had definitely taken a hit.

#32 Kinshasa DRC

July 2010

The mood at breakfast the next morning continued to be conspicuously somber. Greetings lacked animation and table conversations were subdued. It seemed difficult for the reunion crowd to enjoy the moment when their class member's fate was in the balance. As the eating finished, Lawanda rose and clinked her spoon against a glass to summon the group's attention.

"Good morning all. I realize that everyone is worried about Muhammed. Unfortunately, we have no further word at present regarding his situation. We have a call out and we will let you know of any new developments as soon as we hear anything." She remained standing, scooted her chair against the table and leaned back against it. "Because of the ah...unforeseen developments, we did not complete our introductions last night. I'd thus like to invite those of our group whom we did not hear from to briefly introduce themselves now."

A short, handsome, sharp featured Pakistani man promptly stood to his feet, as if anticipating the invitation. He was dark complexioned and meticulously groomed and dressed.

"Morning all. I'm Abdul Malik and this is my wife, Aisha." He gestured to the attractive lady seated next to him. "We presently live in Vancouver, BC. My parents were both doctors at Mama Yemo Hospital here in Kinshasa during our TASOK days. They now live near us, but very much retired these days. You may have guessed...I followed in their footsteps. I'm an orthopedic surgeon. Aisha is a pharmacist. Both of our sons are also medical professionals in Canada." His bright, white teeth flashed a smile. "I guess it's some kind of family script. We have returned to DRC several times for brief periods doing voluntary medical education at the university."

As he pulled his chair back to sit, he added in a quiet voice, "I am worried about my friend Muhammed. We have remained in touch over the years. I pray he's not harmed."

Abdul's reference created a moment of silence in the room. It was broken by the screech of a chair being pulled out as a heavy-set woman dressed in bright colored shorts and a simple print blouse stood to speak. Her choice of attire favored comfort rather than style. She wore no makeup of any kind and her graying hair was pulled back in a bun.

"Hi everyone, I'm Joanna...Joanna Brubaker and this is my daughter, Tiffany." She rested her hand on the shoulder of an attractive young girl of seventeen or eighteen, who was mid-bite with a forkful of scrambled eggs. She turned beet red at the mention of her name.

"I stayed in the Mennonite hostel during TASOK and have shared many stories over the years with my two kids. Tiff here has come along to check things out first-hand. She has an older brother who works on a farm near our home in Pennsylvania. Oh, yes...I am married, and I teach social studies in a local high school. My farmer spouse is averse to travel so it's me and Tiffany on this trip. Do you want to say anything, honey?" The red-faced teen seemed to sink even lower into her tank top as she vehemently shook her head, eyes scowling down at her plate.

A skinny arm in a khaki safari shirt shot up in the air, signaling to the room as its owner slowly rose to his feet. The man's angular face, ruddy from many hours in the sun, bore a short salt-and-pepper beard. Crow's feet creased the corners of his smiling eyes. "Hey everyone. I'm Tim McClennon and this is my wife, Dorothy." His big smile invited the same from others.

"We presently live in Tucson, Arizona, but we've inhabited spots all over the globe at different times: India, Croatia, Sri Lanka, Uganda. I'm an electrical engineer and my assignments have mostly been international. We have two grown kids who can't figure out where they belong." That comment brought nods and new smiles from his audience.

"I guess you could say a close encounter with cancer a few years back scared the hell out of us, so these days we're very involved with our church community." More chuckles. "I'm one of the fellows who returned to Congo soon after graduation and took "the trip" to Muanda with the guys. That tale needs to be told, but that's all from me for now."

The next speaker remained seated but waved an arm at the room to indicate his participation. His attire – a tee shirt, shorts and flip-flops – seemed incongruous with his distended belly and double chin. As he ran one hand through thinning hair, he flashed a nervous smile at the woman next to him.

"Carl and Brenda Cooper here, presently from Chicago. Maybe some of you will recall that I was one of four Cooper kids attending TASOK. Four is a good number. We now we have four grown kids of our own...but thankfully we are presently in possession of an empty nest, yay." That brought new chuckles from the audience.

"My folks were Presbyterian missionaries – both have gone to be with the Lord by now, may they rest in peace. Brenda and I are still active in the church. I'm a travel agent, so we get to indulge our travel passion, only at a discount." Someone across the room called out, "No fair!" Carl glanced up smiling, "Eat your heart out!" and continued.

"It's been a decade or more since we passed through Kinshasa on our travels. Congo is a tough place for tourists. My limited French and Lingala helped out on those past visits. I don't know what we'd have done without it. And by the way, last night's abduction of our classmate really rattled me. It brought back memories of tense times in my childhood. Brenda and I have been praying for Muhammed's safety."

The blonde bombshell next to him then popped up out of her seat. "Have you finished, Carl?" He nodded. "Well, for those who don't know, I'm Shirley Hansen Bond. These days I hail from Tampa, Florida. I have one husband, Michael – at home working – and two kids in college. I'm an X-ray technician. It took me a long time to find myself after TASOK. I was in and out of several colleges, did a stint in the Peace Corps and went through a number – I won't say how many – of relationships. It was only in my late 30s that I finally settled...on my spouse and my profession. I dearly love both of them. It just took me a lot longer than most to figure out."

Shirley had no sooner concluded her comments then the sound of a commotion echoed into the dining room from the hallway. Heads began to turn toward the noise coming through the open door at the back of the room. The volume increased with cries of surprise and excited voices. Suddenly a cluster of chattering, smiling people burst into the dining room. At the center, with huge smiles on their faces, were...Muhammed and his cousin Ali!

Cheers rang out, chairs clattered, and tables were nearly

overturned as the room full of former classmates scrambled to greet the two returning men.

"We thought you were a goner!"

"What happened? How did you escape?"

"Were you hurt? What's that bruise on your face?"

When the barrage of questions slowed and the hugs, backslaps and high fives ceased, Muhammed wearily pulled up a chair and collapsed down into it. "Whew. I'm beat, no pun intended. No sleep for me last night." He leaned his head against one open palm, elbow on the table.

Taking a deep breath, as if to signal to himself that he was up to the task of reporting, he continued. "Okay guys, here's the scoop. The short version of what happened is exactly what Ali told some of you last night. It was basically a shake down. The security forces finally snagged a member of my family – me, regrettably – and my relatives paid up. So...I was promptly released. But not until I was roughed up a bit as a reminder not to cause any trouble over the matter."

A full plate of scrambled eggs, fruit and toast was set before Muhammed and his cousin with instructions to head straight for bed when they had finished eating. The reunion crowd slowly drifted off in much lighter spirits but with greatly diminished nostalgia toward their former homeland. The snapshot of present-day life they had just witnessed was a sobering flashback.

#33 Kinshasa, DRC

July 2010

In spite of the absence of the two sleep-deprived attendees who readily took the invitation to retreat into bed, by mid-morning the reunion had picked up momentum. The entire group headed for the TASOK compound to tour the familiar classrooms and grounds that held so many vivid memories from their high school days. Several of the former classmates merely walked the distance arm-in-arm up the street from the MPH guesthouse; others climbed into the van for the short transfer to the school campus.

Much was made of the expansion and development of the buildings and grounds. Upgrades were evident at every turn: soccer field, basketball court, admin buildings, teachers' apartments and in and around the classrooms themselves. Oft repeated phrases punctuated the superintendent's official tour.

"Will you look at that? We never had those."

"Do you remember when we..."

"The breezeway where we hung out looks just the same. Some things never change."

"Books, science equipment, computers, furnishings...there's so much more now. It's so modern."

At the end of the official tour several of the guys talked the superintendent into finding a basketball for an informal pickup game on the covered court. The lively competition provided plenty of noise, laughter and sweat but not much in the way of demonstrated skill. It all transpired at a far slower pace than the alumni recalled in their vivid memories. Some of the gals even managed to join in with familiar Condor cheers, though none had the courage or dexterity to kick their heels in the air as they had done in high school.

The game ended with the MPH guesthouse van's arrival with sandwiches and drinks for lunch. It was a pre-planned on-campus noon meal, imported from off-site, reminiscent of the weekday practice during TASOK years. Mealtimes were always a school day highlight and this experience proved to be no exception. It turned out to be an effective memory prompt for the former students, triggering a plethora of animated stories and hearty laughter.

In keeping with tropical practice, after lunch the reunion crowd adjourned back to the guesthouse for a siesta break. Those who did not actually nap made use of the Wi-Fi to report back home or visited quietly in twos and threes in the lounge area.

Hal was glad for the down time and for the company of his two reunion roommates. He discovered a new appreciation for their sense of humor from the lighthearted banter they exchanged, and he marveled at the trio's shared perception of their circumstances. It was camaraderie of a kind he had not felt for forty years.

"You haven't lost your touch, Ty. You were awesome in that basketball game. However, you still go left every time after you throw that head fake under the basket."

"Ha. You got lucky on that steal, Schroeder. I *had* to let you think you had me figured. Actually, to be honest...you *did* have me figured. I just didn't think you'd remember my moves." That comment generated guffaws.

"I thought good old Carl was going to split a gut at one point," Paul chimed in. "It'd be a big spill, if it happened...he's grown since high school. An impressive gut, that is. Probably all that gourmet food flying first class on his travels."

Ty stretched out on the bed locking his hands behind his head, elbows fanned out. "Hey Schroeder. Did you catch Carl the Christian cussing in Lingala when Oscar plowed into him? I wonder if his wife – what's her name...Brenda? – knows what those words mean." Another round of chuckles commenced.

Hal sat up on the bunk where he had been resting. Still smiling, he added "I suspect that Tim still knows their meaning since I saw him taking Carl aside for a serious 'come to Jesus' chat after that little outburst of his."

Paul climbed down from the top bunk and pulled his tee shirt over his head. "Did either of you guys notice that the gals seem to be frozen in time...in a clique? Mona, Alice and LaWanda are still hanging together and the other three gals are keeping their distance. I remember that same arrangement during high school."

Hal and Tyrone did not comment, reflecting on Paul's observation. He continued, "Do you recall that one lunchtime in our senior year when Joanna had a meltdown, yelling and accusing Mona of being mean and snobbish. Wow, what a scene! That could have come right out of the "Mean Girls" movie from the 90s. I wonder if those two ever worked things out between them."

"Doesn't look like it," said Tyrone sitting up and bending down to pull on his shoes.

"On a lighter note," Hal chimed in, "I've been impressed with how many of us have moved around a lot, lived in so many different places. And how the majority of us like to travel."

"*Have* traveled, you mean," said Ty as he stood. "It's one of those things we all like to do. It also sounds like quite a few of our number have not found and stuck with a perfect marriage match. Paul here has given up even looking." That remark resulted in a shoe sent flying across the room. Ty adeptly ducked.

As the hazy afternoon shadows lengthened, the reunion crowd made their way back to the lush TASOK grounds, this time for a refreshing swim in the school's 25-meter pool and for a BBQ event that lasted well past a diffuse orange sunset and on into the evening hours. A case of cold Primus beer unique to Congo and an ample supply of both red and white wine elevated the spirits of the group and levity of their interaction. Tiki torches surrounded the pool area creating an ideal atmosphere for conversation and reflection. It ended up nearly 11 P.M. when the last vanload exited the TASOK gates and returned to the guesthouse for the night.

Hal was exhausted as he shed his clothes and climbed into his bunk. The gecko on the bedroom wall had already begun his nightly rounds of hunting mosquitos in the pitch black, warm and humid night. As he pulled the sheet over bare shoulders, Hal mumbled a sleepy "Good night, guys," to his roommates. Their silence suggested that both had already checked out for the night. The day's food, conversations, warm sun and swim had all added up to bodies aching for sleep and minds fully shut down. Unfortunately for Hal, his mind did not remain in the "off" position.

Somewhere in the still early morning hours vivid images began to form in earnest. It was one of "those" nightmares. The mental video commenced on a cloudless, stifling hot day among golden sand dunes that lined the raging waters of the mighty Congo River. It was a social outing. Hal's reunion classmates and their guests were spread out along the expansive beach, some wading in the shallows, some sitting on rocks visiting, others lounging in beach chairs or sunbathing on blankets.

Without warning, a cry of alarm sounded, jolting the beach's relaxed occupants into instant action. It appeared that everyone was in motion, agitated, rushing in the same direction. Something serious and compelling was unfolding, but what? A cluster had formed around one of their number who was lying very still on the ground at the center, in distress. It was...Hal himself! As if accelerating the video's speed, Hal saw himself first bouncing in the back of the MPH van, then being transferred on a gurney into a hospital and finally lying in bed in a dimly lit room...in agony. Was he dying?

As he pondered that thought, a shadowy backlit figure appeared in the bright doorway. To Hal's surprise, his anxiety seemed to evaporate with this unannounced appearance. It was replaced with a deep sense of peace that slowly spread over him. Who *was* that person? Hal struggled to conjure up a clear image in his dream. It seemed the individual must be a nurse, at least it was obviously a "she" in nursing garb, but he couldn't make out her face.

As the figure slowly approached his bedside the thought flashed, *"Good, now I'll get to see who it is."* At the very moment he sat up in the hospital bed to greet the mystery person, Hal's head hit the mattress springs above his bunk, and he awoke with a start.

Hal rubbed the sore spot on the top of his head. He was breathing hard. Sweat was pouring from his forehead, dripping off his ears. He carefully swung his legs off the edge of the bed and placed both feet on the ground, covering his face with his hands. As his newly conscious mind attempted to process the disturbing sleep images from just moments earlier, he discovered his emotions were tangled in a knot: disappointment, curiosity and alarm. He was disappointed to have failed to identify the arriving figure, curious about the theme of the crisis and alarmed that he was at the center of the drama.

There was no returning to slumber for Hal the rest of the night. "Why me?" and "Why now?" kept cycling in his head. At last the faint gray of approaching dawn turned into a bright new day.

#34 Kinshasa, DRC

July 2010

Hal was uncharacteristically silent at breakfast the next morning. He picked at his French toast and bacon and his coffee became cold before he attempted a first sip. Paul, sitting next to him, finally noticed. He had been enjoying an animated conversation with Patty, Oscar's significant other. Her breakfast was in "pause mode," mouth ajar with a horrified look on her face.

Paul turned to Hal to confirm the "eaten by a crocodile" story he had been telling his enthralled listener. "Isn't that true, Hal? They cut open the stomach of that huge croc and found the missing embassy guy's watch." When he received no reply, he turned toward Hal and did a double take.

"Hey, buddy, what's going on with you today? Don't you feel well?"

"I'm okay," Hal managed. "Just had a restless night."

"Is that the same place we're going today, I mean by the river where the croc ate that guy?" Patty asked with a shaky voice, still processing the tale she'd been told.

Paul was frowning, eyes remaining focused on Hal who had resumed his distracted picking at his plate. A dismissive, preoccupied reply to Patty signaled he was done with their conversation. "Yeah, same place. Don't worry; there are seldom any croc sightings there these days. We'll check it out before anyone swims in the shallows."

"What's going on, man?" Paul asked again. "Talk to me." He searched Hal's face as he laid a light hand on his arm.

Hal looked up from his engrossed reflections. A quick apologetic smile flicked across his face. "I had another one of "those" dreams last night, Paul, the kind I occasionally had during our hostel days. This time it was *me* at the center...in trouble. I don't know what to make of it. It wasn't very clear. It concerned our trip to Ngombe Beach later today. If trouble awaits me there, I'm tempted not to go at all, but if it's like past dreams I can't change the overall reality. Maybe by anticipating it, I can modify the outcome a little."

166

Paul sat silently for a long minute, deep in thought, forehead creased. "I...I don't know what to say, man. I never did get that premonition stuff, but I do remember it was spooky-real whenever you had those dreams. I hope this time it just turns out to be leftovers from bad barbeque."

***

The early morning haze, a daily occurrence during the dry season, had mostly lifted by the time the vans exited the guesthouse gate. They headed for the day's planned outing at Ngombe Beach, a favorite picnic site for expatriates. It was a short drive. Cooler temperatures near the river made it a welcome destination on a warm day.

Large rocks bordered a broad golden sand beach that led to shallow still water inlets. Behind them roared the wild waves of the Congo River's main channel. Large floating mats of water hyacinth, dense enough to walk on, clung to the edges of the quiet riverbank pools. Above the group's sandy destination, deceptively smooth waters that stretched across the wide river allowed a select few wary Congolese fishermen to ply their craft in their long pirogues. A handful of young children could be seen wandering slowly along the beach; others splashed in the shallow waters, their dark forms visible in sharp contrast to the bright sand.

The reunion crowd exited their transports and quickly dispersed along the sandy beach. Since there was virtually no available shade, large sun umbrellas were set up with portable chairs and blankets spread beneath their welcome shadows. Coolers with food and drink quickly followed. While this set up was occurring the two guesthouse van chauffeurs strolled slowly along the river's edge near the shallows, scanning the surface for any signs of danger. Since there were local children splashing about here and there, their level of concern was relatively low. Any crocs lurking nearby would surely have set off alarms.

As Hal made his way from the van to the beach, he leaned close and spoke to his roommate in a lowered voice. "Paul, I really don't know what to expect of this day. Don't think of me as too big of a wuss, but I'm not planning to go swimming. I'm wondering if I might ask you to keep an eye out for me from time to time. Just in case trouble shows up. I think I'll hang out over there by those big rocks at the end of the beach."

"Last night's dream really shook you, didn't it? Well, you got it mate! Safety first. I, however, am presently headed for the water." And with that declaration he dropped his towel and took off at a trot for the water's edge.

Hal found a flat spot and a bit of shade at the base of some large rocks. On his head was a woven grass hat he had purchased from a vendor by the parking area. His shoulders and arms were protected with a light, khaki long sleeved safari shirt worn over swim trunks. After a lifetime of anthropology field trips to the South Pacific he really didn't need more sun exposure. In his hand he carried a recently published copy of Christopher Ryan's "Sex at Dawn: The Prehistoric Origins of Modern Sexuality," which he had brought along to read and review for *American Anthropologist* magazine. *It should be a good afternoon*, Hal thought as he settled down to read and relax.

It indeed began as a very pleasant afternoon. Interesting reading, friends cavorting about nearby, the scenic beach and soothing background roar of the mighty Congo River all generated a kind of internal contentment and peace that made Hal smile as he looked up from his book. It was soothing to the soul to be back in Congo with *his people* again.

It was also, however, plenty warm even in the shade. Several of the guys tossed a Frisbee back and forth down by the water's edge. They spotted Hal, yelled and motioned for him to come join them. *It would feel good to cool my heels in the water*, he thought as he rose and headed toward the river. Lining the water's edge was a thick mat of water hyacinth. Here and there, its characteristic pink flowers bloomed, incongruous with the large solid green platform that held them.

Hal stepped down into the foliage, enjoying the soothing coolness of the river water on his feet and ankles as he sloshed along toward his friends. The big leaves impeded his progress, however, so he stepped out on top of them to see if they might support his weight. Surprisingly, they did or very nearly so. He slowly picked his way forward, arms out to keep his balance as he walked, each sinking step generating a puddle at his feet.

Someone yelled, "Hey Hal, catch this!" and launched the Frisbee in his direction. As he looked up to catch the flying disc, the corner of his eye caught a gray flash rising before him.

"Ow!"

A sudden sharp pain midway up Hal's right calf made him instinctively kick out. As his leg jerked up, with it came a writhing gray form. Hal's reflex action detached a thick meter-long snake from his calf. It flew through the air, splashed back onto the hyacinth mat and immediately slithered away, disappearing beneath the leaves with a final flick of its tail.

"Snake!" came an alarmed cry.

"I saw it. It had a hood."

"Cobra! Water cobra!"

It all happened so fast that Hal had little chance to react at first. Suddenly, it seemed the entire reunion gang was headed in his direction, running, calling out. He waded out of the hyacinths onto the sand and carefully sat down as a crowd gathered around him. Everyone chattered at once in excited and concerned tones.

Hal finally spoke up. "No, it's okay, guys. It just smarts a bit there." He pointed to two clear red fang marks about an inch and a half apart, midway up his right calf. Each puncture had a little trickle of blood beneath it. A second flurry of suggestions immediately erupted.

"Cut the bite marks."

"Make X-slices and suck out the poison."

"Get him to the clinic."

"Here's my belt. Wrap a tourniquet above his knee."

The dark form of Abdul Malik rushed up and pushed through the circle. As he knelt in the sand next to Hal, he waved a raised hand at the onlookers bending over the two of them.

"Hey! Hey! Stop everyone! Move back! Someone get me a cloth to wipe the wound." Startled, the circle moved back a half a step.

"I'm a medical doctor." The wiry figure spoke with authority as he leaned forward to get a closer look at the bite marks. "We studied Christy's Water Cobra in our tropical medicine course. That's likely what bit you, Hal." He glanced up to make brief eye contact with his patient.

To the circle he intoned, "No cutting or sucking the poison. That doesn't work. It can harm the tissue and cause problems. Immobilize his leg...no moving about at all. Flexing the muscle increases venom absorption."

Someone handed Abdul a cloth. As he carefully dabbed at the blood spots, he continued his explanations. "I'm just removing whatever venom might remain. No massaging the tissues here...including use of a tourniquet. Now," he looked up and around the circle once more, "we need to get Hal to a van and to a hospital...right away! Time is critical with snake bites."

Tim had already run to the vans to alert the chauffeurs. Tyrone and Paul created a fourhanded seat by grasping each other's wrists with both hands. They slipped their base beneath him while Hal looped his arms over their shoulders; as they rose, Carl and Oscar each carefully supported Hal's feet and legs to keep them as still as possible. The human litter moved steadily across the beach to the vans. Surrounded as it was by the entire alumni group, it resembled some kind of strange, giant centipede moving across the sand.

At first Hal felt only a bit of stinging at the site of the snakebite on his leg. *Much ado about nothing*, he thought, a little embarrassed by all the attention he had generated. As he was placed in the van, however, Hal started to feel dizzy. His throat felt dry. It was hard to swallow. "Water?" he asked, in a croaking voice. It took effort to get the word out.

What's happening to me? A sudden shudder of fear swept over him as the van began to bounce and rock its way up the dirt road heading for the hospital.

#35 Kinshasa DRC

July 2010

The van roared away from its shady parking spot under large trees, turning onto the city's paved but rutted streets. *"Tokai wapi?"* The chauffer called for the destination over one shoulder as the van careened around huge potholes. *"Kenda na CPU (Centre Privé d'Urgence), noki!"* was the shouted reply from the back of the van as both Abdul Malik and guesthouse host, Darrel Baylor, yelled out in unison. The two men clutched Hal firmly attempting to prevent him from bouncing off the seats as they tore along. Their best efforts, however, barely held him in place.

The CPU was a full 18 kilometers from their location, a voyage of nearly an hour. Hal felt increasingly strange as the moments progressed. Saliva had begun to dribble from the edge of his mouth. He was having difficulty swallowing. When he reached up to wipe off the moisture, his hand and arm felt like they were moving under water, sluggish and slow to respond.

Abdul's face was creased with worry. Bending over his afflicted classmate, he kept repeating in an even, low voice, "Just keep still, Hal. We're getting you to help. Keep as calm as you can. We're right here with you." The comforting words seemed far away to Hal, as if spoken from another room. Waves of fear swept over him. *Is this it? Am I dying?* He groaned at the grim thought.

It seemed no time at all before the van turned off crowded Avenue Wagenia, just a few blocks from the U.S. Embassy and arrived at the emergency room of the Centre Privé d'Urgence. Upstairs loomed the four-story, 80-bed Centre Medical de Kinshasa (CMK) Hospital. Hal was hastily transferred to a waiting gurney and whisked into the facility. A Belgian doctor and several Congolese nurses were waiting to take vitals and assess the new arrival. Abdul's articulate description and diagnosis in fluent French placed Hal at the top of their triage, prompting immediate action.

As the medical staff began to work on him, Hal was not faring well. His heartbeat was rapid, he was nauseated, and his head throbbed. His throat felt like it was closing up; his mouth felt dry and his lips were flaccid. Ironically, saliva was drooling out the side of his mouth. He tried to ask for water, but this attempt to speak only generated guttural noises.

The nursing staff took Hal's blood pressure, noted his rising temperature, and carefully swabbed the fang punctures on his calf with alcohol while the clinic doctor conferred with Abdul in rapid French. "The immediate danger at present for your friend is flaccid paralysis including respiratory paralysis, a process that has already started as you can see. The neurotoxins from the cobra venom have begun their work in earnest. We must intubate him immediately and get him on a ventilator. We have antivenin ready to administer but it may not be effective with this particular venom."

Hal was conscious and could hear the conversation going on around him, though he couldn't speak and found it increasingly difficult to move. Nothing he heard was reassuring. His face felt like it was melting. He wondered if he might drown in his own saliva. Hal's chest was heaving with the effort of breathing, prompting the beginnings of panic inside. It felt like he was drowning.

The insertion of a breathing tube and the accompanying thump, thump of a respirator brought relief of sorts, but it was worrisome relief at best. At last the clinic doctor injected something and Hal's worries came to an end for that day as he drifted into a semi-coma state. His physical battle, however, was far from over.

It was completely dark when Hal once again regained consciousness. It took a while for him to figure out where he was: in a private room in a hospital. As his head began to clear slightly, he could make out a rhythmic thump, thump sound adjacent to his bed. He became aware that his throat was sore. It had a tube in it. He could not swallow.

In response to his stirring, he detected a movement in the darkened room. A white clad figure rose from a chair. He approached Hal, placed a cool hand on his forehead, and spoke quietly in French.

"*Bonjour mon ami.*"

Hal tried to raise one arm to point at a clock on the wall and find out what time it was, but he could only move the limb slightly and make grunting noises. The nurse, sensing his quest spoke softly. "*Il est deux heures du matin. Monsieur, vous devez dormir.*" (It's 2 A.M., sir. You must sleep) He straightened the sheets, patted Hal's arm and returned to his chair.

At least I'm still alive, thought Hal, *though who knows for how long*? He listened to the thumping of the ventilator for some time, watching his chest rise and fall in rhythm until he finally drifted back to sleep.

When Hal next awoke the room was brightly lit. To his right, the early morning sun streamed in the window creating a brilliant yellow rectangle on the opposite wall. The ventilator still thumped away, and he could now see he had an IV hooked to a port in his arm. The private room was sparsely furnished with a bed, two chairs and a small table. A curtain rod circled overhead and a collection of medical machines stood against the wall behind him. Standing at the foot of his bed were two figures engrossed in serious conversation. He recognized them as the Belgian doctor from the CPU and Hal's classmate, Abdul.

Seeing his friend's eyes opened, Abdul interrupted his conversation and came around the bed to speak with him. "Good morning, Hal. It's much too early to ask how you're feeling, but I'm glad to see you awake." Hal managed a weak smile, raised his eyebrows and moved one hand in response.

Abdul placed a hand on Hal's shoulder. "Dr. Bernard, here," motioning toward his medical colleague, "reports that your vitals are good. It's likely you are responding well to the antivenom you were given. It was a Christy's Water Cobra that bit you as we suspected. It's an Elapid snake whose venom fortunately doesn't cause serious damage at the bite site. It does, however, create moderate to severe neurotoxic paralysis. That's what you're experiencing at present. Hopefully, it will be short-lived. You were most fortunate to get prompt medical attention. We'll watch things here for a couple of days. As soon as you're breathing on your own, we'll pull the tubes. Maybe even later today."

Hal nodded acknowledgement and offered another weak smile. This was good news, indeed. He was still mute and mostly immobile, but these were words of hope. "*Thank you, God.*" The phrase came almost automatically to mind. *Wait*, he thought immediately, *do I really mean that?*

He did not have time to reflect further on the matter as a noisy commotion in the hallway outside his room revealed itself:

reunion friends had arrived for a visit. Tim and Dorothy, Carl and Brenda, plus Kasandra and Joanna all chattering away as they entered, surrounded Hal's bed. Smiling and talking over one another, they exclaimed positive surprise at his condition and peppered him with questions he could not answer.

Abdul smiled and greeted the visitors. "Hal can't speak right now but that should change by the end of the day. We're pretty hopeful he'll make a full recovery...eventually. It was very fortunate he got medical help so promptly."

"It was good *you* were there," Tim clapped Abdul on the back. "We believe the Lord was watching out for Hal. We're here to pray for his healing." Abdul just smiled.

Hal lay silently, taking it all in, his mind whirling. *How do I decline this well-meaning action? I can't say I put much stock in the prayer thing. If a sovereign all-powerful God really does exist, why did He or She allow the snakebite to happen in the first place?*

He of course did not voice those thoughts, but rather managed yet another weak smile. The six former TASOK classmates bowed their heads, closed their eyes, placed their hands on his prone body and prayed for his healing.

#36 Kinshasa DRC

July 2010

Just as Abdul had predicted, by that evening Hal was able to breathe normally and the tube and respirator were removed. Much to his great relief, by the end of the day he was also able to move his limbs. With assistance he even took a few faltering steps from his bed to the adjacent bathroom.

The day had been filled with visitors though Hal had been unable to speak for most of it as the tube was still in place. That suited him just fine. He really didn't want to rehearse the events of the previous day and he wasn't ready to analyze their meaning. Nearly all of the 40th reunion attendees showed up at one point or another to check on his well-being and to express their relief at Hal's rapid recuperation. By mid-afternoon the hospital staff finally called a halt to visitors. He needed to rest and recover.

At Hal's special request, however, Paul returned to the hospital soon after dark. It was still early evening when he finally appeared. Congo's proximity to the Equator meant sundown came at the predictable six o'clock hour. As sore and scratchy as his throat felt and as achy and weak as he was, Hal needed to talk.

"Hey, roomie how's it goin'?" Paul strode through the doorway, his big smile lighting up the dimly lit hospital room. Hal was sitting up in bed reading "Sex at Dawn," the anthropology book that someone had retrieved from his rocky retreat spot at Ngombe Beach. Paul approached the bed, reaching over to check out the book title.

"Ha. Already into sex, I see. Things are lookin' up!"

That brought a chuckle from the patient who promptly slammed the book shut and motioned for his visitor to pull up a chair. "Sit closer. My voice is still scratchy from the tubes. I want to talk."

Paul pulled a chair close to the head of the bed and sat down, his smile fading into an expression of concern. "Is something wrong? What's going on, Hal?"

Hal closed his eyes and took a deep breath before speaking. When he opened them again Paul could see they were swimming.

A single drop coursed down his cheek and off his chin. "The dream, the snake bite, the quick medical help, the prayers, the paralysis, my recovery from near death...it's, it's too much to take in. I don't know what to make of it."

Paul leaned forward to take in Hal's croaky words, spoken at a near whisper.

"It has the feel of something spiritual. I'm sure my mother would say it was...and probably Dad too. But that's a world I left many years ago. I mean, we both grew up hearing things of all kinds, especially dramatic ones, attributed to God and prayer, right? Do you still believe in that stuff, Paul?"

Paul's hand went reflexively to his forehead massaging his temples as he reflected on Hal's question. "Well..." he began slowly, drawing out the word. "My path in life has taken me a long way from the 'faith of our fathers.' I wouldn't, however, say I've rejected it all. It's more like I've just...neglected it. I have had my faith moments, though. Like when I was in the hospital after my racing accident. I prayed then. Boy, did I ever! But later I sort of forgot it again." He lifted his gaze back to Hal's face. "What about you, Hal?"

"All the Kisambo Station stuff that happened to me and my family growing up..." Hal shifted the pillow behind his back. "By the time I got to college I thought, how could a loving God – the one my parents worshipped – allow such bad things to happen to good people, to innocent people? When everything works out well, God or Jesus gets the credit. Answered prayer, right? But clearly *everything* in life doesn't *always* work out well. It sure hasn't for me. What, then am I supposed to believe about God?"

The single tear had now become streams running from both eyes, though Hal's voice remained steady. "And why do I have those dreams? I used to pray earnestly for the bad things from the dreams *not* to happen, but they always did. In my case, they just did again. So where is God and prayer and divine protection? I don't get it."

"Maybe I can help."

Both men jumped at the sound of the voice in the doorway, their eyes and heads snapping to face a backlit figure standing there. They could not make out the person's face, but it appeared to be a nurse, and it was clearly a woman's voice. She seemed in no hurry to enter but remained standing quietly.

"May I come in and join your conversation, Hal?"

Hal did not immediately recognize the voice, but it carried a tone of familiarity and intimacy that sent a chill up his spine. *Who is this person and why do I feel like I know her?*

"Um, enter...er, I mean yes, come on in," he managed to blurt out after a moment's pause.

A slender, petite woman dressed in white nurses' attire moved quietly to the far side of the bed. Her short blonde hair framed a square jaw with even teeth that appeared in a widening smile. "Hello, Hal," came the soft voice. "It's good to see you again. It's been a very long time."

"Who? Whaa...? Barbara!

The visitor chuckled at Hal's recognition. "Yes, it's me all right. Still in Congo after all these years. Word travels fast in Kinshasa's small expatriate community. I heard about your little encounter with our local wildlife and decided to check on you firsthand."

Hal was still aghast at the unexpected appearance of his childhood neighbor and playmate. Turning to Paul, he managed, "You remember Barb from the hostel, don't you Paul? We grew up together at Kisambo. She was a year behind us. She returned to the states with her folks on an extended furlough our last two years at TASOK."

"That's right, Hal. Mom had developed breast cancer and so I missed graduating from TASOK. I understand your class is presently having a reunion and that's what brought you back here. It looks like you got a bit more adventure than you planned on."

Paul got up and found another chair for Barbara.

"But what are *you* doing here, Barb?" Hal's question had an incredulous tone.

Barbara leaned forward and reached out to squeeze his left hand with her right, smiling in reply. "It's so good to see you again, my friend." She sat down and scooted her chair closer to the bed.

"I've actually lived in Congo most of my adult life, Hal. I first returned with my husband after college and medical school in the early '80s. James and I worked in our mission's medical clinics – he as a physician and me as a nurse – for fifteen years, until his death in 1995. That happened during Kikwit's Ebola outbreak." Her eyes teared up and her voice caught. She paused briefly before continuing.

"After a year or so of bereavement leave in the States, my daughter and I returned to Congo. We came back on our own this time, however, not under the mission. I have worked in various hospitals here in Kinshasa ever since. So that's my story. I'd like to hear yours, as well, but I interrupted a significant conversation. I'm more interested in returning to it."

Hal's mouth stood half open as he absorbed this new information from his childhood friend. "Oh, Barb. Jeez...Um, I don't know where to begin. So sorry about your loss, your husband, what was his name...James? And you have a daughter? Other children? You've been here in Congo for years? I had no idea."

"I probably know more about your life's journey than you do mine, Hal, since my mother and yours used to be in regular contact with one another. Mama was good at passing on news of our former Kisambo Station colleagues. She passed away a few years after you and Phyllis divorced, some time after you moved to USC. I've not been updated since then. I did hear that your mother died recently, however. I'm sorry for that loss and for the breakup of you and Phyllis as well."

"Bonsoir madame et messieurs."

All three occupants of the room turned toward the figure entering the doorway. Paul scooted his chair back as Dr. Bernard strode directly up to Hal placing one hand on his forehead grasping his wrist with the other to check his pulse.

"Ça va bien," came the conclusion after a brief pause.

Barbara then initiated an extended conversation with the doctor in rapid French that Hal had a hard time following. After several long back and forth exchanges, Dr. Bernard gave Hal a brief tobacco-stained smile, patted his arm and turned to leave.

"Dormez bien, M. Schroeder et bonne nuit à tous."

"What was all that about?" Hal inquired after Dr. Bernard's departure.

Barbara stood as she replied. "He said that you are doing remarkably well and that he intends to send you home – back to MPH, that is – tomorrow. He also said that you've had plenty enough conversation for one day and that we should leave...now."

Hal frowned and raised a hand in protest. "Wait...we're not done yet. Don't I get some say-so here?"

Barbara smiled. "No, not this time, I'm afraid. But we can continue our conversation at MPH. Dr. Bernard indicated you need several days of down time to fully recover. I told him I will check in on you daily at the guesthouse and give him a report. He agreed. So, I guess I'll say good night now and see you later." Barbara gave a friendly pat to Hal's foot as she headed for the door. Hal's mouth was ajar.

"Ah...well, okay I guess. Thanks for coming by, Barbara," he managed to stammer out.

Paul was on his feet by then. "I'll walk you to your car, Barbara." Looking back from the doorway, he called out, "Good night, Hal. I'll be back in the morning to take you to MPH, OK?"

Hal listened to the footsteps as they retreated down the tile hallway. His room was still and the shadows, deep. He reached up to turn off the light over his bed. Full darkness closed over him. As he settled down for the night his mind replayed the last part of the evening.

Barbara...what a surprise. What a pleasant surprise! A deep sense of peace settled on him as he drifted off to sleep.

#37 Kinshasa, DRC

July 2010

Bonnie Baylor, MPH hostess, arrived in the guesthouse infirmary carrying a tray containing a mug of tea, a plate filled with mango, papaya and pineapple slices, and a still steaming cream-filled beignet liberally crowned with powdered sugar. The pastry's savory aroma brought a smile to Hal's face before he actually laid eyes on the mid-morning treat. He was surrounded by well-wishers. Mona and her ever-present lieutenant, Alice, were both seated on the edge of the bed. Tim and his wife, Dorothy, plus former classmates Kasandra and Shirley had all found chairs; Muhammed, Ty and LaWanda stood behind them, visiting among themselves. Mona's husband Bradford, stood by the window chatting with Alice's partner, Rodney.

A collective "Ooh!" went up from the room's occupants as Hal's tray arrived. "There's a plate of warm beignets and a pot of tea in the dining room for everyone," Bonnie announced, motioning with her chin for the two gals to slide off the bed for her delivery. As she placed the tray on Hal's lap she continued. "Let's give Hal a little breather now. He was sent here to recover, not to hold court. He'll still be around later."

A subtle flash of relief flickered across Hal's face, but no one seemed to notice. As the others filed out, Kasandra lingered behind. Hal placed a spoonful of sugar in the mug and looked up as she rested her hand on his shoulder. "Your recovery is a real miracle, Hal," she said quietly. "Several of us who have been praying consider it a clear answer to our prayers."

Hal stopped his stirring and looked directly up into the eyes and serious face of his visitor. "Kasandra, I'll probably not say this well, but I'm going to just put it out to you as best I can. While I genuinely appreciate your concern and the prayers you and the others have offered, I don't share your spiritual perspective. Did God really answer your prayers or were circumstances just in my favor? What would you and your prayer partners have said if things had gone the other way, or even if I had died...that God willed that as well? It's just not clear to me how that all works."

Kasandra had stiffened and stepped back from the bed. The frown on her face approached a grimace as Hal finished speaking. Her eyes became glassy and her voice wavered as she finally responded. "I...I'm sorry you feel that way, Hal. We thought you'd be pleased. We didn't know you had..." She caught herself mid-sentence. "That you felt that way. I hope you'll give it more thought. It seems like a God-thing to us." With that, she backed away, turned and hurried out the door.

Hal sat there staring at the tray in his lap with a sinking feeling, thinking guilty thoughts. *What should I have said? Probably nothing. She meant well and I just had to be honest. I hurt her feelings. I probably disappointed the others as well once she reports to them.*

Hal was so focused on his reflections that he hadn't noticed the quiet figure in a crisp white nurse's uniform that had entered the room. "I couldn't help overhearing, Hal. It appears once again I've interrupted a spiritual discussion."

Barbara's calm demeanor and slight smile provided a sharp contrast with Kasandra's pained expression as she made her exit. Hal considered it a welcome exchange. In spite of his intense reflections, he couldn't help but smile.

"Ha. You sure have a unique sense of timing, Barb. Good to see you again."

"I'm here to check on you, friend. How are you feeling by now?" Barbara pulled a chair closer to the head of the bed and sat down.

Hal took notice of Barbara's calm demeanor and unthreatening manner. It was refreshing. *How did I lose contact with this lady?* He wondered to himself, immediately dismissing the thought.

"I'm actually doing well. I'm moving about fairly normally by now but still feel weak. To tell the truth, I feel like I survived a train wreck or something." Hal smiled and held up the fruit plate offering to share. She declined with a raised hand. He popped some fruit slices into his mouth. "I have a slight headache and my snake bite still hurts a bit, but everything considered, I'm good."

Barbara pulled a blood pressure sleeve out of the bag at her side and slipped it over his arm. "BP looks good!" she declared shortly. Hal had begun his attack on the beignet as she put the equipment away.

"So, what's this about rejecting your friends' prayers? Your

former classmate seemed shaken by your comments just now."
Barbara sat, crossed her legs and settled down for a comfortable
visit with an old friend. At least, that's the impression she gave to
Hal.

"I'd better level with you, Barb...I'm not at the same place
spiritually that you remember from our Kisambo Station
days...from TASOK days as well, to be completely honest." Hal
took a sip of his tea that had become lukewarm by then and
crinkled his nose.

Barbara smiled. "Neither am I, for that matter. Life is a crucible
that refines one's beliefs, don't you think so?"

"Refines or *deletes* them, I'd say." He stuffed another big bite of
beignet into his mouth.

"So, what caused you to turn away from your Christian faith,
Hal?" Barbara put the question directly back to Hal. She posed it
lightly, in such a relaxed manner that he did not immediately feel
defensive. He took note of his internal reaction to what he would
typically have resisted as an intrusive query. *She seems genuinely
interested.* Hal paused and took a deep breath before responding.
His next words surprised him.

"The events that took place around the time we were
evacuated from Kisambo Station affected me deeply, Barb. Seeing
our home burned and my friends killed was horrible. For a long
time I found myself questioning how a loving God could possibly
allow innocent people like us and our friends to suffer...to die! All
of our prayers and petitions at the time seemed to have little
effect on the eventual outcome...death and destruction. I finally
concluded that the kind of religion my folks believed in did not
make sense. I always respected the sincerity of Mom and Dad's
convictions but after TASOK years I just couldn't buy it for myself
any longer."

Hal moved the tray to the side of his bed and shifted to a more
upright position. "My therapist back home claims that those
childhood events may well have caused PTSD of some kind.
Perhaps my loss of faith in God was another of the by-products. If
you don't mind my asking, Barb, how did *you* survive all that
drama in our childhood?"

Barbara had clasped her hands and was leaning forward on
her elbows, listening intently to Hal's comments. At his question,
she sat up. One hand went to her mouth and chin in thoughtful

reflection.

"I was a real scaredy-cat in those days. The events around and during our evacuation traumatized me for sure. I had nightmares and clung to my folks for months afterwards, afraid to let them out of my sight. When we returned to the States for a year, they found a wonderful counselor for me. She was a gentle and wise Christian lady. Together we worked through my fears and reactions to all that violence and loss. It made a big difference going forward."

"But you apparently came to very different conclusions than I did. How can you still hold onto those God-beliefs when even your husband was lost to you...and all the other innocents in the Ebola crisis?" Hal's jaw was clenched, and his forehead creased. "Where was prayer, mercy and a loving God when *that* happened?"

Barbara sat quietly for a time, reflecting on Hal's question. "It sounds like you believe that God is somehow obligated to protect His children from adversity and harm; that prayer for help and rescue should always be answered in the affirmative. And if it doesn't happen, you have concluded He is not real or is not a loving God. Am I hearing you correctly?"

Hal frowned and made a "Hrrumph!" sound. "Not *exactly* my thoughts, but something like that I suppose..." he finally managed.

"The fact that Jesus was crucified, most of the Apostles were eventually martyred and even Paul's prayer for his "thorn in the flesh" to be removed was unsuccessful tells us that sometimes God's purposes are accomplished by loss and suffering rather than deliverance. Does that make sense to you? Admittedly, that's a hard lesson to accept, but I've come to understand it to be very true. It's one of the deep mysteries of faith. In short, God has a different view of adversity than we do."

"So, you're saying that prayer does no good? God will do whatever, regardless?" Hal's frown persisted.

Barbara smiled. "I'm not attempting to defend or explain God, here, Hal. We are repeatedly encouraged in Scripture to pray, to communicate with God, to let Him know our deepest longings and needs because we are His personal concern. Jesus taught that righteous prayer changes things. Note, however, that even He prayed earnestly at Gethsemane for the cup of suffering to be removed from Him, if it be God's will. God did not do so. It's good that He didn't! We understand Christ's suffering to be at the heart of our salvation."

Hal shook his head as he glanced at his articulate companion. A slight smile formed at the corners of his mouth. "I can't say I totally follow your logic, Barb, but you've given me food for thought...a new perspective, new to me anyhow." His fingers automatically ran through his hair and he stretched. "I think, however, I need to take a break from theologizing at this point."

Barbara chuckled in response. "You bet. Glad to change the subject. Now, tell me about your kids..."

#38 Congo to California

July 2010

"Here's to old friends and new adventures!" Tyrone and Hal clinked mimosa cocktail glasses as they settled back in their business class seats for the eight-hour flight from Kinshasa to Paris. "I'm glad you talked me into upgrading my ticket. It gives us more time to debrief."

Before Hal could respond, their conversation was interrupted by the formalities of departure instructions delivered in French and English. Hal's mind and emotions were swirling. The airport gauntlet of security checks and hypothetical infractions was a final reminder that he was passing from one kind of reality to another. It was certainly a relief to be past the tensions and uncertainties of urban Africa. However, at the same time a kind of inexplicable sadness welled up deep inside, a reminder that Congo remained a part of his core identity, rediscovered but presently about to be stripped from him once again. Hal's class reunion experience had turned out to be a mixture of pain and pleasure, distress and delight. *How can one measure the value of such things,* he pondered to himself as he settled in for the long flight home.

Once they got underway, Tyrone was in a chatty mood. Person by person he commented on each of their classmates who had attended the reunion. Overall, Ty considered the range of home locations, lifestyles and accomplishments, impressive. He found it fascinating that familiar TASOK patterns of behavior and friendships had seemingly persisted over the span of forty years.

"Some things and some people never change. I remember thinking when I left after that summer visit in college that the whole country was on the verge of collapse and I was lucky to get out when I did. Now, here we are nearly forty years later, and life has gone on, but I still feel like I did then."

Hal smiled. "That comes from comparing our affluent, well-ordered western world with life lived on the margins, like most Kinshasan's experience. It's actually pretty remarkable that Congolese find a way to survive, given all the challenges they face even today."

Hal raised the leg support of his seat. It felt more comfortable to elevate his injured limb. Ty took notice of the action. "So, how's ye ol' leg doing by now? And how are you feeling overall? That was some close call you had with the snake bite, buddy."

"I'm doing well, just about back to myself again, thanks." Hal drained the last of his drink and placed it on the steward's tray as he passed by. "It wasn't the reunion experience I was expecting to have, that's for sure!"

As Ty reached over to do same, the corners of his mouth hinted a smile and his eyes crinkled at the edges. "That good-looking blonde nurse who showed up...what's her name, Barbara? She appeared at just the right moment, didn't she? You two seemed to hit it off. Anything up with you and her, any follow up?"

Hal did not immediately reply, but sat staring ahead, unfocused, unsmiling. Finally, he turned a serious face to his seatmate.

"Barb's world and mine are on opposite sides of the planet. It was nice to meet up with her again, an unexpected pleasure actually. By the way, she's not had an easy time of it, losing her spouse to Ebola and raising her daughter in Congo as a single parent. But it's a stretch to imagine our paths might cross again, let alone that anything more would develop."

"Well, Fate has some strange and mysterious ways of invading our lives. Never say never, buddy." The smile persisted on Tyrone's face.

***

Lyndsey Franklin sat quietly behind her desk, elbows resting on the arms of her chair, fingers forming a tent before her, a pleasant expression across her face. Hal was seated on the edge of the facing chair, eyes flashing and arms working the air in animated discourse. Scheduling an appointment with her was one of the first actions he had taken after arriving home from his Congo adventures. His report was fully in progress.

"In sum, Dr. Franklin, so many of the things you told me about TCKs – well, by now they are ATCKs, Adult Third Culture Kids – were clearly present in my TASOK classmates. A broader worldview, multicultural perspectives, deeper relationships with other ATCKs and foreigners, struggling with being misunderstood and feeling different in our various home cultures, feeling rootless, treasuring travel and change…all those TCK markers were present in my classmates' stories."

"It must have been satisfying to discover so many of those qualities that were once causes of self-doubt are in fact sources of validation for you." Lyndsey briefly shifted her attention to a piece of paper where she jotted some notes down. Looking up over the top of her glasses she asked, "What were some of the *differences* you discovered between yourself and the others? Surely some divergent things emerged along with all the commonalities."

That question caught Hal by surprise. He had not anticipated being asked about differences. Looking down, he pondered a response as he ran nervous fingers through his hair.

"Well, for one thing, some of our number have had long term marriages while others of us have gone through multiple partners. A few of us have struggled with drug and alcohol dependency. And then there is the matter of religious values. Several of our number have kept the faith, perhaps becoming even more devout than their missionary parents. Others of us have drifted away or abandoned the church."

"You say 'others of us'…do you place yourself among the latter?"

"I do but some of the things one of my former classmates had to say made me wonder if I shouldn't reconsider my beliefs, or rather my non-beliefs." Hal settled back in his chair.

"Would you care to say more about that?"

Hal frowned, not really wanting to pursue the topic. "I don't think so. There's actually not much to say at this point."

"So, which of your classmates was it who challenged you in this area?" Lyndsey inquired, continuing to pursue the topic.

"Um, it was actually a friend from the past, from my childhood. She is a nurse who still lives and works in Congo. She came to see me when I had a health problem that I'll tell you about on another occasion. We got reacquainted a bit. She seems as settled in her beliefs as I am *unsettled* in mine."

"Was it *her* or *her message* that got your attention?" Lyndsey asked with an ironic smile.

Hal looked up briefly, shaking his head, rolling his eyes and returning the hint of the smile. "Next subject, doc."

Lyndsey paused to take a sip of tea from the cup at her desk.

"Speaking of your past history, prior to your trip you expressed a good deal of ambivalence about returning to Congo. I identified some of that resistance as constituting a PTSD defense. What do you make of the class reunion experience along those lines as you reflect on it now?"

Hal sighed deeply before he answered. "You were probably right about PTSD as well. I felt pretty nervous the whole time. Several situations were particularly stressful. Going through customs on entry and exit was one. Then, a second spike came when a small squad of soldiers burst into our reunion session to arrest one of my classmates. I froze up big-time. I wanted to be anywhere but there. Overall, however, I'd have to admit that it was good to go back. I feel far more settled inside now than I did before my visit."

"You declare that with such hesitancy, Hal. I am assuming there still remains some apprehension on your part regarding Congo. Am I right?" Lyndsey took another slow sip of tea, signaling she was expecting further elaboration from her patient.

Hal was quiet for a long minute, studying the floor. His reply came in a subdued voice. "While it's true that my guts no longer tie into a knot when I just think about Congo, since I've returned, I have had several flashback dreams that have placed me right back into the scene of our evacuation. They were disturbing. They've left me with a lot of negative thoughts about myself. I still feel guilty, depressed."

Lyndsey briefly jotted notes once again before looking up to view Hal's troubled demeanor. "You had another premonition dream during this trip, didn't you Hal?"

Hal's eyes widened and his mouth opened. "Yes. Yes, I did. How did you guess that, doc?"

"Do you remember our conversation about well-traveled emotional pathways? PTSD patterns carried through life are not all that easy to shake. Yours have included those troubling premonitions. They, in turn are inevitably accompanied by a distorted sense of responsibility and guilt. It's not so difficult to figure. So how did you respond to the dream?"

Hal's hand went to his hair once again. "I didn't let it stop me. I continued on in spite of my apprehensions. I'm just saying I realize I've still got emotional baggage."

Lyndsey slowly rose to her feet. "You're not finished with

PTSD and it's not finished with you. Not yet. I'd say progress is clearly being made, however. You faced your fears head-on though your mind and emotions were flooded with Congo stimuli. Let's expect things to settle down for you in the coming days."

"Deal," replied Hal with a smile as he rose to leave.

PART III:

Transformation

#39 Kisambo, DRC

October 2010

The dissonant whine of the two Land Rovers as they slowly climbed the hill did not go unnoticed. A small collection of children appeared as if by magic, dashing out from between the village huts and heading toward the moving dust cloud marking the arrival of visitors to the settlement. An infrequent occurrence in the isolated community, any new arrival was occasion for interest and attention, a sure magnet for the children.

The arriving transports cast long shadows across the yard in the late afternoon sun. Low shafts of light lit up the accompanying dust cloud creating a colorful yellow-orange ball that slowly faded as it drifted to the side. The high-pitched squeal of Land Rover brakes prompted echoing squeals of laughter and exclamations from the young reception committee. The late day sun reflected off the arriving vehicle windows blurring the identity of their occupants. The tiny mob quickly surrounded the vehicles chattering to one another, craning their necks and jumping to peek in the windows to discover who the visitors might be.

Michael Friesen opened the door of his vehicle and unfolded his cramped legs, stepping down into dust that nearly covered his feet. The drive from Gungu had taken much longer than expected. The ruts and mud pits along the way were deeper and more extensive than anyone had imagined, let alone described. Passage had required shoveling sand, cutting logs from the forest, shoring up broken bridges and repeatedly employing the motorized winches and cables from the front of the Land Rovers to extract them from the mire. He was exhausted.

Michael's deeply tanned face, forehead creases and crinkles at the corners of each eye hinted at years of responsibility as well as a good sense of humor, badges of long-term service in equatorial Africa: Mozambique, Angola, Mali and now Congo. His short, closely cropped beard was flecked with gray as was his hair, markers of his five plus decades of life. The sleeves of his tan safari shirt were rolled up to his elbows. He was solidly built, neither slender nor stocky, of medium height and weight, blue eyes conveying both a friendly demeanor and an alert appraisal of whatever came into view.

As the Country Director for Mennonite Central Committee's relief work in the Congo, one of Michael's many duties was to monitor the distribution of medications to outlying clinics. His assignment included a far more challenging task: to inventory clinic supplies. It was an expected form of accountability that nearly always turned out to be an awkward and tense experience, certainly not a favorite duty. This, however, was the purpose of the present Kisambo visit.

Michael and his wife Shirley were accompanied on this occasion by Bobozo Henri, a government education official, Mukana Jonas, the Legal Representative for the region's church organization plus an army escort, Sgt. Mpika. Both vehicles were driven by Congolese chauffeurs.

"Mbote na beno." Michael's chipper Kituba greeting to the minions was met with a chorus of *"Mbote's"* in reply. The dusty crowd of smiling barefoot greeters giggled and chattered in delight at the attention he gave them. The doors of both Land Rovers squeaked open as the other members of the delegation exited their vehicles. As they stretched aching limbs, they caught sight of several adults rapidly heading their way from the village to offer an official welcome.

"Well, Shirley we finally made it to Kisambo. How about that?" Michael looped an affectionate arm around his wife's shoulders for a short hug as they scanned the scene.

Shirley's dishwater blonde hair, softened by streaks of gray, was pulled back into a bun. The sleeves of her pale green safari shirt were rolled to her elbows like that of her spouse. At just shy of six feet, she nearly matched the height of her husband. Her long limbs, slender frame and smooth, easy movements resembled those of a ballet dancer, or an athlete. She put her arm around Michael's waist and leaned her head on his shoulder in response to his hug. They stood arm in arm surveying what used to be Kisambo Station.

The burned shells of three former missionary residences stood silent and empty in the deepening shadows of the afternoon. The roofs of each dwelling were missing. Vegetation had grown tall enough inside each to be visible through empty window frames. The remnants of small outbuildings behind the homes stood in piles of crumbling cement block and rubble. Across a field the stately, graying Kisambo church dominated the scene, its red roof still very much intact. The surrounding yard, however, showed signs of neglect. Uncut grass grew right up to the wall's edge and weeds appeared to overtake the path leading to the main entrance. On the other hand, in the opposite direction a well-worn path lead to the stained walls and faded blue door of the medical clinic suggesting that it was still very much in regular use.

Shirley glanced up at her husband. Gesturing toward the abandoned residences, "I suppose this means we'll be staying in the village tonight."

Returning her cynical smile, Michael commented, "That's a safe bet, Sweetheart. Woven mats, thatched roof and dirt floors...the real Africa. But you know, I find it curious that after all these years the missionary dwellings here have not been rebuilt."

By that time the first of the local officials had arrived on the scene. Enthusiastic welcomes and introductions were being exchanged with their visitors. Men, women and children continued to stream from the village, surrounding the vehicles. Many helping hands reached out to assist in carrying the delegation's luggage back to where guest huts had been carefully prepared in anticipation of their arrival.

Soon afterwards, Michael and Shirley settled down for the evening next to their assigned hut. They sat on carved chairs; low two-piece innovations shaped like reclined letter "Ls." Next to them Sgt. Mpika relaxed, legs crossed, munching on a handful of peanuts. The twilight's short appearance had already darkened the shadows between the village dwellings. What meager light remained was fast departing. All about the tranquil threesome swirled delicious aromas of food cooking and the homey clinks and chatter of evening meal preparation in the village.

"This place has a lot of history, Shirley. It was once a thriving mission station. In addition to a primary school and medical clinic, there used to be a regional Bible school. The story goes that back in the mid '60s during the Simba Rebellion the followers of Pierre Mulele attacked and burned the station. The resident missionaries were even taken hostage for a short time."

"The rebels were successful in destroying things, all right" Shirley said, glancing back toward the shells of former residences. "Were any of the people harmed?" She turned to face her husband, concern in her voice.

"My recall is that the UN eventually rescued the mission folk, but that some of the rebels and villagers were killed during the rescue. I'm not clear on the history. Let's ask Sgt. Mpika."

At the sound of his name the relaxed soldier turned his gaze to his two companions with raised eyebrows. In French, Michael asked him, "Sargeant, are you familiar with the history of Kisambo, with what happened during the Simba Rebellion?"

Mpika smiled and sat up. "*Bien sûr.* I grew up in a little village just across the river. You can almost see it from here. I know all about Kisambo. Some say this place is cursed by what happened."

"Did you say, cursed?" Michael asked as both he and Shirley sat up, fully attentive.

"*Aeye,*" was the reply. "There were at that time two spirits in Kisambo at war with one another. People followed one or the other. One spirit supported the church and the missionaries and the second supported the rebels. At the time of the rebellion some of the sons of both sides left the village to secretly train with the *Jeunesse* in the forest. Both sides hid this fact from the missionaries, but for different reasons."

Mpika paused to throw his remaining peanut shells into the darkness and brush his hands, giving him a chance to gather his thoughts before continuing.

"Kisambo was eventually attacked and burned. The *Jeunesse* took the missionaries captive. Their friends in the church did nothing to prevent it, though they had assured them all along that they would keep them safe if rebels came near. UN helicopters and soldiers rescued the *mindeles* but some villagers and *Jeunesse* were killed in the process. The Kisambo Bible school students who were not Bapende fled for their lives. Some were eventually caught and tortured."

Sgt. Mpika shifted his position to fully face his speechless, spellbound listeners. He spoke rapidly, excitedly, arms gesturing, and face lit up as he finished the story.

"It was a major betrayal. It's been over 45 years, more years than I have even been alive, but the mission never returned to Kisambo. Not even for a visit."

Shirley expelled the breath she had unconsciously been holding in and put a hand to her forehead. "Whew, that's some tale. The former mission station is like a...a ghost town, *un ville morte.* After all these years has no one tried to repair the broken relationships? By now, I suppose most of the original parties have died."

Sgt. Mpika nodded somberly. "Kisambo people say they do not feel right using the church that the mission built, so these days they worship under the trees by the village. And no one wants to rebuild the homes that were burned. Some say it would be bad luck, that it would anger the ancestors."

The three sat quietly for several long minutes before Mpika finally broke the silence. "There are recent signs that things may be changing for Kisambo."

"What sort of signs?" asked Michael, perking up.

"Well, a wealthy Kinshasa merchant recently put a new roof on the school. His name is Kuyantika. I know him. He grew up here. He also paid to have some things fixed in the church so it can be used again. It is rumored that he intends to contact the leaders of the mission to see if they can be persuaded to return. That's a good sign."

"That sounds very hopeful," Shirley chimed in, smiling.

Mpika held up a hand. "*Attendez!* Not all agree. Local shaman, Kamanga Nsapo, is strongly opposed to any new missionary influence in Kisambo. Women's leader Muzele Zacharie has also voiced caution. She is the niece of former shaman Muzeka Andoko. She is worried that the embers of the Kisambo curse may be stirred by any return of *mindeles*." He sat back, smiling. "So...the Kisambo divisions continue to this day."

At that point out of the dark appeared Mukana and his government colleague Bobozo, interrupting the conversation. *"C'est l'heure du dîner. Venez manger."*

As Michael, Shirley and the Sergeant rose to join them for dinner, Michael first thanked Mpika for his explanations. Then, turning aside to Shirley he remarked quietly in English, "I have a feeling the Kisambo story is far from complete."

#40 Rancho Palos Verdes, CA

October 2010

Kisambo village was dark and quiet. It was the silent hour just before the first rooster calls beaconed the faintest grays of new morning light. Even the earliest risers had yet to stir and escape from the clinging tentacles of pre-dawn slumber. The village dogs were strangely silent, in a deep sleep as if drugged. But something, someone was moving about: a soundless, stealthy, sinister presence slipping between the deepest shadows, moving across the village. The ominous figure glided purposefully between the huts finally coming to a stop at one particular dwelling. Ever so slowly, with virtual invisibility the shadowy character slipped through an open doorway, made a deposit and re-emerged only to vanish back into the surrounding darkness. The stillness remained undisturbed.

A loud shriek startled the stirring community to full alert. The sun had not yet lit the tops of the tallest palm trees, but villagers were already moving about here and there in the grayness lighting fires, visiting latrines, clanging pans and chiding little ones in typical early morning fare. Repeated shrieks attracted scurrying feet in the direction of the sound. In no time a small crowd surrounded the entrance to the hut where a prone figure lay face down in the dust. A shattered drinking gourd was clasped in one of the fallen man's hands. The young girl who had made the discovery and broadcast the alarm buried her sobbing face in the breast of a pagne-clad woman with a baby on her back who had wrapped her in an embrace. The bundle of sticks the girl had been carrying on her head was scattered under the feet of the gathering crowd. Other adults knelt by the motionless figure attempting unsuccessfully to rouse the man. He remained still, limbs flayed out at awkward angles.

Hal let out a loud cry and a gasp as he sat straight up in bed. His heart was racing and sweat was pouring from his forehead. He was surrounded by a deep sense of dread, a foreboding that left him shaken as he slowly swung his legs over the edge of the bed and attempted to breathe evenly once again. He was gasping.

Had he been holding his breath?

In the weeks since his return from Congo Hal had experienced repeated flashbacks to his childhood and the dark days of Kisambo Station. Alarmed, he had reported these recall experiences to Lyndsey Franklin. She had reassured him that they were most certainly positive indicators. According to her, Hal's travel to the DRC for his class reunion was paying dividends. It was allowing him to safely surface formerly dangerous PTSD memories. The flashbacks were signs of healing.

Fine and good as an interpretation, Hal thought seated on the edge of his bed, *but this was not a flashback. It was one of "those" dreams.* With that realization, waves of guilt and angst coursed anew through his system like an electric current. He shuddered.

By nine o'clock that same morning Hal had showered, dressed and managed to gulp down a piece of toast and jam with his first two cups of coffee. That would have to do for breakfast. He had no appetite for more. He turned on the computer in his home office and clicked on the Skype icon.

I don't know whether it's fate or coincidence that I have an appointment to talk with Barb this morning, he thought to himself, *but I'm glad I do.* In the back of his mind he knew that the time had finally arrived to confide in her. That, and he really needed to figure out what to do about the dream. Especially *this* dream!

Barb's smiling face appeared on the screen. In spite of his troubled mood Hal could not help smiling a greeting of his own in return. In the three months since his return from Congo he and Barb had been in regular contact with one another, Skyping once a week and emailing in between, often daily. He discovered that she knew a lot more about him and his checkered history than he did of her. Barb's mother and Hal's had clearly been in far closer contact than he had ever been aware. He wondered if the two former Kisambo Station matrons had had some sort of premonition of their own, or perhaps shared a hidden aspiration that their two children might someday find one another? *Well, we have,* thought Hal glancing upward, *and I imagine you are somewhere above flashing that knowing smile of yours right now, Momma.*

Barbara was already in mid-sentence when Hal left his private musings and mentally joined the conversation. "...and as I mentioned, Michael and Shirley have become good friends in the last year or so since they arrived as MCC country directors. Two nights ago, we had dinner together at that little Italian restaurant near the Memling. They had just returned from of all places, our childhood home...Kisambo. They had some interesting things to share that I thought you'd like to hear."

The blood drained from Hal's face at Barb's mention of Kisambo. "Ah, yeah, for sure..." he stuttered. "Tell me more. What did they have to report?"

Barb immediately noticed the change in Hal's demeanor. "Hal? Are you okay? Is this not a topic we should discuss right now? I do remember that you have been processing PTSD with your therapist in recent days."

Hal tried his best to recover lost composure. "No, no...it's fine. I was just reminded of something that distracted me. What did your friends have to say about Kisambo?"

Barb's face bore a dubious expression and she paused as if deciding whether to pursue the matter before continuing. "They...they described the station as appearing like time has stood still. Our burned-out former homes stand as empty shells; the church is intact but mostly unused and the clinic provides only the most minimal of services. Apparently, many local residents believe the place is cursed. In addition, they were told that no one from our former mission has even visited the place in well over forty years. Michael thinks that some kind of reconciliation is overdue."

Hal shifted his position at the desk and leaned forward running his fingers through his hair. "I never realized that our former mission had so totally abandoned Kisambo after the rebellion. I know my folks were deeply disappointed, deeply hurt by what they considered a major betrayal by their friends. Dad's Congo assignment changed dramatically after our evacuation...he and Mom were totally preoccupied in starting the theological school in Kinshasa. I imagine he took his Kisambo wounds with him to the grave."

Barb's eyes had a faraway look. "I think my folks had a similar experience. I remember my father declining to meet with one of the Kisambo church leaders who had come to see him in the city a few years after our evacuation. The rebellion was a painful experience for the folks. It almost became a deadly experience. Mom had nightmares for years, even after we returned to the

States for her cancer treatment."

Brightening up, Barbara shifted the conversation. "On a positive note, Shirley indicated that there are glimmers of hope for Kisambo. Recently, someone you know, Kuyantika – your childhood buddy Tika, the pastor's son – has funded a couple of economic development projects. It seems he is now a successful Kinshasa businessman with interests in revitalizing the home community."

Hal froze at the mention of Tika's name. His eyes grew wide and he gripped the edges of his desk. Barb didn't know what to make of this sudden change.

"It was Tika I saw," he blurted out in a hoarse whisper. "Tika is in grave danger. Someone must warn him." Hal's eyes had pooled, and deep furrows appeared between his eyebrows and across his forehead. His chest was heaving.

"What, Hal? You saw Tika? Where? How? What's going on?" Barb's voice rose in alarm. "What do you mean, danger?"

Hal took a deep breath. "Okay...okay, I'm going to tell you something that I have shared with very few people." He paused to sort out his thoughts.

"Since I was a child, I have periodically had these disturbing...dreams. They are vivid images of something that will happen in the near future. I guess you could call them clairvoyant visions. I...I've never known what to do when they happen. The responsibility of...of this awareness of pending harm has driven me crazy. Well, it's driven me to drink, anyhow...in the past. This probably sounds nuts to you. You're wondering now if I've really lost my marbles." He looked up to read Barb's reaction.

"No, Hal. I actually heard about your dreams years ago. Our mothers talked. Go on." Her face had softened with his disclosure, but her eyes were intent on his words.

Hal paused again, startled by this revelation. "Then you...you probably think I'm demon possessed or...or something diabolical. I sometimes feel like I've been cursed."

"I do *not*," Barb declared with certitude. "What I think is a topic for another time. Now continue with what you were telling me."

Though still distracted, Hal returned to his comments. "The reason I was especially looking forward to our visit today, Barb, is because I had one of those dreams last night. I wanted to tell you about it. The dream took me to Kisambo village." He paused and took a deep breath. "I think I saw someone killed or injured. That person was Tika! I'm sure of it."

Hal's voice had gotten shaky and so he blurted the last declaration to just get it out. As he did so, he unconsciously pushed his chair back from his desk. He exhaled, a far-away look in his eyes.

Barb's response surprised him. "I think you should warn him, Hal. Yes, warn him...don't you?"

"Warn him? I have not even *seen* him since we were kids. I know *nothing* about him or even his whereabouts. You said he is now a Kinshasa businessman. Have *you* run into him in all your years in the city?"

Barb smiled and beaconed with her hand. "Hal, get closer to your computer screen. I can hardly hear you. There. That's better. No, I haven't seen Tika, but I will look him up and see if I can get some contact information for you. But when I do, Hal, you need to prepare yourself for what you will say to him. And then, say it!"

Barb's suggestion was at the same time encouraging and disturbing to Hal. He was surprised and flattered that she believed him so readily, but the thought of contacting Tika directly and delivering a warning sent chills down his spine.

Barb added an afterthought. "And, oh yes...I intend to *pray* for you, Hal. Count on it. And also, for Tika."

"Pray? What would you pray?" Hal uttered the response without thinking.

"My prayer will be that the Lord will use this situation for good in both of your lives; that He will bring healing and reconciliation – both are clearly needed – but most of all that His purposes will be accomplished."

Hal didn't know what to say in response. He managed to mumble, "Um, thanks, Barb. Those are noble thoughts. I guess we'll be in touch some more about this later," and they signed off. He sat at his desk for a long time afterwards, mind spinning.

"What should I say to Tika if she locates him? What *will* I say to him?"

#41 Kisambo Village, DRC

October 2010

It was midafternoon in the village of Kisambo. The women were still busily cleaning pots and wrapping leftovers in banana leaves, the surpluses to reappear for the evening's repast. A semicircle of a dozen plastic chairs stood before the fire ring marking the center of the settlement. Occupying each chair was a chief from nearby villages. All of the seated dignitaries carried or wore some symbol of their authority: horsehair fly switches, colorfully beaded ceremonial hats or hatchets with beaded shafts. Additional white and blue plastic chairs were set up in a haphazard manner three or four deep behind the semicircle. They were occupied by elders and advisers who had accompanied their headmen to this special gathering. A large crowd of onlookers surrounded the seated visitors. Its number included not only the entire Kisambo village – men, women and children – but also scores of others who had made the trek to the meeting from throughout the region, anxious to witness the proceedings.

Mansuaki, the current chief of Kisambo village and eldest son of legendary chief Ntotilla, stood to address the assembly. In deep baritone locutions he welcomed the visitors to his village and immediately launched into a graphic history of Kisambo. He identified, with reverence, the ancients who originally occupied the site and their descendants who first granted land to the missionaries – Baptists in 1928 – to establish a mission station. These *mindele* built the first structures at Kisambo Station. He reminded the group that the Mennonites then purchased the station from the Baptists in 1954. It was under their watch it thrived for the next ten years. A church, Bible school and medical clinic were added serving the needs of the entire region. He concluded, "the *mindele* mission station brought prosperity and resources to our community."

The crowd murmured their approval at various points of emphasis in Mansuaki's speech, responding in such a way that his resonant voice resembled a soloist leading an echoing choir. Thus encouraged, the Kisambo chief became even more animated and the crowd, more engaged. Little ones unable to follow the content of the speech giggled and poked one another adding their high-pitched squeals to the "Ohs and Ahs" of the adults.

At the dramatic high point of his history lecture Mansuaki turned and extended his arm to one side in a sweeping gesture, beaconing to a well-dressed bystander to come forward. A distinguished looking man in his 50s emerged from the crowd and stood by the village chief. He was of medium height, had salt-and-pepper hair, and was attired in a dark sport coat and slacks with a white shirt open at the neck. His ample girth, well-trimmed goatee and careful haircut implied wealth and sophistication. All eyes turned his way as Mansuaki proceeded with an introduction.

"Kisambo's favorite son, Kuyantika, will tell us of his dream to restore prosperity to our community. He is the one who just last month paid to replace the roof on the schoolhouse and to repair our church benches and the broken wall in the health clinic. He has a new plan to share that goes far beyond a few building repairs."

There was scattered applause around the circle but widespread curiosity as the crowd pressed forward to hear what this successful son of Kisambo might have to say.

Slowly and confidently positioning himself before the seated row of chiefs, he smiled and scanned each face, looking directly into their eyes as he began. "I am Kuyantika, son of Kinbumba. You will remember my father the former pastor of Kisambo village. After his many years of service, he has now departed to be with the ancestors...and with Jesus. I left the village as a young man to make my way in the city. I was well prepared by you, my teachers and elders. With your help and God's blessings I have found success in life. I am therefore indebted to you my people and I hope to pay you back. I wish to see Kisambo prosper once again."

Murmurs of approval rippled across the audience. The row of village chiefs smiled and exchanged acknowledging nods with one another. Kuyantika had hit a resonant chord with his audience.

"As the elders and those of my generation will recall, trouble visited Kisambo shortly after Independence. Mulele charmed the sons of Kisambo as well as those of many of our sister villages." Gesturing to the seated guests, "Sons from your homes, honored chiefs. Our *Jeunesse* were trained for war in the forest and one day they turned on us, attacking and burning our village. They destroyed Kisambo Station. We knew of their threat but hid this knowledge from the missionaries. Their lives were endangered, their homes were burned, and they fled, never to return. Kisambo has never been the same. We told them they were safe from harm, that they had nothing to fear, that we would protect them. We failed them on each promise. Had the U. N. soldiers not arrived to rescue them they would surely have been killed."

By this time, no one was smiling. No one moved. The entire assembly was completely still. No one had ever spoken of these events in such a candid way in any gathering since the night of the fires forty-six years earlier.

"I propose we make contact with the Mennonites and invite them to come to Kisambo, to be reconciled with us once again. To do so would mark a new beginning. However, we must be willing to confess our wrongdoing. Our fathers betrayed them. We have never owned up to it."

A buzz of many voices began across the gathering and grew in volume. The chiefs turned to one another and their elders rose to crouch by them to discuss this matter. Kuyantika watched this spontaneous activity quietly, arms folded.

After several minutes of animated interaction, a slight, scrawny figure emerged from the crowd. His bushy hair was gray and long, his deep-set eyes were small and close together, and his face bore a wispy mustache and goatee around stern, unsmiling lips. A faded, threadbare sportscoat several sizes too large hung loosely over the man's bony frame and above ragged shorts and sandals. He moved with surprising ease to take his place by the speaker. A beaded cane in one hand signaled his authority. Squaring his shoulders and looking about, he held up a hand. He was Kamanga Nsapo, Kisambo's current shaman. The crowd's chatter dropped sharply as all eyes turned in his direction.

"No! This is wrong! It is all wrong!" Kamanga declared in a loud, raspy voice. "We do not need *mindele* support to prosper. They invaded our land and robbed us of our freedom, first the Belgians and then the missionaries. They want to change us, to control us, to steal our wealth. Our fathers were right to be silent and allow the *Jeunesse* to do what they could not...rid us of them. But the Kinshasa thieves with their *mindele* partners were too strong for the people's revolution to succeed. We do *not* owe the missionaries an apology. We should *not* invite them to return to our community. No, *never!*"

A loud response erupted from the throng. Many voices shouted for Kamanga to be silent, others bellowed agreement with his comments. Several shoving matches broke out and everywhere animated exchanges took place among the now milling horde.

Finally, pastor Lumingu came over to join Kuyantika and Kamanga who were themselves locked in an agitated exchange in the center of the crowd. He turned to the throng, waved his arms and shouted in a loud voice, continuing to yell until heads finally turned his way and the noise level lowered enough for him to be heard.

"I cannot speak for all...but for those of us who follow the Jesus Way, when wrong has been done, we are called to humble ourselves, to repent, seek forgiveness, to forgive and be forgiven. Our brother Kuyantika has pointed out a clear path to right a wrong. Chief Mansuaki has also spoken well. Our community has suffered for many years. The return of missionaries will birth new hope."

Kamanga shook his head vehemently. "Kisambo was cursed, *that's* why we have not prospered. And it was the *mundele* missionary child who did it, the one known as *Lumwenu*. His words brought about the death of your cousins, Nsukula and Biungu," he said, pointing directly to Munzele Zacharie seated nearby. "He surely cursed this place." He spat to the side. "I do *not* welcome missionaries to return. Kisambo has had too much *mindele* religion. I say, good riddance!"

The roar of the crowd's response resumed and with it the meeting disintegrated, the audience dispersing in small clusters still agitated, debating. As Kamanga disappeared back into the crowd, Lumingu and Kuyantika were joined at the fire pit by Mansuaki. The three of them conferred further in quiet somber conversation.

"I believe it is up to us to complete what our fathers lacked the courage to do," volunteered Kuyantika at last to the somber nods of the other two.

"Yes," Mansuaki offered, after a short pause, "but perhaps the goal you propose is too big to accomplish all at once. We all can see that strong resistance still remains here. Perhaps some still lingers on the missionary side as well." He paused to kick a smoking ember back into the fire. "An old saying of the elders tells us *the only way to eat an elephant is…one bite at a time.* Reconciliation is our elephant. Perhaps, therefore, we should first invite the return of the former missionary children. The parents are gone but the children – now adults – may be willing to meet with us. Success with them could very well clear a path to the mission officials."

"Wait…that's not the reason to reconcile, is it, *mbuta* (brother) Mansuaki?" Lumingu, frowning, reached out as if to touch his arm, then withdrew his hand. "If we are insincere, if it is only access to resources the *mindele* will notice."

"No, no…restoring a broken relationship, healing, forgiving, all the things Kuyantika here pointed out," he replied hastily. Perhaps a little too hastily. Turning to his childhood friend he hinted at a next step. "You were once good friends with the one Kamanga named…*Lumwenu*, yes?"

"It is true, but we have had no contact over the years." Kuyantika reached up to stroke his goatee, adding pensively, "Clearly, *some* still believe him to have cursed Kisambo. I will have to give it some thought."

Lumingu concluded their exchanges with a note of caution. "My friends, we must pray…for wisdom. I fear some among our brothers and sisters may yet hold the burning coals of bitterness after all these years. Kamanga is no friend of the church. The wounds of our fathers have been passed to the children. They are still in need of healing."

#42 Kisambo Village, DRC

October 2010

The scent of charcoal fires, palm oil stew, fried plantains and warm manioc balls filled Kisambo village. Dinner was being prepared. Light was fading and the shadow-darkened parameters focused light and activity around the cooking fires in front of the huts. The chatter of children, calls of parents and occasional peals of laughter here and there from family banter joined with the thumping and pot clanging sounds of food preparation to create a cozy, familiar feel to Kuyantika. He sighed deeply, leaning forward on a reclining wooden chair to stir the crackling fire before him. It was good to be home in familiar environs.

His sister, Claudine, quietly stepped beside him, placing a gentle hand on his shoulder. Shy, smiling eight-year-old daughter Marie, arm around her mother, peeked at her uncle from the safety of her mama's side. "It's so good to have you here, Kuyantika," she spoke softly, patting his shoulder affectionately. "The children miss you. I miss you. I just wish Kinshasa wasn't so far away."

Tika smiled and looked up to reply, but halted mid-sentence, the smile quickly evaporating. A scuffling commotion behind them announced the unexpected arrival of several persons.

"There you are!" called out a throaty male voice. "I wondered if you'd be sleeping in the village tonight. I thought perhaps you'd consider us too primitive here for your wealthy Kinshasa bones."

Kuyantika recovered his wits and resisted reacting to the barbed greeting. *"Mbote Tata Kamanga Nsapo, 'kele?"* He observed that his visitor was accompanied by a half-dozen smirking companions, men and women, lined up like a chorus behind their leader.

Kamanga, ignoring the greeting, wasted no time getting to the point. Leaning forward into his face, he stabbed his forefinger at Kuyantika's chest. "I've given the matter more thought since your speech. You are *half right* about what's needed to restore life to this struggling village. We don't need a return of missionaries, but we *do* need to bring *Lumwenu* back so we can settle things, once and for all. We need to confront the curse that has settled on our people like a toxic cloud. *His* curse."

"What makes you so sure *Lumwenu* – Hal Schroeder – is responsible for Kisambo's ills?" he asked in an even voice.

"We all know of his gift to foretell the future. My mentor Muzeka, our shaman, first recognized it and trained him as a youth. You were his friend, so you know this is true." He did not wait for an acknowledgment before continuing. "*Lumwenu* cursed Kisambo when his family was taken captive by the *Jeunesse* with the other missionaries. He was responsible for the death of Tata Muzeka and his sons Nsukula and Biungu, as well." His voice shook with anger. "It is *he* who needs to repent and cancel the curse, not us!" The others behind Kamanga murmured their approval. Kuyantika remained silent, thinking.

"What do you want from me?" he finally asked, quietly.

"You were once friends with him. You want to see Kisambo restored. That makes *you* the one to see that he returns here," was the vehement reply. "*You* find a way to bring him here."

"And if I refuse?" Kuyantika looked up into the shaman's dark eyes and scowling face made even more menacing by the flickering firelight.

"Test your loyalties, Kuyantika," Kamanga replied evenly, arms now folded across his chest. "If you are *truly* a son of Kisambo, you will make it happen. If not..." His voice trailed off.

"If not...what?" he replied, rising to his feet. "Are you threatening me?"

"Let's just say, things will not go well for you and your family, both here and in Kinshasa. You may encounter the power of curses, yourself...firsthand," was the reply. With that declaration, Kamanga turned on his heel, entourage closely following, and headed off into the dark shadows.

"What will you do, Tika?" asked a shaken Claudine, clutched tightly by her young daughter.

"I will invite the former *mundele* missionary children to come to Kisambo," he replied evenly. What choice do I have?" Kuyantika shrugged, palms up. "I can't say for certain that *Lumwenu* did *not* curse this place. Nsukula and his brother and father did indeed die. Maybe if he returns..."

Tika did not finish his sentence but kicked another coal back into the fire.

***

As Hal sat at his desk working on his next day's lecture, his computer chimed – a Skype invitation. His face broke into a smile as he saw that it was Barb in Congo attempting to reach him. He had not been expecting her call but given their previous contact he was eager to respond. *To process things with...with my friend. Yes, I guess I do consider Barb a real friend*, he thought to himself as if that particular epiphany had just occurred to him for the first time. It had not.

As soon as the connection was made, Barb by-passed any small talk greeting and excitedly launched into conversation. "Hal, "I met with Kuyantika here in Kinshasa this week. He wants to hear from you. He has invited the two of us to return to Kisambo for a reunion of sorts in January. I think the two of us should go."

"Whaaa...Tika?" Hal gasped. "Where? How? When? What did he have to say?"

"He told me he had known for years that I was living in Congo. He said he had learned from Internet searching that you were a professor and knows where you live and work. Tika confessed that for many years he has been too embarrassed and ashamed to attempt any contact with us. Only recently through what he described as "a spiritual awakening" in his life has he begun to take steps to reconnect with Kisambo, with his past. He thinks that he and others from Kisambo need to formally apologize and to be reconciled with us as the surviving *mindele* members of the mission."

"That's pretty amazing information," Hal managed, still stunned. "How did you locate him?"

"I didn't find him, he found me! According to Tika, it wasn't all that difficult. He was acquainted with a couple of Bapende nursing colleagues from the surgery team at the hospital. They directed him to me. Incidentally, Tika was most delighted to see me, even tearful by the time I left. We spent over two hours visiting and reminiscing at his place of business. It's located in the Kintambo sector near Joli Parc. You may recall we had TASOK friends who lived near there."

Hal shook his head, feeling somewhat overwhelmed by this news, not sure what to make of it. He finally managed, "If you have contact information for Tika I'll at least begin by emailing him."

Barb's tone turned serious once again. "One other thing I need to tell you about my conversation with Tika. It's a little disturbing. He told me that not all in the Kisambo community may be excited to see us. One strong voice of opposition whom he identified as Kamanga Nsapo – the successor to Muzeka Andoko as village shaman – recently spoke up in public denouncing the *mundele* whom he claims placed a curse on Kisambo...*Lumwenu*. That was *your* Bapende nickname, wasn't it Hal?"

Hal paled and swallowed hard, the lump in his throat providing hearty resistance. "I...I need to find a way to warn Tika. My dream...He's in danger."

"But from Tika's report, so are you!" Barb declared. "Dangerous though things might be, in my view that fact makes an even stronger case for us to participate in a reunion of sorts at Kisambo. Darkness and misunderstanding that have plagued our childhood home for a generation need light and clarity...healing. I'm praying for all of us and especially for this opportunity. It seems to me to be just the kind of thing Jesus would endorse. Peacemaking."

Hal did not know what to say. "Um, thanks Barb. You're probably right. I don't know how I feel about returning to Kisambo, however. I'll...I'll give it some thought. Now if you have that contact info for me, I am serious about firing off a warning to Tika."

Barb supplied Tika's cell phone number and email address to Hal and with promises to be back in touch in the next few days, they signed off of Skype.

Hal settled back in his recliner, nervously running a hand through his hair. The creases on his forehead and distant look in his eyes were a sure sign his thoughts remained far from the quiet environs of his comfortable foothill home.

The reunion, the snakebite, Barbara, the dream, Tika's invite...what can it all mean? Some sort of strange, eerie saga! Barb would probably label it "a God thing." Hal continued to mull these reflections over for some time trying to decide if he should close the book on Congo, forget it all and get on with his life, or pursue these developments further.

A loud thump on the sliding glass door in front of him roused him from his musings. A dove that had flown into the glass lay quivering on the ground, a faint smudge of feathers marking its point of collision. The dazed bird slowly regained its senses, hopped a few feet on the slate patio and, furiously flapping its wings, resumed its journey in a different direction.

That's like me, Hal thought, *in danger of flying into something I can't even see. If it brings me down, I just hope I'll be able to recover in a like fashion.*

With a sigh and new resolve, Hal turned to his computer and immediately began scripting an email message to his former friend.

> *Cher frère Kuyantika,*
>
> *C'était bon d'entendre parler de votre visite récente avec notre amie Barbara depuis notre enfance à Kisambo. Je vous demande pardon pour mon absence de votre vie pendant ces nombreuses années. Les circonstances de mon départ de Kisambo m'ont profondément blessée. Je ne vous en veux pas. Je réalise que je leur ai permis de me séparer de mon passé...*

[Dear brother Kuyantika,

It was good to hear of your recent visit with our mutual friend Barbara from our childhood in Kisambo. I ask your forgiveness for my absence from your life for these many years. The circumstances of my departure from Kisambo wounded me deeply. I don't blame you for them. I realize I allowed them to separate me from my past. Your contact with Barbara opened the door to renewing our friendship. I eagerly anticipate meeting with you to restore something precious that has been lost for so long. I will accept your invitation to return to Kisambo.

I reluctantly remind you that since childhood I have had unusual dreams that sometimes predict danger. I recently had one in which you were the subject of mischief in the village of Kisambo. I therefore urge you to avoid visiting Kisambo until we meet in January. I could not bear to learn that you had been harmed. Please assure me you will not return in person prior to that time. I know it is an unusual request, but I ask you to trust me on this...]

#43 Kinshasa, DRC

January 2011

The tables and chairs in the shady outdoor café faced a low wall, beyond which flowed the mighty Congo River. Its location offered a distinct advantage over other daytime dining spots in Kinshasa, refreshing its patrons with cooler temperatures and light afternoon breezes due to its proximity to the rushing river waters. Waiters dressed in crisp white serving jackets glided silently between the tables, balancing drinks and clearing dishes.

Hal sat in the very center of a group of seven diners, smiling broadly. Next to him, addressing the small group in deep lyrical tones of French was the distinguished appearing Kinshasa businessman, Kuyantika, attired in a dark blue patterned wax print matching shirt and pants. At his other side sat an attractive middle-aged blonde woman, Barbara Clausen Jones, also smiling warmly in response to the speaker's monologue. Periodically, she leaned in to whisper a comment to Hal, placing her hand across his shoulder in a familiar manner.

The circle of listeners was completed by a second white couple, husband and wife, and two Congolese men, one wearing a stylish sport coat and tie and the second dressed in military garb. In addition to former MKs Barb and Hal, the listeners included MCC Country Co-Directors, Michael and Shirley Friesen, Sergeant Mpika, a friend of Kuyantika and finally, Muwana Pierre, a member of the DRC National Assembly, also a friend and colleague of his.

"I have become convinced that the Spirit of Jesus is calling us to demonstrate God's power to bring healing and renewal to this land. The Evil One has bound us with guilt and shame for far too long. He has separated brothers and sisters in the faith and stirred the smoldering embers of hate and fear for many years, for the length of a generation. Perhaps my father, Pastor Kinbumba, foresaw this day when he named me Kuyantika ('*the beginning'*). It will require humility, confession and a willingness to embrace the Spirit's prompting to bring about a new day in Kisambo. This is the spirit I hope to carry to Kisambo."

Kuyantika's words were met with an enthusiastic round of "Ummms" and "Amens" from his listeners. His remarks were concluded with a personal reference. Turning to the two next to him, "I believe your return to Kisambo with me – professor Schroeder and nurse Jones – will prove to be the needed bridge to forgiveness." Hal lifted a hand to acknowledge the comment.

When Kuyantika's speech-making finally came to an end, the group rose, and exchanging warm farewells, slowly headed for the exit. Barb and Tika remained by the table sporting broad smiles as they engaged in animated reminiscence in a mixture of French and Kituba.

Hal returned to the pair after thanking the Friesens for joining them and trading farewells. Tika reached out to offer a two-handed shake with a hearty, *"Lumwenu. Ngolo ikele?"* Hal returned the clasp and enthusiastic greeting, responding in kind: *"Eaye...'Kele."* The brief pause that followed hinted at a strain between them, or perhaps a natural awkwardness at conversation after a gap of so many years.

Barb smoothed the way forward. "It warms my heart to see the two of you fellows together again, embracing. It seems so natural, all three of us in the same place," then adding as an afterthought, "Except that we're occupying well-seasoned bodies these days."

That comment prompted smiles from all three. "A lot has happened since we last spoke," Hal volunteered. "My recall is that our last contact, Tika, was during my high school days at TASOK. You had come to Kinshasa with your father." He ran a hand through his hair, adding, "As I think about it now, it seems like we didn't have much to say to one another at the time."

Tika's smile faded, replaced by deep creases across his forehead. "Those were still tense times in Kisambo village and also between our parents." Tika stroked his goatee, a faraway look in his eyes. "I think your father was still angry with *tata ya mono* (my father) and the other village elders. I remember that he did not want to hear my father's apologies. Neither of your fathers did," flicking a glance toward Barb. "My father was anguished by this, tormented by all that had happened. Our visit to Kinshasa ended up being a short one since my father was forced to head back to Kisambo heavy-hearted and, in terms of his objective, empty handed. The fact that we had no MMC contact for years afterwards only confirmed the worse to him. All love and trust between the missionaries and our people had been lost."

"Let's sit, shall we?" Hal gestured to his two childhood friends and all three returned to their table and pulled the chairs to face one another. "It appears that we have some history to rewrite together, Tika." Hal looked his childhood friend directly in the eyes, while Barb sat back with a slight smile on her face, arms folded across her chest signaling that she intended to serve as a witness in this exchange.

Tika leaned forward and lowered his voice so others nearby would not hear him. "*Lumwenu*, I have respected your warning to me and have not returned to Kisambo since receiving your message. We need to speak more of your visions. But I first have a question for you, *mpangi* (friend). It has waited almost fifty years to be asked. Here it is. Since you possess the ability to see the future, why did you not warn your father and the other missionaries what would happen? They blamed my father and the elders for keeping the rebel threat from them but you, their child, knew about it all along. We, your friends – Nsukula, Ilunga and me – informed you. Isn't that so?"

Hal remained silent staring at the floor as if he could see through its surface, to a scene at its depth, a scene occurring over forty-five years ago.

Tika continued with an edge to his lowered voice, "And why did Nsukula have to die, *Lumwenu*? His relatives are convinced to this very day that you cursed him and Biungu...and Kisambo. Didn't you foresee harm coming to them? Didn't you even think to warn them?"

The question caused Hal to wince, a grimace forming on his face. His eyes became moist. A single wet line formed on his cheek as he finally looked up to speak. He started to reply but the words caught in his throat, in a choked groan. After a deep breath he began once again.

"No, Tika...no, that's not it at all! Perhaps you have forgotten. You and our buddies swore me to secrecy about Biungu and about the rebel threat in general. We all agreed to silence. I kept my promise about Biungu. I was very afraid to tell my father about my visions. I was sure he'd think I was demon possessed. Besides, I didn't think he'd believe me. Still, I *did* attempt to warn him of coming trouble but as a young child he didn't take me seriously. He and the other missionaries strongly suspected they were not being told the truth, but they trusted your father and the elders. I think the final straw that broke that trust was your father, Pastor Kinbumba, promising the church's protection but then hiding from the rebels when they actually attacked and took all of us *mindeles* captive."

Tika's eyes were now moisture filled as were Barb's as the memories of Kisambo Station's final days surfaced for the three childhood friends. "My father was heartbroken over his betrayal," Tika offered in a quivering voice. "He fully expressed to us children his remorse. I don't think he ever got over it, not to his dying day. The same could be said of others of the village elders as well. He told me there was a time he even considered taking his own life."

Hal resumed his reflections. "While we were held by the rebels, Muzeka Adoko sent Ilunga to inquire of me what was to happen. I had a dream that revealed things to come. I warned Ilunga to tell Muzeka that under no circumstances should he or any member of his family set foot on Kisambo Station as long as any *mindele* were present or great harm could come to them."

Hal began to sob. "Tika... I saw them killed in my dream. Then, I saw them killed in reality. It was awful! It has plagued me for a lifetime. I owe my life to Nsukula who somehow chose to show up at the evacuation in spite of my warning. He jumped one of the rebels trying to prevent me from escaping. He was killed for his efforts to rescue me. I still bear the scars of that day." He held up his arm showing the marks of the arrow that had hit him.

Barb had moved over to Hal and knelt, wrapping her arms around him as his shoulders shook. Tika reached out to rest his hand on Hal's arm. No one said anything for several long minutes.

Tika finally broke the silence in a trembling voice. "I'm sorry, my brother, for this burden you have carried since childhood. I can see those dreams of yours have created great turmoil for you. I had not before this day, heard of your warning to Nsukula's family. You may not know of it, but Muzeka Adoko was also killed by the rebels shortly after Kisambo Station burned so your warning was very real. It was, however, never reported in the village. I fear that in the coming days you may find that some there still harbor resentment toward you."

That pointed declaration came as a sobering revelation to Hal. He had not imagined that his clairvoyance was known in the first place, let alone that he represented a lingering symbol of brokenness and loss in his childhood home. These new shadows cast the whole return visit into a different light.

#44 Kinshasa to Kikwit, DRC

January 2011

The pre-dawn back-and-forth concert of mourning doves and neighborhood roosters had only just begun but Hal was already wide awake, elbows out and hands clasped behind his head as he lay in bed, studying the gray shadows on the ceiling of his MPH guesthouse room. A kaleidoscope of images swirled in his mind's eye as he anticipated the day's journey ahead. Drives upcountry in the Congo were always a combination of beauty, adventure and threat. How would the three balance out today? Vivid memories of past trips into the bush, danced on the ceiling above. With them came waves of excitement and dread. *What will it be like to revisit Kisambo once again? Will I be welcomed as a native son or viewed as the symbol of rejection, a curse on the community?* Tika's words of caution comingled with his own recent warning to his friend causing Hal to shudder, involuntarily. *What will be waiting for us at the end of the long drive?*

Breakfast was set out on the counter: toast and jam, cheese and bananas, accompanied by orange juice and a steaming cup of coffee all designed to send Hal and Barb on their way without delay. The sun had just lit the tops of the backyard mango trees as two Land Rover-type vehicles entered the guesthouse yard to pick up their two additional passengers. Barb had spent the night there for convenience sake. She greeted Hal with a warm smile and a hearty hug. "Good morning travel mate! Are you ready for the day?"

"As ready as I'm going to be," he replied, extending the embrace just that little extra. *'Travel mate, eh?'* he thought to himself with a smile.

The vehicles were quickly loaded with food and baggage and onto the busy boulevards of urban Kinshasa the two-car convoy headed. The timely departure meant that they managed to clear the downtown streets before the first sleepy-eyed traffic cops found their way to their posts. That proved to be a strategic move that got the travelers off to a good, unimpeded start.

They headed east on the Boulevard Lumumba, aka N1, the

African nation's major east-west highway, continuing past the Ndjili International Airport and on through several additional miles of a densely populated *cité*. The sun had fully risen by that time. The morning commute into the city had begun in earnest. Scores of pedestrians filled the roadsides, some carrying large loads on their heads, others flagging down packed taxis and still more, waiting in clusters for trucks and other forms of transport into Kinshasa central.

With the windows partially down, a strong aroma of rotten garbage, diesel fuel, body odor and smoke filled the vehicle. Hal took a deep breath. Reflexively coughing, he could not resist a smile. "Something incredibly familiar and satisfying about that smell," he commented to Tika who was at the wheel of his personal Land Cruiser.

"What? You mean our Kinshasa pollution? What could be positive about *that*?" came the driver's incredulous response.

"Just...nothing else like it, Tika, anywhere on the planet. At least nowhere I've visited." Hal gestured at the colorful roadside drama taking place on all sides as they whizzed by. "And look at the crowds! How do so many people ever survive in this place? It's remarkable!"

Tika flashed a cynical smile. "We Congolese are a resilient lot, it's true." That comment – made in Kituba – triggered a chuckle and back poke from Barb.

A Congolese chauffeur was at the wheel of the lead vehicle in the mini caravan, with Assemblyman Muwana Pierre occupying the adjacent front seat. As a well-known National Assembly member, Tika hoped his friend Muwana's presence along with that of Sgt. Mpika riding in the back, would be their key to smooth passage through an anticipated gauntlet of barriers and DGM (*Direction Génerale de Migration* or security police) roadblocks along the route. Undoubtedly, tolls would have to be paid, but the presence of high-profile persons would surely reduce time delays and the price of passage. Hal was seated next to Tika in the following vehicle. Barb occupied the back seat.

As they approached the outskirts of the city entering the quarter called *Kingasani ya Suka*, the traffic slowed. Tika turned slightly to his companions, "Quickly, roll up the windows!"

"What's going on?" Barb asked, puzzled.

As they inched forward in a line of vehicles, scores of women rushed into the street, many of them vendors with arms full of bread, bananas and other food items. These were thrust into any open windows on the stalled vehicles in an attempt to secure a sale. Some were thrown to the tops of huge transport trucks mounded with produce and passengers who shouted their encouragement.

"This is where the transports purchase bread for their journey upcountry," Tika explained. "It's always chaotic along here...a favorite spot for light-fingered thieves as well," he added with a chuckle.

The N1 paralleled the broad Congo River for several miles before crossing the muddy brown Nsele River and turning abruptly east crossing flat, richly cultivated fields of manioc to begin its ascent up the escarpment to the broad Plateau de Bateke. At one point, when the vehicles geared down to climb through a dry, steep-walled canyon, Tika motioned with a hand sweep, "*Voila, le Grand Dibulu* (the big hole)." Turning to address both passengers he added, "The locals say that God originally planned to put a river here but changed his mind."

"Judging from what we're seeing, one might imagine God was pretty distracted when He made Congo," Hal quipped. "Or angry!" Tika chimed in. chuckling. "Stop it, you two!" Barb said smiling.

It was nearly mid-morning when the two vehicles approached the Bombo River bridge. The descent to the river was steep and both vehicles geared down, following a line of overloaded transports creeping slowly down the slope. With the windows down the sound of singing carried back to the Land Cruiser.

"Listen, they're singing...hymns!" Barb exclaimed, straining forward in her seat to get a better look.

Tika shot a quick sideward glance, his eyes crinkled in a smile. "*Eaye.* It's a tradition born of experience. The brakes of many a *camion* have failed on the descent, tearing through that sharp right turn down there at the bottom. Lorry and load have ended their journey in the Mai Ndombe. Permanently. Thus, we witness hymns on the descent, quiet prayers of thanks on the other side."

Turning at the base of the hill, they encountered their first DGM roadblock, marked by several huge tractor tires rolled into the center of the road. As they pulled to a stop behind a line of vehicles, they spotted a disturbance taking place near the barrier. A circle of soldiers, rifles in hand were gathered around two of their number who were repeatedly beating and kicking a crumpled figure on the dusty ground. The bloody victim was curled in a fetal position, arms clutched protectively over his head. The soldiers and other on-lookers were clearly enjoying the brutal entertainment, laughing, jeering and cheering-on their two stick-wielding comrades who were busily thrashing the hapless man.

Hal and Barb stepped out to stretch their legs and checking out the commotion, they quickly determined what was happening. Barb gasped, "Oh my! Someone's got to do something. They're going to kill that man. Hal, Tika...someone, stop them!" Her companions remained still, unmoving, watching.

Barb turned to Hal with an imploring look, but Hal stood in place, shook his head slightly and lifted a hand to halt comment. "Wait, watch," he whispered motioning with his eyebrows in the direction of the commotion.

The circle of soldiers had finally noticed the two vehicles stopped at the back of the line. Taking note of white faces among the new arrivals, they quickly lost interest in the dusty action at their feet and headed toward them. Tika, Sgt. Mpika and Muwana promptly advanced in the soldiers' direction, greeting the military men warmly and engaging them in conversation. The two soldiers with sticks left their crumpled victim on the ground and after delivering parting kicks, hurried to join their comrades interacting with the visitors.

Shortly, Muwana approached Hal and Barb with one of the fatigue-clad soldiers in tow, a somber looking fellow he introduced to the group as the DGM *"Capitaine."* He asked for their passports and papers, indicating with a slight smile that "some negotiation will be required," before they could be on their way. Both handed over their passports to Muwana who carried them safely in hand as he and the DGM official walked to a small thatched roof booth by the side of the road.

Meanwhile, Tika and the Sargeant appeared to be successfully entertaining the soldiers, as gales of laughter emanated from their circle of banter.

Noticing that the Congolese man who had been beaten had quickly disappeared from view, Barb let out a sigh. "Whew, that was nasty! Why didn't you intervene, Hal?"

Hal ran a hand through his hair. "Power and justice are

inflicted here in Congo quite differently than elsewhere. I was always told it's best to use care in what we *mindeles* say and do. Otherwise, a mere disturbance – like the one before us – can escalate into a full-blown crisis. Did you notice the African solution demonstrated by Sgt. Mpika and Tika? A timely distraction is priceless."

Barb shook her head slowly. "You're right, Hal. You'd think after all my time here I'd recognize that. It's just hard to witness violence and injustice firsthand and refrain from intervening."

True to Muwana's prediction, the two negotiators carried on a lengthy, animated negotiation before money exchanged hands and the travelers were free to be on their way once again, moving to the front of the lineup. It paid to have influence, especially influence that paid.

The two vehicles made good time across the plateau on newly paved tarmac, courtesy of Chinese road builders. Hal mused out loud that their smooth going on this section of recently surfaced N1 was likely to be short-lived. The combination of a sandy base, thin paving material, heavy vehicles and tropical rains predicted an early demise.

At the next river bridge a second DGM roadblock awaited their arrival. This time, however, they were simply waved through without a check of papers.

An hour later they passed into Bandundu Province and soon after that they arrived at the wide Kwango River bridge. Hal noted to Barb as they exited the Land Cruiser, "I remember this river crossing quite well from upcountry travel in my youth. We used to have long waits for the ferry that kept breaking down. You can still see at least three old concrete access ramps from different seasons when the river was flooding or low. The Japanese also made this bridge in the 1980s." They had a longer wait at the bridge barrier and money changed hands once again before the two-car caravan continued on.

Cruising along a flat sandy stretch, Tika pointed to deep ruts on either side of the tarmac. Parallel lines of gouged earth extended out for over a hundred yards on each side. "This section of road used to be known as the '*mille chemins*' (thousand roads). The earth is so bad here that vehicles carved a new path with each passing. It presented a real challenge especially during the dry season with all the loose sand. Let's hope this pavement stays in place."

The mini convoy encountered two more barrier stops by midday. At one village barrier an enterprising fellow with fake DGM credentials attempted to collect a toll. It first appeared that this might turn into a major delay, but in the end, Muwana's savvy recognition and confrontation sent the "official" fleeing. On they went.

As they entered the outskirts of the town of Kenge the vehicles pulled to the side. Tika briefly conferred with the chauffeur in the lead vehicle. Climbing back into his Cruiser, he informed Hal and Barb that since Kenge has the only gas station between Kinshasa and Kikwit, they would need to refill their tanks there.

Refueling, however, proved to be no simple matter. A long line of waiting vehicles and the station's rules predicted an unwelcome time delay and frustration. Tika explained. "It is illegal to fill jerry cans directly from the pump. We must first fill our tanks, drive off, siphon the gas into our extra containers, get back in line and fill up once again in order to have enough fuel to reach Kikwit." He paused before adding, "There is another option, however."

Hal gave Tika a quizzical look.

"He's talking about the *"Kadafi,"* Barb chimed in. "They sell petrol in jugs along the side of the road. You buy from them if you don't want to wait in line."

"Kadafi?" Hal puzzled.

"Eaye." Tika explained, smiling once again. *"Kadafi* are family of military. They siphon the fuel out of army vehicles at night for sale during the day. Simple Congolese ingenuity."

Hal just nodded, offering a flicker of a smile in reply.

In spite of purchasing *Kadafi* fuel to top off their supplies, it became early afternoon before the refueling process was complete. The delayed departure included a short detour to purchase a popular local delicacy from a roadside vendor: *brochettes de chèvre* (goat meat shish kebabs). Tika explained, "We never pass through Kenge without a *chèvre, oignons et pili-pili* treat." This comment was met with a hearty *"Eaye!"* from the other Congolese.

Barb looked at her watch with worried eyes. "We're going to be hard pressed to make Kikwit by dark. I thought we'd be much further along by now."

"As you can see, backcountry travel in Congo is no simple matter, but hey...patience builds character, right?" Hal quipped with a chuckle and a one-armed hug.

Smiling, Barb just rolled her eyes.

#45 Kenge to Kikwit & Kisambo, DRC

January 2011

The long afternoon trek east from Kenge carried the vehicles over yet another river and onto the sandy Kenge plateau. It proved to be a continuation of the travelers' morning experience, only by this time their enthusiasm and energy level had plummeted. Silence replaced storytelling and any exchange of clever quips. Travel in hot, cramped vehicles interrupted by repeated roadblock delays and numerous off-tarmac detours around monster chuckholes...all began to take a toll.

Here and there along the road, rusting, well-scavenged frames of Ford or Mercedes trucks lay where they had crashed or broken down, the iron skeletons sometimes partially blocking the roadway and at other times lining the ditches on the sides.

In response to Barb's question about the number of rusting hulks, Tika observed, "The shell collection you see is one result of Chinese road building. New tarmac invited our chauffeurs to drive much faster – sadly, not with greater skill – on the narrow paving. Our generously loaded trucks are not often in good repair. You can see for yourself the results: terminal encounters."

"What is the reason for all these groups of people camping along the roadway?" Hal asked Tika, as they slowed to pass two successive lorries resting part-way on the road. Weary passengers sitting in the shade of wax print canopies waved arms in a half-hearted attempt to flag them down.

"Our people pay the transport drivers up front for their passage. If a *camion* breaks down along the way, no refunds are issued. The passengers must simply wait for repairs. It can take days, even weeks for parts to be sent for, delivered and installed. So, they sit and wait."

A short time later, Tika startled his drowsy companions by repeatedly honking his horn. Both Hal and Barb jumped and grabbed for support as the Land Cruiser braked sharply to a stop.

Pointing to the vehicle ahead, Tika stated the obvious, "Flat tire."

As they disembarked to inspect the Land Rover's tire, a man

walking along the side of the road rushed up and approached Muwana, addressing him with animated gestures. Tika offered a synopsis of the monologue. "He says if we drive him to the next village, he will arrange for his cousin to take care of our problem. He has a *quado*.

"*Quado*?" Hal asked. "I'm not familiar with that one."

"*Eaye, nduku*. It's a roadside tire repair shop. I'd say...good timing." An hour later, tire repaired, they continued their journey.

Four more bridges and a like number of roadblock negotiations later, the pair of vehicles at last approached the outskirts of Kikwit. Darkness had settled fully upon them like a heavy blanket, the black night broken only by dancing headlights of the vehicles as they dodged and bounced along the potholed highway. Hot, dusty and tired from the day's journey, Hal, Barb and their traveling companions were greatly relieved to finally enter the courtyard of the mission guesthouse for the night.

***

The two weary figures, bags in hand, slowly shuffled their way down a dimly lit guesthouse hallway. The florescent bulb at the end of the hall emitted just enough light to create long silhouette shadows that disappeared into the darkness behind them. Barbara paused at the door to her room. "Well, that's the longest day I've had for some time," she said with a sigh. She looked up, smiling. "Good night, Hal. Sleep well."

Hal set his bags down slowly and with one hand reached out to gently cradle Barb's jaw. Her eyes widened, mouth parted, and she began to inhale in surprise, as Hal drew her to him, bent down and pressed his lips to hers. She managed an "Oh!" at the end of the embrace before releasing her bags, with a thump, and on her tip toes, reached up with both arms to return the kiss. Their passionate exchange continued for several long moments before they finally broke off, clutching each other tightly and gasping for air.

"Oh, Hal...I've wanted that to happen for so long. Imagined it, dreamt of it," Barb gasped, her eyes closed, face turned to one side and pressed to his chest.

"As have I," replied Hal in return. He gently lifted her chin and kissed her once again, slowly, tenderly. For the second time, passion flared, and their soft kiss again became all consuming.

When they finally stopped to take a breath, Hal spoke gently, "You know, Barb, this moment doesn't have to remain a hallway event. We're both adults. Why don't we...spend the night together...your room or mine?"

Barb resumed her hug, face to one side and let a full minute pass before replying. "A part of me is more than willing to say yes to that invitation. Another part – the practical part – tells me the time is not right. It's not right on several levels. Let's celebrate this "hallway event" as a new chapter, Hal, and see what happens going forward. Okay?"

She released him, stood back, smiling, then reached up with both hands cupping his face. Looking Hal directly in the eyes, she gave him one more quick kiss on the lips before turning, picking up her bags and entering her room.

Hal stood in the hallway staring, mesmerized. When the latch on Barb's door clicked shut, he sighed deeply and reached for his bags.

Though exhausted, both Barb and Hal found sleep elusive.

#46 Kisambo Village, DRC

January 2011

A dancing crowd of cheering and jumping children met the two vehicles as they squealed to a stop by the edge of the village the next day. "Look, Hal...our Kisambo welcome committee," Barb pointed out with a big smile. Tika was well prepared for the encounter. He produced a large sack of hard candies from under his seat and flung handfuls to the overjoyed greeters as he opened the door and stepped from his vehicle. The crescendo of squeals rose as did the cloud of dust from the scramble for the sweet prizes. "It's one of my traditions," Tika chuckled to the echoing grins of his two passengers.

A collection of adults was gathered behind the melee of children, waiting to offer their greetings to the new arrivals. One figure broke from the rest and dodging between the still writhing brown arms and legs of the children, headed straight for Barb and Hal.

"*Mbote, mpangi* Hal. It is me, Ilunga! And Mademoiselle Barbara. *Bienvenue*! Like the *Mabamba* you have both returned to the site that nurtured your youth...returned to your Kisambo home."

Hal opened his arms wide as Ilunga rushed up to him, the two figures enveloped in a vigorous hug. Exuberant grunts, misty eyes and chuckles of pleasure came from both childhood friends separated by a lifetime but finally back in contact once again – physical contact, no less.

When the two at last released their grip, Ilunga turned to hug Barb. "It has been so long. Too long," he said. She nodded, voiceless, wet streaks on her cheeks. By then the crowd of children had drifted off, savoring their treats. The adults now surrounded the vehicles. Greetings and introductions were exchanged, and luggage was unloaded to be moved to the visitors' lodgings.

Pastor Lumingu and Chief Mansuaki lingered close by Ilunga, Tika, Hal and Barb while the others in their party proceeded to make their way toward the village. "It was good of you both to make the long journey here," Chief Mansuaki declared. "We had all but given up hope that it would ever happen. My father, Chief Ntotilla would have loved to see this day. He expressed great sadness and regret over the years that he and the elders had wronged your families so badly, fearing that *ndolula* (forgiveness) was not possible."

Tika spoke up. "My father also predicted that he would never see the missionaries in Kisambo again. Sadly, he was correct. But now – today – we, their children are witnessing what our fathers only hoped for, *mambu ya kuyituka* (a miracle)." Hal and Barb acknowledged the affirmations with smiles.

The small group slowly headed toward the village. As Ilunga walked beside Hal the two eagerly exchanged updates: their mutual calling as teachers – village and university – numbering children and grandchildren, identifying familiar sights, past and present and noting milestones of village life.

As they made their way along, at one point Ilunga's expression faded from upbeat and warm to dark and concerned. He grasped Hal by the arm and pulled him aside. Lowering his voice and looking him directly in the eyes, he quizzed him bluntly, "*Lumwenu*, tell me from your own mouth...have you cursed Kisambo village? That's what the family of Muzeka Andoko and Nsukula have told everyone. Is it true?"

Stunned by the blunt question, Hal stopped walking to gather his thoughts. He ran his hand through his hair, eyes and face revealing both surprise and alarm. "No, my friend. No...I swear I have never done such a thing, or even thought of it." Hal proceeded to retell his warnings to Muzeka and Nsuka. "Why would you ask me this?"

"I never believed it," declared Ilunga, looking relieved, "but many have. Muzeka's successor, Kamanga, has insisted for years that Kisambo's troubles are due to a curse, *your* curse! He has stirred Muzeka's family against you. In fact, some say that Tika was persuaded by him to bring you here for the sole purpose of confronting you so that the curse could be broken."

"Confronting me? What does that mean?" Hal asked, anxiety creeping into his quiet question.

Ilunga shrugged. "Just consider this a friendly warning. Stay alert during your visit here. Trouble may be waiting for you in disguise. Perhaps a different sort of reconciliation will be necessary than that which you expected when you agreed to come."

Several huts had been prepared for the visitors' stay. Chief Mansuaki pointed out the location of each person's accommodations and directed their luggage to be deposited accordingly. "We will call you when the evening meal has been prepared. A basin of water and cloths are there in your hut for you to use. Settle in. Welcome."

Hal stepped into the doorway of Barb's hut after first checking both ways to see they weren't being observed. He swept her into a quick embrace and she eagerly returned his kiss. "I've been looking forward to that all day," he whispered in her ear. Barb wrapped her arms about him in a tight hug, "Mmmm, me too!"

Stepping back, with his hands on her shoulders, Hal looked Barb directly in the eyes. "There's something I need to tell you." He quietly informed her of Ilunga's warning. "His advice to stay alert makes me wonder if I can trust Tika, if I *should* trust him. Do you think it's possible this whole reconciliation thing is actually a set-up, some kind of a trap?"

Barb stepped back and sat down hard on the cot behind her as if her legs had given out. "Oh my!" One hand brushed her hair back out of her eyes, as she stared at the dirt floor in deep thought. An anxious moment later she looked up. "It's possible I suppose," she said slowly, "but...he seems sincere, so...cordial. How will you sort it out, Hal?"

"I'm not sure," he said carefully, scratching a bug bite on his arm, "but I plan to follow Ilunga's advice. I'll keep a watchful eye on Tika. I intend to note who he speaks with and who approaches him. Will you help me as well with a second set of eyes and ears?"

"Count on it," Barb replied, standing to hug him once again. "Now, go before any curious eyes see us here together."

#47 Kisambo Village, DRC

January 2011

The evening began with a traditional meal that instantly took Hal back nearly fifty years. A series of tables had been spread with colorful cloths near the fire circle at the center of the village. The familiar blue and white plastic chairs lined both sides. The usual rice, *luku* (manioc balls), *poulet à la muamba* (chicken in palm oil gravy) and *pondu* (manioc greens) were supplemented with a variety of additional delicacies: smoked caterpillars, fresh grubs, fried plantain, *dongo-dongo* (okra soup), peanuts, *mikate* (fried dough balls), *mfumbwa* (forest leaf & dried fish), *makayabu* (salted fish) and other delicacies, difficult to identify in the dim light of the roaring fire and kerosene lanterns that hung from poles placed at various intervals behind the tables.

Pastor Lumingu said a long blessing for the meal. His conclusion was followed by loud and enthusiastic "Amens" by a hungry audience and the feasting began in earnest. Tika had arranged for Muwana to transport three cases of Primus beer, so that thoughtful addition, along with the village's best palm wine added an upbeat element to the meal, raising the level of enthusiasm across the tables.

Hal, seeing alcohol being distributed and eagerly received, turned to Tika, sitting next to him. With a feigned look of surprise and a half-smile he observed, "Primus and *malafu* (palm wine) at a village feast? *Incroyable!* That'd never be seen back in the day!"

Tika returned the smile. "Well, *mpangi*, let's just say that since our parents are presently feasting with the ancestors in their preferred way, we are free to do the same. It's a new day in Kisambo, *oui*?" Hal chuckled and rolled his eyes.

A short while later Tika, who had been sitting next to Hal, rose and joined several persons standing near the fire circle. Barb, who had been seated on Hal's other side, leaned over to him, to speak quietly in his ear. "Look who Tika is visiting with. Isn't that Kamanga Nsapo, the shaman? And it looks like Munzele Zacharie the niece of Muzeka's, is with him."

Hal stared intently at the dim figures standing across the way by the fire. Tika seemed caught up in agitated speech but the principal recipient of his attentions, Kamanga, stood facing him with his arms crossed, frowning and intermittently responding. "What do you think they're discussing, Hal?" Barb asked. "You don't suppose it's something about you, do you?"

"I wouldn't be surprised," he answered. "Let's find out when he comes back."

A few minutes later, Tika returned to the table. He was obviously upset. "What's going on, *mpangi* (friend)," Hal asked as Tika sat back in his chair and poked at his food.

Tika took a long time to reply, staring at his plate, deep in thought. Finally, he looked up, deep worry lines creasing his forehead. Barb thought that in the dim, flickering light of the fire and lanterns he looked as if he had aged a decade since he stepped away from them. She leaned forward to hear what he had to say.

"It would seem our reconciliation event must begin with you and me, *Lumwenu*." Tika sighed in a resigned voice, thumb and forefingers massaging his slowly shaking forehead.

"When the idea first came to me, I dreamed it might be possible to heal the great rift between Kisambo and the MMC mission by bringing both parties together face-to-face, confessing one to the another. It seemed like an idea that would...would please God. When the shaman, Kamanga heard of this, however, he came to me." Tika sat up on the edge of his seat, hands pressed to his chest. "He threatened my family with harm if I did not first invite you and Mme. Barbara to return here in person. I was surprised but I agreed to do so since it seemed like a good first step to healing. I knew Muzeka's family harbored some bitterness toward you as well, but I figured they might be able to resolve it once and for all with your presence here. It would also boost the success of a larger reconciliation."

Tika sat back hard and sighed deeply once again, hand back to his head. "Now, it appears that Kamanga and the others do not wish to talk or reconcile at all, but to do harm. He did not say so directly, but just now he dismissed my offer to set up a meeting. He demanded I tell him where you are sleeping in the village. I do not think he means well."

Hal sat in silence, unsure how to respond. He exchanged a worried glance with Barb.

Tika continued, his voice trembling. "I am so sorry, *mpangi*. My actions have placed you in danger. I should have realized this and told you...told you long ago. It seems we are repeating history, not changing it."

"What are you going to do, Hal?" Barb asked, alarmed, grasping his arm.

Before he could answer her, Tika interjected once again. "I have a suggestion. No...it is a request, a demand! You and I will exchange sleeping huts this night. That way should some attempt at harm take place, trouble will find me, not you. But I will be watching for it. You will stay with my sister Claudine and her family."

Hal pushed back his chair and started to rise. "No, I cannot let you do this, Tika!"

Tika grabbed him by the arm, pulling him back down. "I won't take no for an answer. I will be watchful. It was I who brought you here. It's only right that I now protect you in some way...by taking your place."

More words of protest and concern were voiced, but Tika was insistent, determined in his stated action, to which he added one additional caution. "At the end of the evening, we must be careful to slip away without being seen." And that is just what they did.

Sleep was elusive for Hal, Barb and Tika during the early hours of the evening. Each found themselves straining to pick up any sounds or indications that trouble was stalking them in the moonless darkness that shrouded Kisambo village. As the night progressed into the still, early morning hours, sleep finally descended on each one. The tension of their circumstances combined with full stomachs and libation from the village feast caught up with them and they drifted off.

A loud shriek brought the sleepy village to full attention. The solo shriek was followed by several more as villagers ran toward the sound from all directions in the gray, pre-dawn light. The young girl's bundle of sticks that had been balanced on her head were strewn about the still figure of a fallen man, lying face-down at the doorway of a small hut. A broken water gourd was in his hand. He was not moving.

The young girl tightly clutched a pagne-clad woman with a baby, her face pressed into the older woman's side. Several of the first arrivals were crouched near the fallen figure, probing and checking on his condition. Barb rushed to the scene with her medical bag in hand and dropped to her knees by the fallen man. "Move back!" she called out in Kituba, "I am a nurse. I need space to work." She immediately checked on the unconscious man's breathing and pulse, turning him to one side.

Hal rushed up, parting the crowd that surrounded the nurse and patient. "Oh no! Tika...no!" He fell to his knees bending over his fallen friend's body. "Is he still alive? What's his condition? What's happened, Barb?" Tika's sister Claudine arrived close behind Hal, asking the same questions in Kituba.

"Poison," she said, still working on Tika. "His breathing is shallow, but he still has a strong pulse. I suspect something was placed in his drinking gourd. It's right there on the ground. I have some meds in my bag that I think will help. Your dream alerted me to come prepared. Hal, this was intended for you." Barb looked up directly into Hal's shocked and alarmed face before resuming her duties.

In a short time Tika was carried to his sister Claudine's home and made comfortable there. Barb stayed close by as he slowly regained consciousness, retching and coughing for an extended period of time. She had water and medications ready. Claudine brought warm compresses and a basin to contain Tika's spew. Hal sat next to his friend's bed. *He did this for me!* kept echoing in his head. He found himself praying for the first time in many years.

A sizeable crowd gathered in front of the small cement block residence that Claudine and family called home. Angry murmuring swept through the gathered villagers.

"This is the work of those who would keep us from reconciling with the missionaries."

"Kamanga and his friends are behind this! He opposed Kuyantika's ideas from the start."

"No, he intended to kill the *mundele*."

"He will have to pay!"

The murmurs grew to shouts, the noise and commotion increased in volume. Finally, a sudden crescendo of loud shouts prompted Hal to get up and check on what was happening outside the front door.

The crowd was focused on three figures who had been dragged to their center and who were being vehemently pummeled with sticks and fists by those that surrounded them.

Kamanga and two others were crumbled into balls on their knees, arms covering their heads, enduring a hail of blows and kicks from the angry villagers.

Ilunga was at the center of the disturbance delivering some of the most punishing wallops. Kamanga finally collapsed into an unconscious heap. His two friends continued to receive the crowd's abuse. At that moment a figure appeared in the doorway, bent and grasping the door frame for support. He held up a weak and trembling hand as he croaked, "Stop! No more."

The blows and tumult came to an instant halt and the noise suddenly dropped as if a plug were pulled. All eyes turned to view Tika, standing barely upright, signaling for them to halt with a wave of a wobbly hand.

"Enough," he croaked. "I invited the children of our missionaries to return to Kisambo. It was something God stirred in my heart. These three intended evil, like Joseph's brothers in the Bible. But I think God intends it for good. I forgive them. Now let them go."

And with that, Tika's legs buckled. Hal, who had been standing by the door, reached over to catch his friend and guide him back to his bed. The crowd slowly dispersed. Kamanga's friends helped him up onto his feet and the trio limped off.

Ilunga remained standing silently in front of the residence, his face filled with confusion and amazement.

#48 Kisambo Village, DRC

January 2011

The remainder of a day that began with Kuyantika lying near death's door was one that would be remembered for some time to come in Kisambo Village. Sgt. Mpika, together with Chief Mansuaki and several of the men from the village went after Kamanga Nsapo and his two friends to arrest them. A dramatic search that stirred up the entire village ended in vain, for the three potential assassins fled their pursuers and made a successful escape to some unknown location.

Barb continued her nursing care for Tika, who had a rough morning edging away from death's door. Between having his stomach pumped, followed by plenty of retching on his own, he was an active though uncomfortable recipient of her ministrations. There were ample witnesses to his misery as well. Scores of visitors turned up with food, expressions of concern and well wishes.

Muwana, Tika's esteemed political friend, summoned the chiefs from the nearby villages to gather on short notice. With Pastor Lumingu taking the lead, they planned a formal ceremony to coincide with the next Sunday service two days hence. Choirs, speeches, food and an elaborate sermon about reconciliation and forgiveness all made the list. In sum, it was a busy day for the normally quiet village community.

By mid-afternoon, in the heat of the day, when the last of the visitors had drifted off Tika lay exhausted, sweaty and drowsy on his cot in his sister's home. Both Barb and Hal had maintained their vigil, wearily watching over the patient from chairs near his head. Periodically, they waved at flies buzzing their faces and fanned the still, humid air with small hand-held palm fronds. No one spoke. The dimly lit room was illuminated principally by the bright sunlight from the dwelling's open doorway. Its one small window was covered with a shutter of woven bamboo leaves, emitting only tiny shafts of light around the edges.

Without warning, a dark shadow blocked the bright doorway interrupting the serenity of the moment. All eyes shifted in that direction.

Ilunga stooped over to enter the low doorway of the dwelling, calling out softly "Ko-Ko," in the African version of a doorbell. Behind him was the colorful pagne-clad form of Munzele Zacharie.

"*Entre!*" Both Hal and Barb replied in unison, weary smiles of recognition and surprise lighting up their faces as they stood to greet the visitors. "*Ngolo ikele?*"

"*Eeye,*" was the reply from both, "'*Kele.*"

"Munzele Zacharie, we are surprised to see you!" Hal blurted out in an unplanned remark. "I...er we had thought...we assumed..." His voice trailed off.

She moved closer in the dim light to address him, speaking in a soft, solemn voice. "I'm here on a mission of peace. I have spoken with Ilunga, M. Schroeder. He explained your part in my family's past. I confess my heart – my whole family's – has been filled with fear and bitterness toward you for many years. We were wrong. I want you to know I did *not* encourage Kamanga and the others to do you harm. I wish only to ask you to forgive the words I have wrongly used against you. I am deeply saddened by my error."

Hal was speechless. He had been convinced that Munzele and her family were part of the plot against him, and now he was being asked to reverse his conclusions, to offer forgiveness?

"Er...*certainement! Bien sûr!*" was all he could manage after a delay. "*Merci.*"

"How is our brother doing by now?" Ilunga finally inquired, breaking the awkward pause.

Before either *mundele* could reply, Tika croaked out a response. "I'm not finished, brother. Don't start digging my grave yet! God has used the healing hands of these friends to pluck me from the edge of death. Munzele, thank you for your words, and your courage. Tell us...what news do you have of my *real* enemies?"

A quick smile flicked across Ilunga's face at his friend's reply. "We turned the village upside down looking for them but as wounded as they were, somehow all three managed to escape. We even scoured the forest near here but there was no trace. I suspect it will be a long time, if ever, before they are seen again at Kisambo."

"I'm sorry to hear that," Tika rasped. "They were misguided, made a mistake, but I hold no remaining anger or ill will. I meant it when I said I forgave them for what they did, or at least for what they tried to do."

Ilunga briefly stepped outside the doorway to pull two more plastic chairs into the room. He offered one to Munzele and scooted the second up close to Tika's cot as he sat. "You must say more, Kuyantika," he crooned in a soft and earnest voice. "I don't understand how you can just dismiss the acts of those who tried to kill you. How can you do that, brother? *Why* do you do that?"

Tika raised up to reply, leaning on one elbow. Barb reached out with a protective hand, but he waved her off with a small gesture. Hal and Munzele leaned in to hear what he would say.

"The strength of a tree is only revealed when the tempest wind bends its branches to their limit. My willingness to forgive this threat to my life tests the strength of my faith. Jesus taught that God forgives us as we forgive others who sin against us. So, my declaration confirms to my soul – and perhaps to yours as well, brother – that my faith is sincere. It is not a noble gesture; it is an action that reveals truth."

Ilunga dropped to his knees by Tika's cot, grasping both of his friend's hands. "I am shamed by the anger I carry toward others. I don't have your strength. If you are a tree, I am a sapling, a palm branch."

"Not so, Ilunga," Tika managed with a slight smile. "Let's just say your faith has not been put to the test. And I hope it never is, not this way," he added, gesturing toward Barb's medical equipment. "If my name means 'a new beginning,' yours is significant as well, 'Ilunga: one ready to forgive.'"

***

Later that evening, after Hal and Barb had eaten their evening meal and transferred Tika's care to Claudine, they sat together quietly by the fire ring at the village center. The flickering flames danced shadows across their faces as they sipped steaming cups of tea and stared into the fire, deep in thought. Surrounding them, here and there across the village came the comforting clinks of pans being cleaned and stored, cries of infants being put down, clucks and crows of poultry, all familiar sounds signaling the end of the day.

Hal finally broke their reverie. "It's pretty overwhelming,

Barb...all that has happened. I mean, it's one thing to organize a reconciliation event, but to put his very life on the line, to readily take my place in harm's way? Tika is a remarkable person." He took another sip of tea. "Overwhelming."

"I agree, Hal." Barb lowered her cup and turned her head to search his face. "But did you grasp his explanation? That's what impressed me."

"You mean, the part about Jesus teaching forgiveness?"

"Yes, that and his viewing the dangerous situation as an opportunity for good, a chance to demonstrate the validity of his faith. That struck me as mature and courageous...and insightful."

"Hmmm," was Hal's muted response as he pondered her words.

"I'm going to take a risk here, to speak boldly, Hal." He turned to give full attention to her words.

"I wonder what God has to do to get your attention, for you to recognize His reality in your life. Ever since you returned to this land every move you've made has had His fingerprints all over it. Your willingness to participate in the TASOK reunion was prompted by your therapist, someone sent your way who could relate to your TCK roots. Your experiences with former classmates, your miraculous survival from a snake bite...God things. Our meeting and relationship after all these years...in my eyes, it was a divine appointment. This Kisambo event...Tika's act of sacrificial love? Munzele's request for forgiveness? Illustrations of God's transformation power. Don't these things add up for you as more than just good luck or coincidence?"

Hal stared at Barb, frozen in thought. Several times he started to say something and stopped. Finally, he managed to utter "I...I suppose you're right. When you put it that way..." his sentence drifted off.

"So, tell me...what keeps you from just acknowledging the truth, Hal?" Barb inquired in a soft voice.

"The dreams, Barb. The dreams." Hal blurted out, wincing his reply.

"I keep thinking that the curse isn't on Kisambo, it's on me! Perhaps evil dwells in me, *has* dwelt in me for my whole life. How do I reconcile my clairvoyance with any hint of God's favor?"

"While in my mind the answer to your question is clear, it's not an original thought with me. If you recall, the Apostle Paul tells us in I Corinthians that there are many different kinds of gifts or as he calls them, '...*manifestations of the Spirit for the common good*, but it is the same God at work in them all.' Those are *his* words."

Hal's eyebrows raised. "Sooo...you think my dreams are a *spiritual gift* of some kind?"

"Something like that!" was Barb's reply. "Just think...virtually every time you've had one of those dreams, your foreknowledge made it possible to influence the outcome, to prevent greater harm, even to save lives. They did not prevent the event from occurring, but most certainly softened its impact. I came to Kisambo prepared because of your most recent dream-fed word of knowledge. Now, doesn't that sound like a gift that serves the common good?"

Hal sat back in his chair, reflecting on Barb's words as he stroked the evening stubble on his chin. Barb waited for his reply with an expectant look.

He remained quiet, staring into the dancing flames.

Finally, impatient for a response, she added, "It's what your mother believed, you know."

Hal sat up, startled. "W-what? What about my mother?"

"As I told you before, your mother and mine had many discussions over the years, especially after our fathers had passed away. Mom told me Martha was convinced that your special abilities were a unique gift of the Spirit, though your father thought otherwise. That's where I first got the idea."

"Mom actually told her that?" Hal sat dazed, taking this in. "She was always supportive and sympathetic of me and my dreams, but I never heard..." his voice faded out as he slowly shook his head.

Barb continued, "Martha's only concern, at least that she shared with my mother, was back in Kisambo days when she found out that Muzeka had instructed you in throwing bones. *That*, she reasoned, was much too close to the occult and it worried her. But she never shared that worry with your father, thinking he'd overreact."

"I had no idea she ever *knew* about the bones thing," Hal said mostly to himself. "She never said anything to me or corrected me about that."

"Martha told Mom that she had confidence God's Spirit was very much at work in your life and that you'd eventually come to the truth for yourself. She prayed for you daily. In fact, Mom said that *both* of them prayed for you whenever they got together."

Hal's eyes pooled full. He sat very still, staring into the fire. After a long minute he looked up into his companion's concerned face. "Thanks, Barb. Thanks for telling me about that," he said softly. "I think I need some alone time now," and he slowly rose and slipped off into the night.

#49 Rancho Palos Verdes

June 2011

"So, my friend, how are the plans coming along for the big day?" Brad Waterhouse stirred the cream in his coffee mug. Nearby, Hal removed the pod from the Keurig coffee machine, picked up his mug and stepped over to the kitchen island where his friend and colleague was standing. Morning light beams streamed through the windows. Granddaughter Emmie's giggles could be heard coming from the backyard patio where she and her mother were playing with her new puppy. Hal briefly stepped over to the window, stretching to peek over the sill. He returned with a contented smile to reply to the question.

"Things appear to be falling into place nicely, Brad," Hal answered as he stirred his coffee. "So far, it appears virtually my whole family will be in attendance. Cal and Judy and their families are coming down from Portland, of course Tricia and Emmie will be there. Believe it or not, even Phyllis and Greg have indicated they are coming."

"*That* should be interesting," Brad chuckled. Hal ignored the comment. "Both my sisters and their spouses are planning to join us, as is Brian, Barb's older brother, and his family. This will be the first time in many years we've all been together."

Hal picked up his mug and pointed to the next room. "Come on, let's visit in the living room. It's nice enough outside but I think Emmie's having way too much fun to allow for any conversation." The squeals from the patio erupted once again.

"So, are you going to fill me in on what actually happened to you in Africa, Hal? The falling-for-Barb part is obvious. I knew *that* had occurred when you first returned from your reunion. But what else happened in Kibongo – or whatever that village was called – as a result of your visit? What about your PTSD?"

Brad's query brought a smile to Hal's face. "Kisambo," he corrected, "and you can't tell me my interest in Barb was *that* obvious. I hadn't even figured it out for myself when I first returned." Hal took a long sip of coffee. "You know, Brad, the combo of therapy with Dr. Franklin and returning to the scene where my PTSD originated, worked. Those experiences have really resolved things for me, emotionally. I feel different, at peace. Settled, for the first time in as long as I can remember."

"It sounds like you made a good choice of therapists, buddy," Brad observed as he re-crossed his legs.

"Actually, the peace I feel these days is far more than just release from PTSD. I had a...a...*spiritual awakening*, I guess you'd call it. A...heaviness I've carried in that part of my life lifted. Faith-related things came together for me in some unanticipated ways. Barb was instrumental in the process. I owe her a lot. She was insightful and direct with me, but kind, gentle. A perfect combination."

Brad chuckled. "Sounds like *love* to me!"

"Love...yes! But perhaps a different kind than you have in mind. My story is in many respects similar to that of C. S. Lewis in his famous memoir, "*Surprised by Joy*." My spiritual scotosis was a kind of protective cocoon I created early on. It took some tough experiences and Barb's gentle confrontation to break out of it."

"Scotosis?" Brad said, shooting a puzzled sideway glance. "What's that?"

"Yes. You know, it's a form of intellectual blindness, a hardening of the mind against unwanted wisdom. Scotosis nicely describes my posture toward Christianity since childhood."

"And what's different now, Hal?"

"I'm glad you asked, friend." Hal sat forward, elbows on his knees. "Here's the deal: I think God's view of adversity and ours differs sharply. The hard things that happen in life leave their marks on us. We see them as scars, but I now believe that God uses those wounds to remind us of who we are and who He is. We are vulnerable creatures; He is our creator. He desires a personal relationship. When adversity prompts us to finally open our eyes of faith, He reveals He has been there all along. His desires for us are good...to be all we were created to be."

The extended period of silence that followed was finally broken by Brad. "Whew! That's quite a switch, buddy," he said quietly. Then perking up, "But, I'd still like to know what your return to Congo was all about."

Hal flashed a quick grin in response and set his mug on the lamp table. "Sorry about the mini-sermon...but you asked." Brad just raised his eyebrows in agreement, not venturing a further remark.

"The reason Barb and I agreed to go to Kisambo in the first place was to participate in a kind of reconciliation. That community has been estranged for decades from the Mennonite mission that our parents served under. Ultimately, the two parties need to be reconciled. Our visit was supposed to help lay the foundation for that to happen. I believe that's just what it did! We had a bit of drama that I'll have to share with you on another occasion, but in the end, there was mutual acknowledgement of wrongdoing and a wonderful Sunday morning of singing, preaching and worship. Plans are in the works for a U. S. delegation to come to Kisambo in the coming months to expand on our experience. I view it as a remarkable God-thing!"

Just then, the patio door banged open and Trish, Emmie and the pup came crashing into the room in a tangle of legs, yips, giggles and noise. Brad sat up so quickly he spilled his coffee. "Whoa!" Hal yelled, hand raised to stop a collision as the invaders slid to a halt.

Trish bubbled a warm greeting. "Oh, hi Dr. Waterhouse. I didn't know you were coming over. We just stopped in to show Dad Emmie's new puppy and to play a bit in the backyard. There's no green space at our apartment."

Emmie had picked up the squirming puppy and holding it to her chest, staggered over to her grandpa, dumping it in his lap. "Oof! Here, here little fella. Let's look at you." Hal held up the wiggly pup as his beaming granddaughter watched on.

"So, you're going to join the whole Schroeder clan at the big event," Brad observed to Trish.

"Yes, isn't it exciting? It is so amazing that Dad and Barb found each other after all these years. She is an incredible catch: smart, accomplished and beautiful, great personality. No disrespect to Mom, but Barb and Dad are just made for each other. It's obvious."

Hal stood to hand the puppy back to Emmie, frowning. "Trish, you know when we were young, things were different. I loved your Mom..."

Trish interrupted him, "Dad! You don't need to explain. That's ancient history. I'm just saying Barb is a good thing and I'm happy for you. For both of you. Changing the subject...have you heard from your African friends yet?"

"Yes, as a matter of fact, I have." Hal stepped over to place his arm around his daughter's shoulders. "Both Tika and Ilunga are coming! They're bringing their wives as well. It will be a trip of a lifetime for all of them, but especially for Ilunga who has been much more isolated in his home village."

"Where will they stay?" Brad queried.

"They'll all stay here at my place. My sister Rhonda and her husband are coming down from San Jose and they will remain here with the two couples to show them around LA while Barb and I are on our honeymoon."

Tricia smiled with a twinkle in her eye, "And where are you two going?"

Hal returned the smile. "Wouldn't you just like to know?"

Just then, Hal's cell phone rang. "Excuse me, please," he said rising and heading for the back room, "I have been expecting this call. It's from the Protestant University of Kinshasa regarding next year."

Hal had no sooner left the room when Brad leaned toward Tricia and in a lowered voice asked, "Is this whole spiritual thing with your dad for real?"

Trish immediately brightened up. "It sure seems that way to me! Hey, Dad's marrying Barb, isn't he? That's a big deal. He's also going on sabbatical to teach in Congo for next year, right? That's after he avoided going there since he was a kid. And, furthermore, these days he just sounds and looks like someone who's had the weight of the world lifted off his shoulders. His Congolese friends have even given him a new name...*Lumwenu Abongwami*, the seer who has been healed, who is whole. They see a difference! What more evidence do you need?"

Brad was unsmiling but nodded somberly. "I just feel like I might be losing a friend. He seems to be distancing himself, though I have to admit I'm happy to see him so excited about life. That part is refreshing. I just feel a little apprehensive. Should he decide not to come back, the department will really miss him. I will miss him, sorely."

Trish reached over to place a sympathetic hand on Brad's arm. "I think the two of you need to talk some more."

#50 Rancho Palos Verdes

June 2011

It was a balmy June afternoon along the coast in Southern California. Light breezes swept up the steep cliffs rising above gently surging waves. A fleet of sailboats caught the summer winds, tacking back and forth further out from the shoreline. Above, the bright blue skies were streaked with wispy clouds as sea birds, making the most of the updrafts, soared back and forth like tiny animate mimics of the sailboats below. The amphitheater at Point Vincente Park was rapidly filling with guests. It appeared that the 150 capacity would be reached...and then some, well in advance of the three o'clock starting time.

The Point Vincente Interpretive Center was a convenient five miles west, just over the crest of the hill from Hal's Rancho Palos Verdes residence. Thus, the extended family had all gathered at his place to caravan to the park for the wedding. Neighbors puzzled at the line of parked cars that filled the normally empty street in both directions. What could be happening in their quiet neighborhood?

As Brad Waterhouse walked to Hal's residence from where he had parked his car two blocks distant, he wondered the same. Children were running in and out of the house; laughter and a cacophony of voices boomed from within. Stepping up on the porch, Brad's senses were filled with strange sounds, bright colors, exotic odors of food. Everywhere, there seemed a sense of celebration. He couldn't help smiling even before Tricia rushed over to welcome him, wiping her wet hands on the apron she was removing.

"Ah, the best man makes his entrance! Welcome to the party, Dr. W." She reached out to give him a hearty hug and peck on the cheek, before stepping back half a pace to look him over. "Yes! The shirt fits perfectly. That color looks good on you. The Kinshasa tailor Dad's friend commissioned to make the wax print garments did a great job with the measurements he was sent."

A loud burst of laughter from the kitchen pulled Brad's attention away. "What's *happening* in there?"

"Well, you know from the formal announcement and from talking with Dad that this is an African-themed wedding. Two of Barb and Dad's friends from the Congo came here with their wives, and the women are in charge of preparing a feast for the reception – Congolese food. The wives recruited most of us Schroeder women – even some of the men – to help them. The cooking started last night, and it's been continuing all morning long. Most of us don't know what the heck we're doing! There's been much giggling and rolling of eyes by the African women. All efforts to translate their directions by our aunts, the former MKs, have involved tons of forgotten or misused words. It's been hilarious."

Hal stepped out of the crowded kitchen to greet his best man, and then put fingers to his lips to emit a loud whistle. "Listen up everyone!" he shouted in a loud voice. "Let me have your attention!" The noise level dropped, and heads turned in his direction.

"It's time to head out. Leave things as they are. I have recruited a whole squad of grad students to transport the food and set up the reception at the Park. It'll be their final exam in Anthro seminar this semester." That brought a wave of chuckles. "We need to leave now, people!"

The crowd poured out of Hal's residence and soon the street was empty of cars. The entire Schroeder clan arrived en masse at the Interpretive Center. The amphitheater, located on the side of a hill facing the ocean, was completely filled with colorfully attired attendees. Latecomers stood or were seated on blankets at the edges. The invitation had stated *"Informal attire is encouraged: preferably African wax prints or Hawaiian-style shirts and muumuus."* The colorful crowd had obviously gotten the message.

Brian, Barb's older brother, walked his sister down the aisle as loudspeakers played a Congo jazz wedding march. Barb wore a fitted African wax print dress with three-quarter length flaring sleeves, silver-gray in color, accented with a tasteful design of small white butterflies. The entire bodice bore elaborate embroidered stitching in a lustrous silver thread. Her wedding garb was accented with a stylish hat that matched the color of her dress. Barb's brother towered over her and she glanced up smiling to him as they walked the aisle. When they arrived at the front of the amphitheater, the crowd unexpectedly broke into applause. Hal's smile was already full. The applause tested its limits. Barb was a beautiful bride.

Barb's daughter, Shawna, served as her maid of honor and Hal's two sisters, Patty and Rhonda stood with her. Hal's USC colleague Brad performed best man duties and was joined by Tika and Ilunga at the front.

After rings and vows were exchanged, the ceremony concluded with a prayer of blessing delivered by Kuyantika and translated by a French speaking anthropology colleague of Hal's.

> *Saint Père,*
> *Vous nous appelle, vos enfants prodigues, comme si venu d'un pays lointain pour nous accueillir dans votre présence. Nos cœurs sont pleins aujourd'hui alors que nous sommes témoins du mariage de Harold et Barbara, ravivant une amitié et se joignant dans une promesse qui a eu son origan il y a bien longtemps et dans une paye lointaine.*
>
> *Nous sommes doublement bénis, car vous avez également ravivé notre amitié avec ce couple, une amitié longtemps considérée comme morte. Vous avez donné à ce couple une nouvelle vie. Que votre Esprit soutienne l'engagement de ces chers amis, l'un envers l'autre. Dieu d'amour, nous vous demandons de leur accorder, ainsi qu'à nous, beaucoup de joie et de paix alors que nous reçevons avec reconnaissance ces dons de votre main généreuse.*
> *Amen.*

> *[Holy Father,*
> *You call us, your prodigal children, as if from a far country to your welcoming presence. Our hearts are full this day as we witness the joining of Harold and Barbara in marriage, reviving a friendship and forming a commitment that had its origins long ago in a distant land.*
>
> *We are twice blessed, for you have also revived our friendship with this couple, a kinship long considered dead. You have given it new life. May*

your Spirit sustain the commitment of these dear ones to each other. Loving God, we ask that you grant to them and to us much joy and peace as we gratefully receive these gifts from your generous hand.

   Amen.]

Author's Notes

Over the years I've had a lot of contact with adult Third Culture Kids (TCKs), including both close at hand friendships and across the globe internet exchanges. Close TCK contacts? I happen to be married to one! My curiosity about the TCK phenomena prompted an extensive review of research on the topic and led to crafting a memoir (*The Mango Bloom*) that explored our experience as hostel parents in the Congo in the mid-70s, a true crucible of TCK development. I have always been fascinated by stories of TCK childhood adventures. The psychologist in me has been equally fascinated to observe the adult life paths of our TCK friends that have unfolded in both predictable and divergent patterns. This novel provided me with a vehicle to explore those interests in depth.

Some of the most colorful stories surfacing from Congo TCKs concern the tumultuous early days following Independence in 1960 when violence and rebellion swept the land. Mission stations were attacked, and expatriate residents were repeatedly evacuated or relocated. Such life-and-death incidents undoubtedly traumatized both parents and children, but during our sojourn supervising MKs, we heard surprisingly few of these stories from our charges. More recently, reading Jim Bertsche's detailed history, *CIM/AIMM: A story of vision, commitment, and grace*, I came across fascinating tales of courage and faith from that era, tales that deserve to be retold. It occurred to me that avoidance was a possible reason we had not heard those stories from the children who lived them. Avoidance is a familiar psychological defense. It protects traumatized individuals from the pain of Post Traumatic Stress Disorder (PTSD). So, my first question: how has PTSD played out in the lives of TCKs impacted by trauma in childhood?

A second question that has challenged me over the years concerns adult TCKs who have rejected the Christian faith of their parents and youth. Surveys reference "missionary life and experiences" as frequent reasons for TCKs abandoning their faith. I have wondered what it might take for a TCK to overcome this spiritual scotosis (hardening of the mind against unwanted wisdom). And how might a PTSD-afflicted TCK ever resolve this lifelong imprint, heal the old wounds? The core of my storyline pursued these questions.

Imagining many of my target readers to be TCKs themselves, I determined to imbue my story with as much authenticity as I could manage, given my distance from the events in time and space. I inserted Kituba and Lingala (trade languages) words and phrases, depicted familiar details in food, landscapes and behavior, all directed toward realism. Many of the African character's names I chose carry special meaning, also true to real life. I made frequent use of consultation with present and former residents of DRC to help correct and embellish my descriptions. The entire story from Part I of my novel closely traces Bertsche's factual recounting of Mulele Rebellion events with respect to details from one mission station's experience. My characters' names, personalities and dialogue, however, are all invented.

The culminating event in my novel, a return to the former Kisambo Station (fictitious name) for a reconciliation event is also based on an actual affair that took place in November 2017 at the same location as Bertsche's evacuation story. I chose to use the inspired idea of the gathering to serve the interests of my storyline rather than attempt to recast details of the actual event. The authentic three-day celebration event differed in details and outcome from that presented in this novel.

Hal's gift of clairvoyance was my way of enhancing tension in his spiritual journey. It polarized the responses of others to him: some sought his counsel while others considered it a curse, a demonic visitation. Hal's gifting ultimately tormented him as well, heightening TCK feelings of not fitting in, of being a misfit, but at the same time providing him special status with Congolese friends. The reframing of his clairvoyance by his mother and Barb in the final section is not intended as a theological statement. Rather, it is presented as a part of Hal's transformation, resolving this lingering dissonant element in his life.

Finally, and most importantly, I want to acknowledge that this novel is presented from a particular point of view, a western or *mundele* perspective. It is intended to illuminate the experience of white American missionaries whose lives were shaped and impacted by their experiences in that beautiful, enchanting and dangerous land. Congolese storytellers utilizing the same facts and characters that appear in my novel would most certainly tell a different story. Their tale would no doubt exceed the depictions of this novel in chronicling danger, courage, compassion and heroic action. The portrayal of *mindele* privilege and character would likely take on a different cast as well. So, there exist other tales of this era yet to be told.

I would like to thank those who contributed descriptions and details from their life experiences in Congo: Larry Prieb, former MCC Country Director; Phil Kliewer's, first impressions from a TASOK class reunion; Laurie Bowers-Connelly Braun's first hand encounter with a water cobra; Rod Hollinger-Janzen and Charity Eidse Schellenberg for reconciliation event details; Pakisa Tshimika for cultural and translation assistance.

My first readers, Chris Duncan, Garry Prieb, Charles Buller and Glen Chapman were especially helpful in reviewing and correcting manuscript errors and omissions. The three former Congo residents – Prieb, Buller and Chapman – are also astute cultural observers, fluent in Kituba/Kikongo. Garry Prieb's gifted artistic skills show themselves in the novel's cover art.

Finally, a special singled out thanks to long-term Baptist missionary, Glen Chapman for frequent emails from his Kikongo home in the Kwilu Province, near where the fictitious Kisambo village is located. His abundant insightful, good-humored advice was invaluable. He and his wife, Rita represent the best of a modern missionary presence in Congo.

CPSIA information can be obtained
at www.ICGtesting.com
Printed in the USA
BVHW071024250820
587150BV00003B/212